JJ RICHARDS

The Pike

DCI Walker Crime Thrillers (Book 2)

First published by Simulacrum Press Publishers 2024

Copyright © 2024 by JJ Richards

All rights reserved. No part of this publication may be reproduced, stored or transmitted in any form or by any means, electronic, mechanical, photocopying, recording, scanning, or otherwise without written permission from the publisher. It is illegal to copy this book, post it to a website, or distribute it by any other means without permission.

This novel is entirely a work of fiction. The names, characters and incidents portrayed in it are the work of the author's imagination. Any resemblance to actual persons, living or dead, events or localities is entirely coincidental.

JJ Richards asserts the moral right to be identified as the author of this work.

JJ Richards has no responsibility for the persistence or accuracy of URLs for external or third-party Internet Websites referred to in this publication and does not guarantee that any content on such Websites is, or will remain, accurate or appropriate.

Designations used by companies to distinguish their products are often claimed as trademarks. All brand names and product names used in this book and on its cover are trade names, service marks, trademarks and registered trademarks of their respective owners. The publishers and the book are not associated with any product or vendor mentioned in this book. None of the companies referenced within the book have endorsed the book.

First edition

ISBN: 9798873208142

Editing by Hal Duncan
Cover art by Tom Sanderson

This book was professionally typeset on Reedsy.
Find out more at reedsy.com

Contents

PROLOGUE	1
CHAPTER ONE	7
CHAPTER TWO	13
CHAPTER THREE	22
CHAPTER FOUR	26
CHAPTER FIVE	31
CHAPTER SIX	38
CHAPTER SEVEN	46
CHAPTER EIGHT	56
CHAPTER NINE	60
CHAPTER TEN	65
CHAPTER ELEVEN	68
CHAPTER TWELVE	72
CHAPTER THIRTEEN	76
CHAPTER FOURTEEN	80
CHAPTER FIFTEEN	84
CHAPTER SIXTEEN	94
CHAPTER SEVENTEEN	99
CHAPTER EIGHTEEN	105
CHAPTER NINETEEN	110
CHAPTER TWENTY	117
CHAPTER TWENTY-ONE	122
CHAPTER TWENTY-TWO	126
CHAPTER TWENTY-THREE	130

CHAPTER TWENTY-FOUR	139
CHAPTER TWENTY-FIVE	142
CHAPTER TWENTY-SIX	147
CHAPTER TWENTY-SEVEN	152
CHAPTER TWENTY-EIGHT	159
CHAPTER TWENTY-NINE	162
CHAPTER THIRTY	172
CHAPTER THIRTY-ONE	183
CHAPTER THIRTY-TWO	190
CHAPTER THIRTY-THREE	198
CHAPTER THIRTY-FOUR	200
CHAPTER THIRTY-FIVE	205
CHAPTER THIRTY-SIX	212
CHAPTER THIRTY-SEVEN	221
CHAPTER THIRTY-EIGHT	233
CHAPTER THIRTY-NINE	241
CHAPTER FORTY	253
CHAPTER FORTY-ONE	261
CHAPTER FORTY-TWO	269
CHAPTER FORTY-THREE	274
CHAPTER FORTY-FOUR	277
EPILOGUE	282
A Note From the Author	287

"It is during our darkest moments that we must focus to see the light." Aristotle Onassis.

PROLOGUE

She shouldn't have come. It was a bad mistake. That much was clear. But it was too late for that now—too late for regrets.

'You're awful,' said Charlotte, her face all twisted up, squinting to see properly in the dark. He'd hurt her, like really properly hurt her, and there was nothing she could have done about it. He was bigger than her, stronger. And she'd been scared. Really scared.

If she'd got the damned bus home, like she'd planned, she'd already be there, tucked up in bed, all comfy, watching something on Netflix, probably one of those crime dramas she enjoyed. But instead, she'd somehow ended up near the Pike Tower on *Rivington Pike*—the well-known high point on Winter Hill near her home in Chorley—become a real-life victim herself.

The truth was, she'd had a crush on him, a big one. He was a bit older than she was, good looking, she thought, just the kind of guy Charlotte went for, a bit edgy, interesting, real boyfriend material. Hanging out with him at a place like the Pike was just too good an opportunity to pass up, to get to know him better. It was like hitting the jackpot. She'd thought she might even kiss him there and then, if he played his cards right; she knew if she played hard to get, like she usually did, then some other girl might get in before her. She didn't want that. It had happened before with other boys she liked, and she'd learned from these past mistakes.

However, it hadn't gone as planned. She'd drunk too much—way too much, because she'd been nervous—and she'd smoked some weed too, the first time she ever had. It seemed it was a night for firsts, but not in a good way. She'd pretended she was alright at first and drunk and smoked more because she'd been embarrassed, didn't want to seem prudish or lame. She just felt a bit funny to begin with, like her body wasn't her own, all fuzzy. It wasn't so bad. But then her head had started to spin, and she felt sick.

In hindsight, going off to the Pike after dark without anyone she was close with to watch her back wasn't her greatest move ever. It was naïve, to say the least. Her parents had taught her better. She knew that, even in her present state, knew all about the importance of the *buddy system*. She'd only actually intended to get a lift home to begin with but had somehow, wilfully, ended up here. Things have a way of quickly spiralling out of control when you're young, her dad had always said, and that's what had happened. She'd agreed to party for a little while, have some fun, relax, that kind of thing. It seemed like a good idea at the time. It sounded *great,* in fact. But now it just seemed stupid. Really dumb. It was a harsh lesson to take—the harshest she'd ever had—and the worst part: it wasn't over yet.

Currently sitting behind the back of the Pike Tower, Charlotte had gone there thinking she was going to get a snog, maybe fool around a bit. But he'd wanted more. Of course, he did. He was a boy. They *always* wanted more. And he'd got more, too, despite her attempts at stopping him.

Sitting in the dirt, her dress half ripped, hair a mess, lipstick smudged across her face, he was now taking photos of her on his mobile phone. Worse still, she was doing absolutely nothing to stop it. She couldn't. He'd already hit her once, in the stomach, immobilised her. What an arsehole he'd turned out to be. What a bad judge of character she was. She hated herself.

He'd already got a few half-naked pics, threatened her if she didn't do what he asked, said he'd 'slut shame' her if she told anyone what happened, tell everyone what she did with him. Then he'd got weirdly apologetic about it, started talking to himself. He was nuts. All she'd done was come up here hoping for a little fun. She didn't sign up for this. She didn't want anything like it.

She'd been going home early at around eight-thirty as she'd got bored hanging out with her friends. There was nothing much to do in Chorley for teenagers, so she'd parted with them, said 'goodnight'. But then, at the bus stop, she'd been asked if she wanted a lift. From him? Of course, she did! At the very least, she could save her bloomin' bus fare! And at best, well, her imagination had run riot—dates, couple rings, a relationship? In the car, the idea of a private party over on the hill soon came up, and since her parents said she could stay out until ten, she figured, *why not?* It was the most exciting thing she'd heard all night. Finally, some real fun. There'd be free booze, music, even some weed. That's what he'd promised her. It was a no brainer. She'd planned to tell her friends in the morning and thought they'd all be so jealous. But she wasn't going to be telling anyone anything now. Not unless she wanted to be *slut-shamed* on the Internet, which she certainly did not. The thought of it made her want to cry—the public humiliation. She'd heard stories about such things before. It could destroy a person's life. It could destroy *her* life. She was in real trouble.

She wasn't really quite sure what had just happened either, whether he'd had proper sex with her, or if they'd just made out. She didn't know as she'd never had sex before, and she was drunk and stoned and couldn't even feel her face, never mind anything else. This was a good thing though—the numbness— as when he'd hit her in the stomach, she really didn't feel much. But it had completely taken her breath away, long enough for him to climb on top of her and do what he wanted to do. It was awful, humiliating. Now it was over, the world was spinning more than it should be, more than ever, and she was sure she was gunna throw up at any second. Perhaps she should, she thought. Maybe he'd leave her alone then.

When he was done taking the photos, he left her there with the bottle of cherry-flavoured vodka she'd been drinking, which he'd bought for her at the shop on the way. She did her best to do up her torn clothes and put herself back together, but she didn't feel well, started to get upset. If he left her there, alone, she didn't even know how she was going to get home. She'd be all alone in the dark. She suddenly felt very vulnerable, like never before in her life, and started to cry. The floodgates opened.

She grabbed the bottle of vodka, taking another generous swig, just wanting to forget the whole thing. The booze was helping at least. Another swig, but this time it caught the back of her throat and she retched, throwing up a bit on the grass. She was all over the place now, not quite sure what was going on, head spinning, trying to get her balance, leaning over to

PROLOGUE

one side when she tried to walk.

Then he came back, doing up the zipper on his trousers. He'd been for a piss, that much she registered, despite her current state.

'I need one more thing,' he said. 'A video.' He pushed her down to her knees. He *was* stronger than her and did it with ease. She had no resistance. She was very wobbly now, shaky, unable to function properly.

He started to take his trousers down, but her pride kicked in, somehow jolted her out of it, a surge of adrenaline kicking in and sharpening her focus a little. She couldn't have that. If he had *that* on video, he'd post it on one of those nasty porn sites, like Pornhub, and it'd be out there forever, for the whole world to see—her family and friends, her future children and grandchildren. No. She couldn't have that. She wouldn't do it. No matter what. She'd rather die.

She clenched her fist as tight as she could, got ready, swung and hit him, right in the balls. He yelped like a wounded animal. She'd hurt him, bad. He hadn't been expecting that! It had taken *his* breath away this time. Served him right too. An eye for an eye. But once he'd recovered a little, cradling his damaged testes, he pulled his pants back up and looked at her like no one had ever looked at her before, pure rage in his eyes.

'You stupid bitch!' he said, lashing out, shoving her, hard. She staggered backwards into the Tower, felt it at her rear; and he came at her again, relentlessly, hands out ready to slam her again, murder in his eyes. In those final few moments, though, those precious final few seconds, instead of feeling hatred and loathing, she was somehow grateful: grateful for the family she'd had, for her amazing childhood, and for all her wonderful friends—for all of it. Life is such a wonderful thing, she thought—the idea flashing through her mind in an instant—

and she'd had one, no matter how tragically short it had been. She was somehow aware, in that split-second, of all the good things that had happened to her in her life, and she already missed it.

And then her head slammed into the stone base of the tower. She immediately knew it was bad, even in that state—knew she was in serious trouble. Her world rapidly started to fade and just as quickly as she'd been created in that miraculous, ineffable spark, it was all over. All *gone*.

CHAPTER ONE

Having made it up the last few steps to the Pike Tower at Rivington, DCI Walker looked up to see DC Briggs staring down at him, arms folded, with a grim expression on her face. He was out of breath, as the steps were bloody steep, but also grateful for any bit of exercise he could get to help him back to full fitness after his latest enforced leave of absence. At least they'd not had to make the full hike, as there was a narrow road up there for emergencies and maintenance only, and for the odd ice-cream van. It wasn't a route that was open for vehicles ridden by the general public. But what they had *was* an emergency, and there were no ice-creams for sale right now. The place had already been closed off as soon as it had become an active crime scene under investigation.

'Well done, Chief. You made it,' said DC Briggs, who'd already been up there for who knew how long ahead of him. She was much smaller and slimmer than him, carried much less weight.

Walker got up on level ground with her and scowled. 'Easy, Detective. I'm not an old man just yet.'

They'd been working together on and off for over six months now, had got to know each other and developed a close working relationship. However, there'd been no big cases during that time, not since the Smith killings in Rufford, when Shelly Briggs had still been a PC. It was working that case with Walker which had convinced her she'd be better suited working in CID.

'What do we have then?' asked Walker as the rain continued to drizzle. He looked up at the sky, hoping it wouldn't start to pour. Heavy rain would compromise the crime scene, and that was the last thing they needed at the start of an investigation. Unfortunately, such rain was a frequent occupational hazard for detectives working in Lancashire; a heavy downpour wouldn't be out of the ordinary. But at least he'd come prepared, had a waterproof poncho to wear over his suit, one of ten he was currently working his way through. This one was *green*.

'Deceased female, approximately fifteen to eighteen years old, looks as if she's been assaulted,' said DC Briggs.

'Have we ID'd the body yet?' he asked.

'Not yet,' she said. 'She didn't have any formal identification on her. But one of the tech lot are working on unlocking her phone as we speak. When they have, they can ring one of her contacts and find out who the hell she is.'

Walker nodded, satisfied things were moving along.

'Right, let's have a look then,' he said, now he'd got his breath back.

They moved around the back of the Pike Tower, which had already been cordoned off with police tape to protect the crime scene—not just from any straying members of the public, but also from some of the more inexperienced police officers on the scene, along with any Police Community Support Officers, who were largely untrained in investigative matters. Walker was also pleased to see that a white forensic tarpaulin had already been erected, which would help protect the crime scene from the elements. And it was under there that he found the victim lying in the dirt, her dress torn, one of her ample breasts visible. She was pale, the colour of Chinese porcelain, but it didn't look like she'd been dead for more than a few hours: any visible decomposition had yet to set in and there were none of the pungent smells associated with decay at twenty-four hours or more. He ducked under the police tape and carefully navigated, scrutinising where he was placing his feet with every step. DC Briggs held back, seemingly waiting to be invited. She'd normally accompany him without question, but this one probably felt different—perhaps more important somehow—and she'd be understandably wary of making any newbie mistakes. Walker liked this caution in her, hated it when officers waded in, all gung-ho. This kind of attentiveness was one of the reasons he liked working with DC Briggs so much.

He looked at her. 'I told you: *you're a DC now*. You need to inspect the crime scene with me in case you see something I don't.'

DC Briggs nodded and started to manoeuvre the police tape in the same way Walker had.

'Just be careful,' he said, even though he knew she would be—perhaps reminding himself as much as anything. 'We don't want to compromise any evidence.'

She nodded. 'Chief,' she said, to confirm her understanding.

Walker bent down next to the body, felt it. 'Body's cold, stiff. Rigor mortis has set in. It's been a few hours, at least, but not more than twenty-four.' It was morning, so Walker presumed she'd died sometime the previous night. 'Who found her?' he asked.

'Early morning rambler,' said DC Briggs. 'Poor sod. Male. Late thirties. He's pretty shook up, apparently. One of the PCs has donated some of the tea from her flask. She's sitting with him down on the side of the hill.'

Walker moved around the body, looking for any sign of a struggle.

'Quite a few marks in the dirt that will need looking at,' said Walker. 'The condition of the dress is also suggestive of a struggle.' He examined the wound on her head, it had been bleeding, profusely, but had stopped post-mortem, the blood now congealed and matted in her long, straight, tied back blonde hair. Next, he went over to the Pike Tower, which was just a couple of steps away from the body. He looked closely, took a pen out from his pocket and pointed with it. 'That looks like blood,' he said. 'You see that, there? If she'd hit her head on this stone structure with enough force, that would be enough to kill her.'

'You think someone pushed her?' asked DC Briggs.

'Quite possibly. Forensics can confirm whether this injury is the cause of death,' said Walker. 'The autopsy will also need to confirm if any sexual activity took place. What else do we have?'

'A few items were bagged when the mobile phone was retrieved,' said DC Briggs. 'We have one bottle of *Smirnoff Cherry Drop* vodka, found near the body, several smoked joints dotted around, a few cans of beer, and one bottle of *Monkey Shoulder Blended Malt Scotch Whisky*, which I believe can be bought in numerous supermarkets and off-licences.'

'A party gone wrong?' suggested Walker. 'Could be an accident. We'll need to find out how much she drank before her death, whether she smoked any weed as well, or took any other drugs. We need a clear picture of how intoxicated she was before this happened, and, of course, who she was with—which may be a little more difficult.'

'Of course,' said DC Briggs, sweeping her hair back from across her face as a gust of wind suddenly buffeted them. The weather was turning, and not in a good way.

'It's possible this young lady came up here alone, to drink, and these other bottles are from previous visitors. It might be the case that young people in the area have recently marked this spot for a place to have some fun, a site to drink and get stoned at night without any prying eyes,' said Walker. 'Or, she could have come with a boyfriend, or even with several people. This is something we'll need to track. But first, we need her ID. Check for any missing persons lodged in the area, see if we can get a heads up before the Digital Forensics Technician gains access to her phone.'

DC Briggs nodded. 'Will do, Chief. I'm on it.'

Walker squatted next to the dead girl. He was suddenly grateful that at least his own daughter was safe and sound, that he wasn't looking down at her. 'Poor girl,' he said, speaking softly. She reminded him a bit of his own deceased sister, despite this victim being older than she'd been when she'd passed. 'What a tragic waste of a young life. If someone did this to you, we're gonna do our very best to catch whoever did it. I promise you that.'

'Sir?' asked DC Briggs, perhaps not quite hearing what he'd said because of the elements, but he wasn't talking to her, of course. He was talking to the dead girl, and to himself.

He stood back up and got close to DC Briggs. 'We need to assemble a team for this one, ASAP. It's going to be another extensive investigation, just like the one you worked with me on in Rufford. Let's get back to the station, get the ball rolling, see who we have available.

'Got yer. Do you need a hand getting back down the steps, Chief?' she asked. She was getting cheeky, but Walker didn't mind that. It was good to lighten things up occasionally in a job like this. It helped keep a person grounded, to prevent them from going completely nuts—himself included.

'Thanks, but I think I can manage it,' he said. 'I can even act as your Guide For the Blind if your hair keeps blowing all over your face.'

DC Briggs took out a scrunchy, put it in her mouth for a second while she organised her hair, and tied it back. She smiled. 'Age before beauty then,' she said.

CHAPTER TWO

Barry Porter was sitting at the dining room table of his modest-sized semi-detached house on Pennine Road in Chorley, head in hands, trying to take in the devastating life-changing news he'd just been told. His wife, Lizzy, was in an even worse state than him, beside herself, on her knees on the carpeted floor, sobbing her heart out. Losing anyone close was tough enough anyway, but dealing with the death of a child was something else completely. Walker knew that all too well. It was seismic. Whenever he'd had to inform parents of a fatal accident or murder, some went numb, unresponsive, others got angry, while some just started to grieve there and then, the floodgates blasted open by the enormity of it all. For the Porters, it seemed like the latter, although Walker was sure anger would come, in time.

The Digital Forensics Technician working the case had eventually gained access to Charlotte Porter's mobile phone and called the number in the contacts list named 'Dad', asking him to verify the user of the incoming number in order to get Charlotte's name and description, telling him that the phone had been found. In the meantime, Charlotte's parents had filed a missing person's report the night before, once it became clear she wasn't coming home. The night staff at

Chorley Police Station had been dealing with it, making no inroads in the short space of time they'd been investigating, until the body had been found, that is. Then they'd matched the description of the deceased to that of a missing person and come up with the same name and the mobile number of the father who filed the report. It was one and the same. The parents had also supplied a photo of Charlotte, which had been digitally forwarded to Walker for final confirmation. It was her. She looked so full of life in the photo, so energetic and vibrant—but it was her: he was sure of it. A PC Jarrad and his colleague had already followed procedure and visited the parents as soon as possible to inform them of the death of their daughter—double checking everything first, of course. Walker had been assured it had all been done properly, as best as it could be in such circumstances.

DCI Walker had been drafted in to lead the investigation of the potential homicide on Rivington Pike due to his extensive experience in dealing with this kind of case—and the fact that Chorley only had two DIs—and he'd assigned DC Briggs to work alongside him once more. Although she had a lack of experience in CID, she did have some fresh insights that only newbies like her could have, along with a certain way with people that Walker did not, which he felt might be useful in this particular case.

Walker and DC Briggs had arrived at the Porter residence just thirty minutes after Barry had been given the bad news. They hadn't been too far away and joined the Family Liaison Officer who was already there, having taken over from the two PCs who'd given the family the bad news—a DI named Sally Keane, an experienced FLO who worked all over Lancashire for the Constabulary, someone who'd seen it all before. The

CHAPTER TWO

Porters also had another, younger daughter, who was sitting next to her father, not quite knowing what to do or how to react to what was going on around her. At thirteen years old, she looked a lot like her sister, with the same straight blonde hair and facial features, only she was a little plumper and more rounded—less physically mature. However, in the last few minutes, she'd probably grown up more than the average thirteen-year-old did in a whole year.

The front door had already been open when they'd arrived, so Walker and DC Briggs had just entered, knowing DI Keane was already with them with her hands full having begun the information gathering process and now providing support to the family.

'DI Keane, Mr and Mrs Porter,' said Walker, to get their attention. 'I'm DCI Jonathan Walker. I'll be leading the investigation to find out what happened to your daughter.'

Barry looked up, taking his head out of his hands, his face ashen. 'We don't even know if it's her yet,' he spat. 'Lots of girls look like her. You could be mistaken. She's just missing, that's all, and she probably lost her phone somehow, or had it stolen. She's never careful with it. She might have just got drunk and stayed at a friend's house, forgot to call us. We told her not to drink but she won't listen. I suppose we were all the same when we were her age. But I'll still bloody kill her when she gets home!' He wasn't quite ready to fully accept it yet, still in the stage of being tortured by hope. Mrs Porter, however, clearly did not have such hope: she let out a louder wail of grief, before going back to the quieter sobbing. Walker waited until the noise had subsided before going on.

'Mr Porter. I saw her myself. It was Charlotte—the same person photographed on the home screen of the phone we called you with, and a clear match on the photo you supplied with the missing person's report. I'm sorry.'

There was a pause while he battled with it. 'Lots of people look like her,' he spat, stubbornly refusing to believe what was staring him in the face.

'Look, Mr Porter, I was at the scene, and I saw for myself. Forensics sent me a copy of the photo on the home screen, along with a photo of your Charlotte supplied for the missing person's report. I'm afraid both were a clear match to the person we found,' said Walker. 'I'm so sorry for your loss.'

'No. It can't be. She was fine yesterday evening,' said Barry. 'She was... *fine*.'

DC Briggs came over, put her hand on Barry's shoulder. 'Mr Porter. After failing several times due to the position of Charlotte's body, our technician was eventually able to open her phone using facial recognition software, scanning her face. The phone with your number in it, the one used to call you: was that incoming call from your daughter's phone?'

Barry started to tear up. 'Yes. I thought it was her,' he said. 'Why didn't they just tell me then? They just said they'd found her phone, that's all, and that they'd be in touch again soon.'

DC Briggs squeezed his arm now. 'Mr Porter, I'm sorry, but our investigators needed to be absolutely sure it was your daughter before they informed you about what happened. But we needed to speed along the investigation, and do what we could. The first twenty-four hours can be crucial in a case such as this. If we want to catch whoever did this to her, I mean.'

Barry looked up at her now, his eyes wide, realising for the first time that she wasn't just dead, but that she may also have been the victim of a crime, that it might not have just been

CHAPTER TWO

some kind of accident.

'What happened to her?' he asked. 'Someone *did* this to her? What the hell happened?'

Walker stepped in now, and DC Briggs eased off, stepping back, letting him take over.

'We don't know what happened to her yet, Mr Porter, but rest assured we're going to do our very best to find out,' he said. 'For now, given the circumstances and the initial inspection of the scene, we'll be treating it as a suspicious death and, with your help, we'll be conducting a formal investigation.'

'Somebody hurt her?' said Charlotte's sister.

DC Briggs sat next to her, put an arm around her as her parents were too overcome with all-consuming grief to attend to the young girl's feelings at the moment, or to notice. 'And what's your name?' she asked.

'Sally,' said the girl.

'Okay, Sally. Here's what we're going to do. DCI Walker and myself will focus on finding out what happened to your sister, and you, you're going to stay here, stay off school, watch some TV, eat some ice-cream or biscuits, whatever you want, and keep an eye on your mum and dad. Can you do that? I'm sure your sister wasn't hurt much. She just hit her head, that's all, and lost consciousness. It's just like falling asleep.' DC Briggs had seen this kind of thing before and knew that children tended to be more resilient than adults. She'd be affected long-term, of course. It would affect her whole life. But in the short term, she'd probably do much better than her parents.

Sally nodded. 'Well, sleep *is* nice,' she said, before going and getting the remote for the TV in the adjoining, open-plan living room. DC Briggs looked at Walker, her eyes going a little wider, breathing a heavy sigh, before turning her attention back to Barry and Lizzy, who were still too overwhelmed with it all.

'Mr Porter, when you're ready, we're going to need to ask you a few questions about what went on last night, where you thought she'd gone, all of that, all the details. Can you do that?' asked Walker. Although he felt for them, would have liked to have offered to come back later when they'd had some time to digest the news, got themselves together a bit, he couldn't do that. He knew that a high percentage of female murder victims were killed by family members, and he needed to very quickly get a sense of whether there were any red flags here. If there was, giving them more time now could provide the killer with a chance to get their story straight, so he had to press on, even if he didn't like it.

DI Keane stood up, having been crouched down nearby Lizzy, offering support. 'I think they may need a little more time,' she said, her face scrunching up in empathy. 'They only just found out. It's too much.'

'No,' said Barry. 'If speeding things up is gunna help catch the bastard that did this, then we can answer any questions you have now. Whether you ask us reet now, or later, really makes no difference. It's still gunna be upsetting for us.'

'Are you sure?' asked Walker, glancing at the FLO for guidance, as she'd had more training than him in this department. What he did know was that if relatives were pushed too much and too soon, then they might resent the investigators and be resistant to working with them, thus compromising the outcome of the case; and he didn't want that.

DI Keane shrugged her shoulders, signalling for Walker to go ahead with his line of questioning, and got back down on

CHAPTER TWO

the floor with Mrs Porter, offering her emotional support once more.

Walker sat down with Barry, across from him, while DC Briggs sat next to Barry, probably so he might feel less like he was being interrogated, and more like he was being supported. DC Briggs was good with such details, Walker thought, and he appreciated it. It was all in the details.

'Okay, Mr Porter. First things first. What time did Charlotte leave here yesterday?' asked Walker.

He gave it some thought. 'I think it was about six-thirty. Lizzy. Did she leave at half six?' Lizzy didn't respond. *'Lizzy!'*

She snapped out of it. 'What? Yeah. Something like that,' she said. 'Went over to Jasmine's and said they were just meeting a couple of the other girls and hanging out at one of their houses.'

Walker looked at DC Briggs, and she took out her notepad and started making some notes. 'And do you know the names of these other girls?' he asked.

Mr Porter looked at his wife again, who had now eased off on the sobbing, and was engaged in the conversation. 'You talked to her before she left, didn't you?' he said. 'I was busy doing some dishes.'

'She wasn't specific about who, but she doesn't have that many friends. It was probably Daisy and Karen, or Lucy-Anne. You'll find their numbers in her phone,' said Lizzy.

'And what time was she supposed to come back?' asked Walker.

'Ten,' said Barry firmly, seeming glad to at least know the answer to that one. 'She always has to be back by ten.'

'And you didn't get any call, or anything. She just didn't turn up?' asked Walker.

'That's right. We started ringing around some of her friends when she still wasn't back just before eleven. Thought she might have missed her bus or something. Jasmine said she last saw her at the bus stop near the town centre, near Booths. About eight-thirty, I think she said. I drove out there, was out for a couple of hours, couldn't find any sign of her,' he said. 'So, when I got back—this was, like, one, one-thirty—we called the police, and some officers came over here to ask some questions.'

'I see. Are you getting all of this, DC Briggs?' asked Walker. DC Briggs nodded.

'And was there anything unusual about your daughter's behaviour yesterday, or in the preceding days and weeks? Anything that gave you cause for concern?' asked Walker.

'No, nothing at all,' said Barry.

'Mrs Porter?' asked Walker.

'No. She seemed fine. She's generally quite a happy girl, isn't she?' she said, realising she'd used the wrong tense now that her daughter was deceased, and correcting herself. 'I mean... she *was* quite happy.' Lizzy's face started to wobble as she held her emotions back for a few more seconds, before it became too much, and tears started to stream down her face once more.

'DCI Walker,' said DI Keane, urging him to wrap things up.

'We're almost done,' he said. 'Could I also ask if you were aware if Charlotte had a boyfriend?'

'No,' said Barry. 'She did not. Not that we were aware of, anyway.'

'She liked some boy who hangs around the town centre,' said Sally, who'd been listening in to the conversation all along and pretending to watch TV.

CHAPTER TWO

Walker looked across at her. 'Do you know his name? Or what he looks like? Anything at all?'

Sally shook her head. 'Sorry. I just heard her talking about him on the phone, that's all. Said he's "fit". That's all I know.'

Walker sighed, knowing they needed more to get anywhere with the case.

'I think we have all we need to be getting on with for now, Mr Porter. If we require anything else, we'll be in touch. I'm afraid we're going to have to hold your daughter's phone for the time being as evidence. However, rest assured you will be able to get it back once we're finished with our investigations,' said Walker.

'How long?' asked Barry.

'I'm sorry?' said Walker, not quite grasping what he was asking.

'How long before you catch the bastard that did this?' said Barry.

'You have my sincere word that we'll do our very best to find out what happened to your daughter, Mr Porter. For now, thank you for the information provided during this very difficult time. It's been very helpful. We'll be in touch.'

CHAPTER THREE

Mo Hussein looked out of his bedroom window from the semi-detached house on Barmoral Road in Chorley that he lived at, the house he'd occupied all his life. At eighteen years of age, he should have been excited about life—thrilled about what it might bring, and what he might go on to do in the coming years. He was undoubtably smart. He'd got good grades at school and was now studying for his A-levels at college, hoping to get into law school at one of the more prestigious British universities. But he'd somehow managed to completely mess it all up; or, at least, he thought he had.

His head was banging; he'd drunk way too much the night before. There were bits he couldn't remember—like how he'd got home at all in that state. He was dehydrated, short of sleep, but he didn't much care about that now. Stood, slumped over, elbows on the windowsill he watched some cars go by— just neighbours and delivery people coming and going. Time seemed to have no meaning. It slipped by without Mo being aware of it, his thoughts churning, obsessing. He wasn't sure how long he'd been there, in that position, but his arms had started to go numb.

When he'd turned sixteen, his parents had given him a

bit more freedom, had allowed him to stay out later and let himself in with his own key. They trusted him. He was a good boy, had rarely caused much trouble growing up, and they'd got used to him making his own way in the world, making his own choices. He was a third-generation immigrant of Pakistani origin, a British Pakistani, and his father had drummed into him from an early age the importance of education. And he'd listened. Not once had he got a bad report at school or failed a test. He was a model student. He did his chores at home without complaint, listened to his parents, took care of his two younger siblings—one brother and one sister—and generally made everyone very proud. However, it was all a hell of a lot of pressure to succeed and do well, and so now and again, he needed to release some of that pressure, to party and let his steady, short, well-groomed hair down a bit; to hang out and be a regular boy, have a drink even, listen to some music. His dad was always saying that alcohol was "the work of Satan", that it was *haram*, forbidden in Islam, that he should avoid it. But he was fed up with all these restrictions. It was taking things too far, he thought. Everyone had to let off a little steam now and again. And it wasn't something that came naturally to him either—having fun—but he was trying, and he thought he was getting better at it. Until last night, that was. Last night. *She* was there. The girl he used to sometimes walk to school with. He didn't really want to think about it, but how could he *not*.

He thought they'd been having a good time. It was great, in fact. For a while. He'd really blown away the cobwebs. Felt free. Felt liberated. But then it all started to turn sour. It had gone horribly wrong, somehow. They shouldn't have gone up there, to the Pike. It seemed like such a good idea at the time, but it was dark there, dangerous—especially when drinking. And then there had been the weed too. He shouldn't have been smoking that. Not with him pursuing a career in law. He couldn't risk getting a criminal record. It had been stupid. He knew that. But he'd earned a little stupid. He'd been too good all his life. Too responsible. He thought he could just be a little stupid, just for once, right? It seemed not. It seemed that one dumb mistake could ruin everything. And he was pretty sure he had.

'Mohammad! Are you not up yet?' It was his mother. It was 11am, which was late for Mo. She'd be getting concerned. If he didn't go down soon, start helping out, she'd come up for him, see the state he was in. And then she'd go get his father. He just needed a few more minutes to get himself together. Who was he kidding? A few more minutes wouldn't change anything. This would never be right. Nothing would ever be right ever again. This was one thing he couldn't fix.

'I'll be down soon, mama,' he shouted.

There was a pause. 'Well make sure you are,' she said.

He needed to talk to someone, get some advice. But he couldn't. It was something he was just going to have to live with.

He wondered if she might be alright—Charlotte. Whether it had looked worse than it was. *Maybe she was just wasted*, he thought. *Banged her head, got a concussion, slept it off.* She'd be fine. It must happen to teenagers all the time. They'd all be laughing about it soon, bragging about the crazy, mad, fun they had. *That's what teenagers do, don't they?* thought Mo. It was true, and would probably always be true, that the young ones tended to mess themselves up in a variety of creative ways, and then wear those scars like a badge of honour. Mo never really quite got it, though, what was so funny about it. But he was starting to think he'd overreacted about what happened. His mistake was leaving her there, all alone. She'd be furious if she saw him again. But he'd been wasted himself—could hardly stand up—his judgement compromised. He must have blacked out at some point. He had a memory of looking down at Charlotte, seeing blood and panicking, and then... things started to get a little patchy. The journey home was a blur.

Now that he'd started to convince himself it wasn't as bad as he'd first thought, Mo started to get dressed, put on some trousers and a T-shirt, ready to go downstairs. He tried to remember something about the journey home last night, anything, but all he could glimpse were the lights of traffic and road signs, and his head spinning and feeling sick.

His phone rang. It was his friend, Ben.

'Ben. How you doing?' asked Mo.

'Mo. We need to talk. Meet me at McDonald's in thirty,' said Ben.

Mo started to get a sinking feeling and his head started to spin again.

'I have to help my mama with some chores,' said Mo.

'*Mo.* We need to *talk*,' said Ben, before whispering, '*about last night.*'

Mo felt the blood drain from his face. 'I'll see you there,' he said, before hanging up the phone.

CHAPTER FOUR

'What am I looking at, DI Hogarth?' asked Walker. DI Hogarth was a largely desk-based DI, overweight and getting on a bit now at sixty-two, and likeable to most. He was normally based at Skelmersdale Police Station but had agreed to join the small team Walker had assembled at Chorley Police Station to work on the Charlotte Porter case. The Murder Investigation Team, for the time being, consisted of just Walker, DI Hogarth, and DC Briggs—who would also be based in Chorley for the duration of the case, having similarly been cherry picked from Skelmersdale, with no major crimes currently under investigation there. They all had experience of working murder investigations, and crucially they'd all worked together before, and Walker trusted them. He had it in mind that he might need to add to those numbers at some point, if the case became too complex for them to handle by themselves, but he'd see how it went first; there was no need to use up valuable resources if it wasn't strictly necessary. Hogarth was sitting in front of his computer, while Walker and DC Briggs hovered over him, hoping he had something concrete to go on to get them started.

'You're looking at CCTV footage of the bus stop where

CHAPTER FOUR

Charlotte was last seen,' said DI Hogarth. His style of speech was slow and laid back, almost lazy, but Walker had long since got used to it and secretly quite liked its calming influence. 'We confirmed with... a *Jasmine Jones*—the deceased's best friend—that she last saw Charlotte and left her alone at this bus stop just across from Booths supermarket in Chorley town centre, a place where the victim intended to make her way home to Pennine Road. Her statement is supported by this footage. See.'

Walker and DC Briggs watched as two girls walked into the frame, one of them Charlotte Porter, and the other Jasmine Jones. They appeared to have a quick chat, before embracing, and Charlotte was left alone at the bus stop, sitting down and looking at her phone.

'I'll speed things up a bit now,' said DI Hogarth, 'as nothing happens for the next few minutes.' He sped up the footage until a car arrived and parked in front of the bus stop. The time stamp on the video said 8:37pm. 'Note that a red Ford Focus, 2011 model, comes into view. Footage isn't great though, very low quality—it's from an old camera—and reflections from the streetlights mean we can't see inside the car, unfortunately, even if we try and clean it up. It's very grainy. However, what we can see is that there's been some damage to the offside front door—a very obvious dent.'

'Yeah. I can see that. And she's talking to someone,' said Walker. Charlotte could be seen getting up into a standing position, moving closer to the car, chatting. After a minute or so, she willingly got into the car and it sped off, leaving the bus stop vacant. 'Wait. Go back.'

DI Hogarth rewound the footage to the point just before where Charlotte got in the car, and played it again.

'She got in the back,' said Walker. 'On the passenger side, but in the *back* seat.'

'She did indeed,' said DI Hogarth. 'I didn't spot that on the first play, from the angle we have. Good catch.'

'So, there was more than one person in the car then,' said DC Briggs.

'It seems that way,' said Walker. 'Unless there was something on the front seat, which there definitely could have been. We can't assume anything. But I would expect a driver to remove any items from the front passenger seat for any guest if the rest of the car was empty. Is there anything else?'

DI Hogarth nodded and tapped a key on his computer to flick to footage of another location. 'Same car going past McDonalds on the A6, headed towards the home of the deceased. Then we have a right onto Stump Lane,' another tap of the keyboard, 'also still going in that direction. Car stops just out of frame of the appropriately named "Stump Lane Store", which sells beers, wines, and spirits. Amazingly, never once do we catch sight of the registration plate of the vehicle; we get side view on all footage. However...' DI Hogarth turned around for a second, which was something of an effort for his chunky frame, his range of motion not being the best, everything creaking and moaning as he moved and looked directly at Walker and DC Briggs. He raised his eyebrows up and down, twice, appearing pleased with himself.

'What?' said Walker. 'Get on with it.'

DI Hogarth turned back and tapped on his keyboard one more time. There was now a view of the *inside* of the shop, showing a customer stood at the counter, paying for some booze—more specifically, some beers, some Smirnoff Cherry Drop vodka, and one bottle of Monkey Shoulder Blended

CHAPTER FOUR

Malt Scotch Whisky. DI Hogarth hit the space bar on his laptop to pause the action.

Walker grabbed the laptop, got the screen right up to his face, took a good look at it. What he saw was a boy, of Asian ethnicity, skinny, short hair, paying for the goods with cash.

'Take it easy with that,' said DI Hogarth, struggling to his feet and snatching the laptop back, a bit annoyed, sitting back down again and putting it on the desk in front of him.

'We need to find out who this boy is, pronto,' said Walker. 'Did you talk to the shop owner yet? Do they know him? Or do any of the deceased's friends know anyone with a car of that description?'

'Shame he didn't pay by card,' said DC Briggs.

'Wait,' said DI Hogarth. There's more. He hit the space bar again and resumed the action. Before the shopkeeper accepted the money as payment, he said something to the boy and the young lad took out something: a *card*. 'I talked to the shop owner. He was asking for ID. The boy had some: a CitizenCard.'

Walker took a deep breath. 'And does the shopkeeper remember his name by any chance?'

DI Hogarth paused, milking the moment like he so often did. He was a tech geek, and he loved his job and finding something to help along a case like this. He lived for it. 'He does,' he said. 'Was easy to remember, memorable,' he said. 'It's *Mohammad Ali Hussein*. Like the boxer meeting the tyrant, the shopkeeper said. Said it would have been a hell of a fight.'

'Mohammad Ali Hussein,' said Walker. 'Address?'

DI Hogarth handed Walker a sticky note with an address printed on it and a telephone number of the landline to that address. Walker took it, had a look.

'You could have just opened with this,' said Walker.

'But that wouldn't have been any fun,' said DI Hogarth, smiling. 'And you needed to see the evidence trail first anyway. It's important. I knew it wouldn't take long.'

'Fine. Right then, DC Briggs,' said Walker. 'You driving again? We've got work to do.'

'No problem, Chief,' said DC Briggs. 'Let's go bring him in.'

'Oh, don't get too excited yet, Detective,' said Walker. 'It's never that easy. Never, ever. We've got nothing yet, just a guy giving a girl a lift and buying some drinks, that's all. Ain't no crime in that, now, is there?'

CHAPTER FIVE

Walker and DC Briggs arrived at Barmoral Road, the home of Mohammad Ali Hussein, in the grey unmarked Audi A6 sedan they were using for field work. Although the semi-detached residence had a paved driveway, there was no car parked in it, no red Ford Focus, 2011 model. DC Briggs parked their car at the front of the house, halfway on the pavement and the road, as there were no parking restrictions. It was a nice-looking street as far as Chorley went, not a bad place to grow up and just a short walk to the town centre.

They got out of the car and as they were approaching the house, the photophobic Walker—wearing Ray-Ban sunglasses despite it being an overcast November—saw a curtain twitch from one of the upstairs bedrooms. He'd been sensitive to light ever since his two bouts of meningitis and associated encephalitis, and it wasn't showing any sign of abating.

'Someone just saw us,' he said to DC Briggs. 'Do me a favour and go around the back, would you?'

'Sir?' asked DC Briggs.

'Don't want any runners. My back is already a bit out of whack from that bloody hike,' he said.

'Hike? We only went up a few steps,' said DC Briggs, looking at him, smiling. 'You need a little gym work, sir. I'll go around, come back in five minutes when you have everything nailed down.'

DC Briggs quietly opened an unlocked low wooden gate and headed around the side of the residence, leaving Walker to knock on the door. He did so with his customary three rhythmic wraps, before spotting a doorbell and giving that a couple of presses as well, hearing it *ding dong*.

A woman of South Asian origin came to the door. She was attractive but getting older now in her forties or more, with a couple of greys showing up in her long, shiny, dark hair.

'Can I help you?' she asked, in a largely local accent, but with just a touch of the cadence of her family's origins, which she'd naturally have picked up as a child.

'Yes. I'm looking for a Mohammad Ali Hussein. I am Chief Detective Inspector Jonathan Walker from Chorley CID. May I come in please?' asked Walker.

'Mo!' shouted the woman. 'What's this all about, Mr Walker?' She was blunt, to the point, no messing around.

'If I could just come inside, we can talk about it. My colleague will also be joining us shortly,' said Walker, 'so you can leave the door open.'

The woman eyed Walker's CID identity card that he had hanging around his neck by a lanyard for convenience. 'May I?' she asked. 'You can't be too careful these days.' Walker removed the ID card and handed it to her for inspection. 'Mo! Get down here, *now*,' she shouted, again, before taking a good look at the card and handing it back to DCI Walker, satisfied with its authenticity.

A young boy came down the stairs, sheepish looking. Walker recognised him as the boy on the CCTV footage at the Stump

CHAPTER FIVE

Lane Store.

'What is it, ammi?' the boy said. 'Who's this?'

'Come in, Mr Walker,' said the woman. 'We can sit at the dining table. I'll make you some tea if you like. I have some doodh pati chai. It's a Pakistani tea you can try, and some sweet biscuits. It's very good. Shall I make two, one ready for your colleague as well?'

'Mama, who is it?' said Mo again. 'One of those salesmen?' he asked, with some hope.

'No. Mr Walker is not selling anything,' said his mother. 'He's a policeman.'

Mo reached the bottom of the stairs and put his head down, avoiding eye contact with Walker. 'Oh,' was all he said, before helping to sustain an awkward silence.

'Some tea sounds great, Mrs Hussein,' said Walker. 'We're just making some initial inquiries about a nearby incident at the moment, gathering some information. Your help would be much appreciated.'

'I see. But my name is Maira Arain. I did not take my husband's family name when we got married,' said the woman, as she took Walker through to the dining room, leaving the front door slightly ajar.

Walker took a seat and got settled.

'I'll make the tea,' said Maira. 'Mo, can you help me, then we can talk to the detective together. Would you mind, Mr Walker? I'd like to be present while you speak with my boy, if that's okay, hear what is said.'

'That would be fine,' said Walker. Mo looked nervous, rattled. 'I see there's no car in the driveway, Mrs Arain. 'Is your husband out?'

'Yes. He's at work. Getting the family restaurant up and

running for the day, "The Blue Elephant" we called it. Have you been there?' she asked. 'It's got 4.7 out of five on Trustpilot, over three hundred reviews.'

'No. Can't say I have,' said Walker, who didn't know what Trustpilot was, but could hazard a guess. Technology wasn't his strongest point, which was why he needed tech savvy people like DI Hogarth around him, along with younger and naturally more tech-oriented folks like DC Briggs. 'Is that near the Stump Lane Store?'

Mo seemed to physically jolt at hearing the name, the very store he'd been seen on CCTV buying the same drinks that were found at the crime scene.

'No. It's over near Hall Bakery, just around the corner from Foster Street,' she said.

'You don't have any other cars? Mo doesn't drive?' asked Walker.

'No. We only have one car, and my husband currently has it,' she said.

'May I ask the make and model of the car, and the colour, please?' asked Walker.

'Yes. Of course. It's a black Volkswagen Golf 2.0, 2015 model,' said Maira. 'It was only two years old when we got it. Mo, come on. Let's get the nice detective some tea and biscuits.'

Mrs Arain and her son went into an adjoining kitchen, leaving Walker alone. He was disappointed not to have seen a red Ford Focus, 2011 model on the driveway, one with a dent in the door, as this could have provided a rich source of evidence for the investigation, given that the deceased had been in that car just hours before her death. However, they had the next best thing for the time being: the young man

CHAPTER FIVE

who'd got out of that car and gone to buy some alcoholic beverages. Even if Mo hadn't been involved in the events just prior to Charlotte Porter's death, he would certainly know something of her whereabouts leading up to that event. They just had to get that information out of him. Walker was pretty sure he was going to bring him in to the station for further questioning, at the very least, but he wanted a more casual chat in the boy's home environment first, just to see if any information could be more easily extracted that way. The boy was nervous, and his mother seemed to have some power over him, so Walker wondered whether that might be an asset he could exploit to get him talking.

While Maira and her son were busy making the tea in the adjoining kitchen, with the door closed over, Walker could hear them having a heated, yet hushed conversation, the sound muffled further by the boiling kettle. In the meantime, DC Briggs returned, closing the front door after her.

'In here,' shouted Walker.

'Oh, there you are?' said DC Briggs. 'He home?'

'Yeah. In the kitchen with his mother, making some tea,' said Walker. 'Something ethnic. Sounds good.'

DC Briggs raised her eyebrows and took a seat next to Walker.

'Anything yet?' she asked.

'No. Not really. The boy looks scared though. Something's definitely amiss,' said Walker.

Maira and Mo returned to the dining room, each holding two cups of doodh pati chai Pakistani tea on saucers, each with two sweet cumin biscuits on the side.

'Looks great,' said Walker. 'Thank you. You get this imported?' He was just making small talk, trying to establish some kind of rapport.

'No. You can get almost anything in England these days. There's an Asian grocer's over near the train station,' she said. 'We get the tea from there. And the biscuits too,' she said, as her and Mo sat down across from them.

'So...?' she asked.

'Mohammad,' said Walker, looking at Mo right in the eyes for the first time. Mo looked at him but couldn't maintain eye contact for more than a second. 'We need to know where you were last night, and what happened?'

'He was studying at a cafe,' said his mother. 'Weren't you?'

Mo forced a smile and reluctantly shook his head. Maira gave him a slap on the head and then looked at the detective, probably not sure if she'd broken a law or not. Walker let it go. She said something foreign—probably Urdu—and Mo responded with a short reply in the same language.

'He told me he was going to a cafe,' she said. 'The Majestic Coffee Lounge. He tells me he can concentrate better there while he studies with some background noise, and that the wi-fi is good. I trusted him.'

'I was there, mama. But I went for a little walk afterwards, to clear my head,'

said Mo, looking at the detective, likely hoping Walker didn't have anything on him, and that he was just making some initial inquiries. But Walker *did* have something.

'Mo, we have you on CCTV at the Stump Lane Store over on Stump Lane, buying a considerable amount of alcohol, seen getting out of a red Ford Focus. Can you tell us about that, please? It's important.'

Maira this time grabbed her boy by his black polo shirt collar. 'What have you been doing? *Budhoo!* Buying alcohol?

You know that's forbidden in the—'

'I didn't do anything illegal,' said Mo, stubbornly. 'I'm eighteen. I was just doing someone a favour.'

Walker stood up. It seemed his mother wouldn't be much help after all. 'I'm afraid we're going to need to take you in for questioning, Mohammad, at the police station in Chorley.'

'What? What for?' said Maira. 'What about the tea?'

'We're going to need to talk to the boy on his own,' said Walker. 'Sorry about the tea.'

'But I'm his mother,' said Maira.

'He's not a minor,' said Walker. 'We can interview him without you.'

'Mama?' said Mo, clearly panicking at the thought of being taken from his mother and his home and being put into a police car—albeit an unmarked one.

Maira now put her arm around her boy, bringing him close, seeing the fear in his eyes that they all saw. 'It'll be okay, Mo-Mo. I'll get a lawyer. You don't say anything until he arrives, you hear me?' she said.

'Okay,' said Mo.

'Nothing,' she said. 'Wait until he arrives, you got that?'

'Got it, mama,' he said, looking at Walker and DC Briggs.

'Time to go,' said Walker, hurrying things along. 'We'll be in touch, Mrs Arain. Mohammad, shall we?'

CHAPTER SIX

Now sitting in an interview room at Chorley Police Station, Mohammad Ali Hussein waited while his lawyer arrived, arranged by his mother. He was with Walker and DC Briggs who were waiting patiently, having purposefully been in the room with Mo beforehand to intimidate him, just a little, saying nothing and staring at him. Walker was hoping Mo would crack under the pressure, tell them everything. What he didn't want was for his lawyer to get any time alone with him, tell him to conduct a 'no comment' interview. However, it was likely the lawyer would request a brief initial private consultation with his client first, although Walker was holding out some hope he wouldn't, probably thinking it was a misdemeanour he was dealing with rather than an investigation into a possible homicide. That would no doubt come as a bit of a surprise. This kind of thing didn't happen too often in Chorley. The boy looked harmless—skinny, shy-looking, way out of his depth. He didn't look long from leaving school, despite their background checks confirming he recently turned eighteen and was already well into his A-Levels at college. He definitely appeared young for his age. Walker's instincts told him that if the boy was responsible for the death of Charlotte Porter, then it was most likely an accident—perhaps some drunken sex gone wrong. But there was a long way to go in the investigation before they could come to such a conclusion.

After some considerable delay, there was a knock on the door.

'Enter,' said Walker.

It was Mohammad's lawyer. 'Sorry I'm late. Traffic on the M6 coming up.' The man was of Asian ethnicity, overweight, sweaty, with a grey pin-striped suit that was a size too small and a touch cheap-looking, and well worn. He spoke with a more refined, southern accent, but with a subtle hint of the typical retroflex of South Asian English speakers, a habit he'd probably tried hard to eliminate, but which was still there for those who paid attention to such things—and Walker did. He seemed clumsy, in a rush, fumbling with his briefcase. 'My name is Hari Singh. I'll be assisting young Mohammad throughout this interview. Is he under arrest or just here for questioning?'

'We've just brought him in for questioning for the time being, under caution,' said Walker, knowing that he would soon upgrade that to arrest status if the boy implicated himself in the death of Charlotte Porter any further. 'Please take a seat.'

Mr Singh sat down and took out some papers and a pen from his leather briefcase. 'I'm going to need a couple of minutes just to discuss things with my client,' he said. 'If you wouldn't mind.'

Walker nodded, and he and DC Briggs stood up, getting ready to leave the room.

'It's okay,' said Mo. 'I know what's going on. I'm going to study law at university. I want to be a lawyer, just like you.'

'I see. But even so,' said Mr Singh. 'It would be prudent if I could just have a little chat with you first, clarify a few things.'

Mo thought for a second and then nodded.

'As you wish,' said Walker. 'We'll come back in five minutes. Is that sufficient?'

Mr Singh nodded, and Walker and DC Briggs left the room, closed the door behind them, waited outside in the corridor.

'A law student, eh? That might make things a little more difficult,' said DC Briggs.

'We'll see,' said Walker. 'Maybe he'll get cocky, trip himself up.'

'Maybe. But I have to say, that boy in there doesn't look like he could hurt a fly,' said DC Briggs. 'And I'm not sure how comfortable he would be around girls either. He couldn't even look me in the eye. What do you think, Chief?'

'I'm thinking... that car he got out of wasn't his, and it wasn't the girl's. So, either he stole it, or someone else must have been involved. I'm thinking the latter. A law student wouldn't risk their whole future on lifting a car for a bit of fun. Not in my book, anyway. We need to find out who owns that car, and at present, only Mo can help us out with that. Perhaps a friend? Or someone they both know?'

The door to the interview room opened again, and the face of Mr Singh was there.

'All ready,' he said. 'My client is more than willing to cooperate with your investigation. He's done nothing wrong.'

Walker and DC Briggs shared a look, re-entered the interview room, and sat down.

'We're going to audio-record the interview, for the record.' Walker switched on a device to begin recording. 'First, the bad news. I'm afraid a young lady who you may know has been found dead—a Charlotte Porter. Our investigation and this interview are in relation to her passing.'

Mr Singh suddenly shuffled around with some papers, seeming a little flummoxed, evidently realising he wasn't going to be having an easy morning with a youth misdemeanour after all.

'I see,' said Mr Singh, eyeing his client for any reaction. Mo already appeared to be in a state of panic. 'Proceed.'

'Mohammad, can you first tell me if you know Charlotte Porter?' asked Walker.

'Yes, I know her,' said Mo. 'We went to school together at Parklands. We occasionally walked home together, but she mostly got the bus as she said it was a bit far to her house. I'm not sure exactly where she lived. Charlotte is *dead?*'

'Yes, I'm afraid so. That's correct, Mo,' said Walker. 'Can you tell me when the last time you saw Charlotte Porter was?'

Mo swallowed, hard, and looked at his lawyer.

'If you've done nothing wrong, Mohammad, you may proceed,' said Mr Singh, 'with caution.'

'I saw her last night,' said Mo, before quickly following up with, 'but she was fine when I last saw her.'

'Well, she's not fine now, Mo. She's currently in a mortuary awaiting a full autopsy. Please could you describe for us the circumstances in which you met Charlotte last night,' said Walker.

'I was walking home from a café. I'd been studying there. I find it easier to concentrate in that kind of environment. Anyway, it wasn't too late when I finished, so I took the long way around as I fancied stretching my legs. I crossed this one road, and a car came around a corner a bit too quickly and almost hit me. The guy driving got out to check if I was okay. He offered me a lift home, and I was a bit shook up, so I thought, *why not?* I didn't feel like walking any more. I got in, and on the way, he stopped again next to some girl at the bus stop. It was Charlotte. Apparently, he knew her somehow, and I did too, which seemed quite a coincidence. He dropped me off at home and went off with Charlotte. That's all I know,' said Mo. 'I'm sorry. I don't know who he was.'

'I see. And you didn't do anything else on the way or stop off anywhere?' asked Walker. Walker knew damned well that he did, of course. He was testing the boy.

'No. I was tired. He just dropped me off near home,' said Mo.

Walker looked at DC Briggs and took out a laptop from his briefcase, removed it from the protective foam sleeve. He opened it up and double clicked on a video file, bringing up some CCTV footage from the Stump Lane Store, and then turned the computer at an angle so Mo and his lawyer could also see, before clicking 'play' on the video.

'For the record, we're seeing CCTV footage of the Stump Lane Store on Stump Lane in Chorley, taken on November 12th, 2022, at 8:42pm. Note the customer being served can be seen to be one Mohammad Ali Hussein, also identified by the store clerk from the National ID Citizencard that was shown as proof of age for the purchase of alcoholic goods,' said Walker. 'Mohammad, can you confirm that this is you? Do you recall being at the Stump Lane Store last night?'

'Oh. Yes, of course. Sorry. I'd forgotten about that. They stopped off at the store to get some beers and other drinks. The driver gave me some cash and asked me to go get it for them. He wanted to stay with the car, as it wasn't parked in the best spot,' said Mo.

CHAPTER SIX

'I see. And yet you just said you didn't stop anywhere else, other than picking Charlotte up at the bus stop,' said Walker.

'Sorry. I had a busy day. It was just a few minutes in the shop and the drinks weren't even for me. I forgot. I'm still a bit tired,' said Mo. 'And it's stressful being here.'

'I see. Do you have a habit of getting in strangers' cars, Mr Hussein,' asked Walker. 'Seems a little ill-advised for a law student.'

'No. But the guy driving was around the same age as me, maybe a bit older, and we got chatting a bit first. He seemed okay. I thought I could handle myself,' said Mo. 'He was friendly.'

DC Briggs leaned forward. 'Mo, is there anything else you're not telling us?' she asked. 'You need to tell us everything you know now, so you don't get in any trouble later. Can you do that for me? Did anything else happen that you've not already told us?' Her voice was soft, caring. It made people want to respond.

Mo thought about it and shook his head. 'No. That's it,' he said.

Walker brought a Google Map up on the computer of the Chorley area and zoomed in on the town centre. 'Mo, can you show me exactly where the café is that you frequented, where this car almost hit you on the way back, where you went next to come across Charlotte, and then which way you drove to the Stump Lane Store?' he asked.

Mo leaned forwards and pointed on the map. I went to this café, The Majestic Coffee Lounge. I left about eight-thirty and walked up here. I crossed the road, a car came around the corner a bit quick and almost hit me. We had a chat, I got in, and then we drove this way, toward the bus stop that Charlotte was waiting at, *here*. We picked her up, drove some more, this way, stopped at the Stump Lane Store, and then back this way, where I was dropped off here near my home,' he said, pointing at different spots on the map as he was speaking.

Walker leaned back in his chair. 'And the make and model of the car?' he asked.

'I'm not sure. I'm not really interested in cars that much,' said Mo.

Walker clicked on a tab on the browser and brought up a picture of a red Ford Focus, 2011 model. 'Did it look anything like this?' he asked.

Mo squinted his eyes, seeming a bit rattled—even more than before. 'Yes. I think so,' he said, his voice shaky.

'You may go soon, Mo. But we may be in touch again if we have any further questions,' said Walker. 'Before you do go, though, I'll need you to provide a detailed description of the driver of that car to my colleague, DC Briggs, and a sketch artist who'll be with her, and tell them any other details you might remember about the car or that person, or any subjects you talked about. Please take your time and provide as much information as you can. You'll also need to provide a swab for DNA testing.' He looked across to DC Briggs to make sure she understood. The cans and bottles they'd collected from the crime scene might have had DNA on them, and he wanted to see if there might be any matches to young Mo. DC Briggs nodded her understanding. 'And I'm so sorry for the loss of your friend,' said Walker.

Mo looked down, sheepishly. 'Yes, me too,' he said, looking genuinely upset and perturbed about the whole thing. But to Walker, something didn't feel quite right about the whole thing, and he was damned if he wasn't going to find out what

CHAPTER SIX

that was.

CHAPTER SEVEN

Walker was sitting in the Incident Room at Chorley Police Station going through some documents for the case when DC Briggs entered, parked herself near him. He looked up at her, over the glasses that rested on his slightly wonky, once broken nose; during his early days of working as a PC, long before he'd joined CID and become a detective and then later a Detective Chief Inspector, he'd been headbutted by a drunk and disorderly. The incident had given him a deviated septum, which occasionally, on a bad day, like this, gave his voice a degree of hypernasality—a slightly stuffy quality, making him sound like he had a bit of a cold, even if he didn't. It was something he'd got used to.

'Get anything more?' he asked, his eyes wide, receptive, hoping for something to go off. He'd asked DC Briggs to talk to the boy to get some more details after the initial interview as he thought the lad might open up a bit more to her and be less intimidated. It was the old *good cop bad cop* routine, which although was a bit of a TV cliché, actually did still work in the real world—although typically to a subtler degree.

'Some,' said DC Briggs. 'Got a good description of the car driver. He remembered quite a lot. The sketch artist is finishing up the visual as we speak. I also took the DNA swab

CHAPTER SEVEN

and sent it off for analysis—so that's done. And he confirmed the car had a dent in the door, but he couldn't remember anything about the registration plate, which isn't surprising. Few people do.'

'He's lying,' said Walker.

'Sir?' asked DC Briggs.

'Well, maybe not about the car registration, but I've been in this game long enough to know when someone is lying,' said Walker. 'And that kid was. At least, he was lying about some of it. Something was off about it—way off.'

'I know what you mean. I felt that a bit too, but I'd just put it down to nerves—what with him being such a young lad and having his first experience at a police station. It can put the best of people on edge, can't it, make them act in a way they normally wouldn't, make them seem guilty of something even when they're not sometimes. Or he's hiding something smaller, perhaps, because he's afraid of his mum, like not studying when he was supposed to be. Anyhow, we have nothing tangible on him as yet, do we, so what are we going to do?' said DC Briggs. 'Should I bring him back? Do you want to question him some more?'

Walker thought about it. 'No. Let him go home for now. We need to corroborate his story, or disprove it, as the case may be. The most obvious place to start is to look at those areas on the map he spoke of, see if there's any more CCTV footage available. We need to see him at those times and places he mentioned, either by video footage, or through witnesses—the latter of which is going to be difficult, so let's try going with the former for now. You and DI Hogarth get on that, share the workload, get it done as soon as possible. Also, talk to the staff at that café, see if they can pin down exactly when

Mo left. In the meantime, I'm going back up to Rivington, having a good walk around, see if I can spot anything, maybe talk to a few people—see if anyone saw anything. Let's meet back here in, say, three hours, and then review, see what we have, formulate a plan of action then.'

'No problem, Chief,' said DC Briggs, looking at her watch. 'Sounds like a solid plan. I'm on it. See you in three then.'

* * *

Walker parked his unmarked Audi pool car in the car park of The Great House Barn tearoom, a 16th century listed building and converted barn in Rivington, a popular base for walkers going to and from Winter Hill and the Pike Tower. The Tudor-style timber-framed porch and mullion windows provided a grand feeling to what was essentially a café and small gift shop, and this contrasted a little with the Go Ape Rivington adventure park office—a much tackier kind of establishment—at the end of the car park, just beyond the barn café. He'd start with the tearoom, have a word with the staff there, see if they'd seen or heard anything, and get a non-caffeinated, lactose-free beverage while he was there. He was parched.

He entered the café and approached the serving desk. There wasn't much of a queue, as it was getting near closing time, so it didn't take long.

'Could I have one decaffeinated coffee please, to go?' said Walker. 'Flat white, made with oat milk, please, if possible. And a quick word as well, if you wouldn't mind.'

'One flat white, decaf, with oat milk coming up,' said the

member of staff serving him, a young male with dark curly hair, typically lean for his age, cool-looking, if Walker even knew what *cool* looked like anymore. 'Sorry. What do you wanna talk about?'

'I'm Detective Chief Inspector Walker of the Lancashire Constabulary,' said Walker, putting his ID card a little closer to the lad serving him, the card that was hanging on a lanyard around his neck as per usual.

The young man, who Walker could now see was called 'Zack' via a sticker he had on his chest, squinted. 'Sorry. I had to take my contacts out today. They were itching too much. Bloomin' things. Is this about what happened up at the Pike?' he asked.

'There has indeed been an incident up near the Pike Tower today, that is correct,' said Walker. 'What do you know about it?'

'Not much,' said Zack. 'Some of the hikers have been talking about how it's been taped off, that's all. Nobody allowed up there, or something. Police everywhere. Has someone been hurt? We do get the odd accident up there.'

'I'm afraid we're not currently discussing the case,' said Walker. 'Just making routine enquiries at the moment. Did you see anything yesterday, anything that seemed suspicious or odd? Anything out of the ordinary?'

'Not really,' said Zack, who continued to prepare Walker's coffee as they spoke. 'I bumped into someone I knew from school. And a woman's dog threw up in the café, which I had to clean up. That's about it.'

'And the person you knew from school,' said Walker. 'Who was that?'

Zack looked up at Walker for a second, before returning his attention to the coffee. 'A guy called Wilko. I forget his real name. A bit of an oddball—one of those outcast types. Hung around with similar oddball kids, geeks and stinkers, as we used to call them. I still said "hi" though, asked him how he was,' said Zack. 'Just to be polite. We are all grown up now, after all.'

'And how was he?' asked Walker.

'Dunno. Said he was bored, needed a party or something,' said Zack. 'Then he left with some snacks he bought. I don't remember what. We get hundreds of orders here every day.'

'And you really can't remember his full name?' asked Walker.

Zack thought about it. 'I'm not that good with names,' he said. 'That's what everyone called him—*Wilko*. I was never actually in the same class as him, just in the same year.'

'And your full name is?' asked Walker.

'I'm Zachery David Statham,' said Zack.

Walker took out a notepad and small pen, made some notes. 'And which school did you attend?' he asked.

'Parklands,' said Zack. 'In Chorley.'

Parklands. The very same school that Mo and Charlotte attended together. Walker didn't like coincidences and wondered whether there might be something here.

'What did he look like now, this Wilko character?' asked Walker.

'Er... I don't know,' said Zack. 'A bit taller than average, I suppose, a bit rough looking, longish hair, a hoodie, I think, and he was wearing glasses.'

'And when did you both leave school?' asked Walker.

'Three years ago,' said Zack.

That meant Wilko was a year older than Mo, and three years older than Charlotte, Walker noted.

'Zack, would you drop by Chorley Police Station after your

shift ends today, so we can get a sketch artist to draw up a picture of this Wilko person, based on your description of him. It's better if you work directly with them, so they can change and fine-tune the image as you go. You're not in any trouble, not by any means. We just need a good picture of this person of interest, so we can track them down,' said Walker, putting his notepad away again. 'It may be important.'

Zack handed Walker his coffee. 'Sure,' he said. 'I can do that. No problem.'

'And what time will that be?' asked Walker.

'Er, I could make it about six,' he said. 'I'll come on my bike.'

'Excellent. I'll see you there myself, personally, at six o'clock then,' said Walker, turning to leave.

Zack nodded. 'Five fifty?' he said.

'Six will be just fine, Zack. I have a few things to do here first,' said Walker.

'No, I mean... the *coffee*. It's five pounds fifty,' he said. 'You never paid for it.'

Walker rolled his eyes, annoyed with himself. He prided himself on noticing the little things, all the little details that most people missed. But since his illness, he'd started to get more forgetful, had periods of the sort of fogginess he was currently experiencing. He took out his debit card and touched the card terminal with it, paying contactless. It bleeped and accepted his payment. 'Sorry,' he said, turning once more, but then stopping in his tracks. 'This Wilko guy—do you remember if *he* paid by card?'

'Ah. That I do remember,' said Zack, 'because not many people pay with cash these days, and he did. I didn't have the right change, so I had to ask a customer to split a five-pound note for some pound coins.'

'I see. And did Wilko say anything else, anything at all?' asked Walker.

'Not really. But he did ask about a map for the Pike, and I directed him to the Visitor Centre on the other side of this building, just a bit further up,' said Zack. 'If that's any help.'

Walker nodded. 'It is. Thank you, Zack. That's very helpful. I'll see you later on then at the station. I'm sure you can find the address online. In the meantime, try to think of anything else that you didn't mention just now, anything at all. It might be important.'

'Will do,' said Zack. 'Will do.'

* * *

Walker approached the Great House Information Centre and sat down just outside on a slightly crenulated, cool and moist stone wall, taking the weight off his feet for a second while he made a call on his mobile.

'DC Briggs? You got anything yet?' asked Walker.

'Chief. Hi. We're doing our best here, but nothing as yet. You?' she asked.

'Maybe,' said Walker. 'I need you to pull some records on Parklands, the school Mo and Charlotte went to. I just met someone else who went to the same school, says he saw another ex-student up here recently, someone called Wilko. I need to know who that is. It would be a person of interest, given their connection at the same school, and the fact that he was seen up here just yesterday.'

'Well, I could do that. But I'd hazard a guess this would be

CHAPTER SEVEN

Alex Wilkinson,' said DC Briggs. 'Ran into him a few times as a PC, some minor offences, but nothing serious. He went to Parklands. Got suspended a couple of times.'

Walker paused for a few seconds, not expecting that. 'Great. Then we need to talk to him,' he said. 'I'm meeting the guy who identified him at the station around six. Try to get this Wilko there as well, for the same time, would you, so we can talk to them both. And find out if he's a registered driver, and if so, what kind of car he owns.'

'Will do, Chief,' said DC Briggs. 'Is that all?'

'Yes, that's all for now, Detective,' said Walker. 'You may go.'

He put his phone away and stood back up, looking at the building of the Visitor Centre—a quaint two-storey stone build with a slate roof. The entrance to the Information Centre consisted of a small door with a steep, slightly winding staircase, but he made it up there with a few deep breaths, resolving to get in shape soon, just as DC Briggs had suggested.

He opened the door and a traditional shopkeepers' bell chimed, and inside, there were various items for sale, along with a collection of information leaflets and maps, some of which could be taken for free. There was nobody in there except for the person behind a counter, a young woman, slim, with blonde hair and a nose stud.

'Can I help you?' she asked.

'Yes. I'm DCI Walker, just making some routine enquiries about an incident on the Pike last night,' he said, holding up his ID card. 'Someone may have come in here yesterday, a young man, looking for a map of the Pike. I know you must get a lot of people in here, but—'

'I think I know who you might be talking about,' she said. 'Some arsehole came on to me, asked me if I wanted to party, was leering at me, looking down at my boobs, not even trying to be subtle about it.'

Walker made a conscious, concerted effort not to look down and kept focussed on the girl's eyes, but even without looking directly, he could see her breasts were ample, and she wore a tight T-shirt that might draw such unwanted attention.

'And what did you tell him?' asked Walker.

'I politely told him I wasn't interested. I was a little scared, actually—the place was empty except for him, just like it is now,' she said.

'And then he left?' asked Walker.

'Yes. Took a photo of a map with his mobile, said he didn't want to pay for it. Then he tried to get a snap of me as well, and laughed, said he was going to deepfake it for being so frigid or something,' she said. 'Arsehole.'

'*Deepfake*? What's that?' asked Walker.

The girl looked at Walker, probably realising just how old and out of touch he was. 'It's when you put a person's face on another person's body, like a pornstar, but it looks really real. I almost rang the police, but decided it wasn't worth it. Anybody can do that kind of thing these days—just grab one of your online photos and make it look like you've done almost anything. It's the world we live in, I'm afraid. There's no point in sweatin' about it.'

'I see,' said Walker. 'Well, we're going to catch up to him soon, have a word about that, and a few other things.'

'Good,' said the girl. 'I hope he gets in trouble.'

'And you are? Just in case we need to contact you again,' said Walker.

'I'm Cindy. Cindy Morrison,' she said. 'Would you like anything else, Detective? A map, perhaps?'

'Yes. I could use a map, actually,' said Walker. 'I'm going to take a walk around.'

'Then take this one,' she said. 'On the house.'

'Much appreciated. Thank you, Cindy,' said Walker, turning to leave. 'Oh, just one more thing: is there any CCTV here?'

'Afraid not,' said Cindy. 'Not much to steal.'

'I see. Well, thanks again. I'll be on my way now. You've been a great help.'

CHAPTER EIGHT

Benjamin Jackson was sitting at a table at the McDonald's in Chorley, nervously twisting a napkin, checking his mobile phone every few seconds for any missed calls or texts. He'd been waiting for Mo for over two hours now and had only stayed there because he didn't know what else to do or where else to go. He was lost, getting sucked into a rabbit hole of his own making, a vortex that just wouldn't let go. In a word, he was *twitchy*, and his anxieties were starting to get the better of him, eating him up from the inside out.

'*Where the hell are you, Mo?*' he muttered to himself, perhaps just a touch too loudly as two diners passed by, a white middle-aged couple who looked at him suspiciously before giving him a wide berth. He fleetingly wondered if they'd have shifted around him quite the same if he wasn't a young black man, but that was the least of his worries now. His racial discrimination paranoia would have to take a back seat for the time being—just as *he* literally had last night. *Stupid*. He wished, so much, that he hadn't gone, hadn't let Mo talk him into it. But wishing wouldn't change anything now. It was too late.

He was uncomfortable in the plastic bistro dining chair he was sitting in, as you're supposed to be in any McDonald's—

CHAPTER EIGHT

what with them not wanting diners to hang around for too long after a meal, like Ben was doing. But that wasn't the main reason he was restless. It was because he was obsessing, going over what happened last night, over and over again, his mind never letting up for a second, the maelstrom getting more powerful by the second, not letting up.

He texted Mo again, for the fifth time since he arrived, this time in all caps: 'MO, WHERE THE HELL R U?!' But just as he tapped on the 'send' icon, Mo finally walked in.

Ben stood up like he'd just sat on a needle—abruptly. Back straight, body rigid, he didn't take his eyes off Mo for one microsecond, never even blinking until Mo reached his table.

'Where... in the shitting hell... have *you* been?' asked Ben.

'Sit down,' said Mo. 'People are looking.' Ben glared at him, just about ready to explode. 'Sit down, Ben,' Mo said, in a calmer tone, so Ben did as asked and Mo followed, sitting in the chair opposite on the uncomfortably small, two-person table.

'So?' asked Ben, feeling his whole-body vibrating.

'Don't freak out, okay?' said Mo. 'Just... when I tell you, don't make a scene. That's the last thing we need.' Ben thought Mo looked shaken up too, and he was usually pretty calm, so that worried Ben even more. They'd been the best of friends since Year 9 at Parklands High School, so Ben knew Mo as well as he knew anyone. The look on Mo's face told him something was very wrong. His complexion wasn't right, his demeanour.

'Come on. What happened?' asked Ben.

'Okay, so, I've been down to the police station—'

'*What?* We all agreed not to say anything!' said Ben, doing exactly what Mo had asked him not to: *freak out*. But he couldn't help it. This was serious.

'I had no choice. A detective came to my house,' said Mo.

Ben stood up, started pacing around, this way and that, hyperventilating, putting his hands on his face and mouth, trying to get to grips with what Mo had just said. 'No, no, no...'

'Ben, sit back down,' said Mo. 'We're getting too much attention.'

Ben did as asked once more and retook his seat. 'This is messed up,' he said. 'We're totally screwed.' But then he realised the obvious—that Mo was no longer at the police station, which meant they'd let him go.

'They haven't got anything yet,' said Mo. 'But she's... Charlotte. She's—'

'Dead, right?' said Ben. 'Like, *really* dead. I told you.' He didn't want to believe it, had tried to convince himself otherwise all night, but deep down he knew.

Mo took a deep breath. 'Yes, Ben. She is.'

They both sat in silence for a minute. Ben so wished, with all his heart, that he'd just stayed at home, or drunk less, or tried to help Charlotte somehow. He wished he wasn't such a coward. But he was, and now a girl was dead, and he was right in it. He didn't know what to do, how to feel.

'What did you tell them?' asked Ben. 'The police. What did they want to know?'

'Don't worry. I stuck to the plan. But they have me at the booze shop, so I had to improvise a bit. I never mentioned you, or Liam or Wilko. You're in the clear, for now.'

'What do you mean, *for now?*' asked Ben.

'They took a DNA swab,' said Mo, looking down. 'They're trying to link me to the crime scene. If they find my DNA there, or on Charlotte, it's gunna be a problem.'

CHAPTER EIGHT

'Please don't tell on me,' said Ben. 'Look at me. I'm just a skinny young black kid. I'll never make it out of prison, not without getting bum raped and beaten half to death, anyway.'

'Just... Look. I'm pretty sure I took the bottle I'd been drinking from back with me, drank more on the way home. I remember that much. At least, I think I do. Any other DNA found on Charlotte, or anywhere else at the Pike, I can just say was transferred to her while I was getting a lift. I should be in the clear,' said Mo. 'I think. If my lawyer does his job.'

'You *think*,' said Ben, unconvinced. 'And what about me? What if they find out I was there? I kissed her. I got blood on my hands and everything.'

'Shh,' said Mo. 'Keep it down.'

'It was everywhere,' whispered Ben. 'They'll find out I was there, and then they'll match the DNA on her body to me.'

'It'll be okay, Ben. We just have to keep calm,' said Mo.

'Keep calm? It was you who thought it was a good idea to go up there in the first place. Why should I trust what you think now?' said Ben.

Mo thought about it. 'It is what it is,' he said. 'There's not much choice. We just lie low, hope this blows over. That's all we can do. Have Wilko or Liam been in touch with you?'

Ben couldn't stand it—the feelings he was having. He felt like he was going insane. It was all so unreal. 'Liam called. Said to stick to the plan,' said Ben. 'Or else.'

Mo took a deep breath. 'So, that's what we do then. We stick to the bloody plan.'

CHAPTER NINE

DC Briggs arrived at The Majestic Coffee Lounge in Chorley town centre with a printed photograph of Mohammad Ali Hussein in her pocket, ready to show the café staff there. Mo's story was that he'd left the Majestic at around eight-thirty on the night Charlotte Porter died, and DCI Walker wanted her to corroborate that, do some fact checking. DC Briggs walked into the café to find that it wasn't much, modest in size, homely, with just a handful of tables for diners to sit at, but it did boast 'Fast Internet Access!' on a poster on the wall, which was perhaps what drew Mo to it, she thought, for his studies. It certainly wasn't the hipness or the trendiness that was the draw card—far from it.

'Can I help you?' said a young man from behind the counter, stood next to an older rough-looking lady, perhaps early fifties.

'Yes. I'm DC Briggs.' She tapped on her ID card hanging around her neck. 'I need to ask you a few questions about someone who frequented your café last night.' She pulled out the photograph of Mo from her pocket. 'A Mohammad Ali Hussein. Could you take a look, please?'

The boy took the photograph and gazed at it, while the woman next to him quickly plucked it out of his fingers and took an even closer look.

'He was here,' said the woman. She was abrupt, but to the point, no messing around. 'Very quiet boy. Polite. What's the problem, Detective?'

'We're not sure yet. He may have been involved in an incident we're investigating, or he might have information that we need. Can you remember what time he left the café, last night? It could be important.'

The woman smiled and looked up at the clock on the wall. 'I'd say it was around eight to half-eight,' she said. 'I remember because the lad suddenly upped and left, like he was in a hurry for something, and he left his pencil case on the table.' She reached under the counter, opened a drawer, and pulled out a black fabric pencil case with a zipper on it. 'This one. I went out after him with the case, hoping to give it to him, but he was already getting into a car just down the road, and it sped off before I could catch up.'

'Into a car, you say? And did you see the make and model of the car by any chance? Can you describe it?' asked DC Briggs.

The woman thought about it. 'It was a red... something. I don't know. I don't know a lot about cars. It was smallish. Small and red. Four wheels, a windscreen, that kind of thing. That's all I can tell you, I'm afraid.'

'I see,' said DC Briggs. The description vaguely matched that of the red Ford Focus, 2011 model, which they had on CCTV, but that wasn't gunna be bloomin' good enough. They needed more. 'Anything else?'

'Actually, I saw another young man get out of the car to let our diner in. He was familiar. You tend to see some of the same faces over and over around here. I've seen him around, passing by and the like, numerous times,' said the woman. 'He has one of those faces that are easy to remember. You know, a bit distinct somehow. Seems like trouble. A tough-looking one.'

'And could you describe him?' asked DC Briggs.

'I suppose. He was...' The woman stopped what she was saying and removed her apron, dropping it on the counter, then strode through the counter swing door, over to the window. Her eyes were fixed on something outside. 'Hey, that's him! I don't believe it. He's right there.'

DC Briggs quickly joined her, ready for action. There weren't many people around, so less chance of confusion. 'That young lad there?' she asked, for confirmation. 'The one who just stopped, looking at his phone. You're sure that's him?'

'Yes, that's him. I'm sure. That's the lad who got out of that car last night,' said the woman, looking dumbfounded at DC Briggs. 'Is he in trouble? Did he steal something? Or hurt someone?'

'Thank you,' said DC Briggs, moving quickly towards the door. 'I'll be in touch if we need anything else.'

She quickly exited the café, walking swiftly towards the male in question. He saw her, appeared a little nervous, went right by her, looking back twice, so she quickened her step, almost breaking into a run, but held back a bit, not wanting to spook him. 'Excuse me, sir,' she said. 'Could I have a word please?'

He ignored her, started to walk more quickly, stuffing his phone in his pocket.

'Sir? I'm Detective Constable Briggs of the Lancashire Constabulary. I need to ask you some questions.'

It was too late. The boy bolted, running off as fast as he

CHAPTER NINE

could, dodging around a couple of pedestrians walking down the footpath as he went.

'*Shit!*' said DC Briggs, and she too started to run after him, almost bumping one of the pedestrians as she went.

'Hey! Watch it!' said the elderly gentleman she'd almost knocked over, but she didn't have time for apologies. She needed to catch up to the runner, find out who the hell he was, see what his version of events were.

DC Briggs grabbed the two-way radio on her belt and called it in while she was on the move. 'Suspect running down the A581 towards Astley Park. In pursuit without support. Require back-up, over.'

'Got you, Detective,' came a reply from a male voice on the other end. 'We've got some PCs headed up there now. We'll alert them immediately, over.'

The boy was getting away from her. He was faster than she was, younger, more agile. But she could already hear sirens from the squad cars that were on their way, so she kept on him, pumping her arms and legs, hoping the gym work she'd started doing would stand her in good stead. He was approaching the main entrance to Astley Park just as two squad cars arrived. The cars pulled over, blocking the entrance to the park, leaving nowhere else to go but further down the A581, which was completely fenced off on the park side, and had a small stone wall at the other side of the road.

Two uniformed male officers got out of the squad cars just as DC Briggs caught up. She was out of breath—spent. 'Get him!' she shouted.

The officers got after the lad, and DC Briggs did her best to keep up. The boy ran down the road, before zigzagging around traffic, making it to the opposite side. He was headed towards the stone wall at the other side, probably intending to jump over it into whatever lay beyond—trees and foliage by the looks of it, probably some unused land that would be more difficult to navigate if unfamiliar and perhaps therefore easier to lose the officers in. Before he could make it to the wall though, one of the officers grabbed him by the back of his pants, pulled him close and twisted his arm around his back. The boy resisted, but the officer who held him was much stronger than he was, and the second officer quickly caught up, assisting, making the boy's plight impossible. They cuffed him with relative ease, despite a brief struggle, and started marching back towards DC Briggs, who waited patiently at the other side of the road.

'Got him, Detective,' said one of the uniformed officers. 'He's all yours. Want us to take him in?'

DC Briggs shook her head. 'No. Just get him back to my car. I'll take him. I want to talk to him on the way.'

The officer nodded. 'Roger that,' he said, dragging the boy along, encouraging him to walk quicker. 'Who's been a naughty boy then? You run again, and I won't be so nice about it a second time,' he warned.

'Easy, Constable,' said DC Briggs. 'There's no need for that. But thank you. I'll take it from here.'

CHAPTER TEN

Having left McDonald's, Ben walked down the street with Mo, along the footpath of the A6 towards Chorley train station. His phone pinged and he checked it.

'Got something from Liam,' he said. 'Wait.' He silently read the message.

PIGS HAVE ME. GTFOH!

'So?' asked Mo, nervously.

Ben stopped walking. 'He says the police have him. He says to get out of here.'

Mo put his hands on his head, paced around, breathing heavily. Ben felt like time was standing still, like he was disassociating from the world, like he was no longer a part of it. His head was fuzzy, his thoughts unclear; it was like he was being sucked into a mental bog.

'Let's just get a train ticket and leave,' said Ben.

'And go where, exactly, Ben?' asked Mo, a bit aggressively. 'Where are we going to go? Blackpool? Take a trip to the seaside? It's not like either of us need a tan now, is it, even if there was any sun around here.'

'This train line goes to Manchester Airport as well. We could go grab our passports, go somewhere, anywhere, until things blow over,' said Ben. 'We could just pick the cheapest place, stay there.'

Mo seemed to think about it, consider it as an option, before his eyes changed, dismissing the idea completely. 'That would be dumb, Ben. We do that, and we just look guilty. We have to ride this out, stick to the plan. We'll get through this. That's not an option.'

'We're not gunna get through this,' said Ben, beginning to break down, beginning to cry in front of his long-time friend, the tears obstructing his vision. 'We're screwed.'

Mo grabbed his friend by the shoulders, face-to-face, looking him square in the eyes just as a car full of youths drove by, one of them opening the window and throwing a half-eaten pie at them. It hit Ben on the shoulder, gravy splattering up on his face and arm.

'What the…?' said Ben, stunned. Mo stepped back, looked at the car that the pie came from, speeding by.

'What are your pronouns, dickheads? Did Allah warn you about *that*?' shouted someone from the car as it disappeared, overtaking a bus at a bus stop.

'Just… ignore them,' said Mo, getting close to Ben again. 'That's not important now. Look… if we don't all stick together, then we're screwed. The only chance we have is to ride this thing out, hope they don't gather enough evidence for a conviction. I study this shit, remember? I know what I'm talking about.'

Ben shook his head, still struggling to think clearly.

'Go home, Ben, yeah?' said Mo. 'I'll call you later. Just watch some TV or something, take your mind of it, kill some time.'

'Don't say that word,' said Ben. '*Kill*.'

He was being oversensitive, he knew, his emotions raw. But

how could he not be? They were in so much shit and he had no idea how they were gunna get out of it. They should never have picked Charlotte up, plied her with drink. He wasn't even sure what had happened—they'd all been wasted—but it looked like they'd killed her, he knew that much. Things just got out of control, somehow. It was tragic.

'You know what I mean,' said Mo. 'Go get some rest.'

Ben nodded, but he had no intention of going home and watching the telly. No intention at all.

CHAPTER ELEVEN

'Right. What do we have?' said Walker.

He was in the Incident Room they'd been allocated at Chorley Police Station—another bleak, concrete block building where even the Union Jack flag outside looked clinically depressed. The room they were in was modest in size—some might say *small*—which was fine, as they only had a skeleton team of three on this one for the time being in himself, DC Briggs, and DI Hogarth, although Walker felt they'd soon need more help as the case was growing and becoming increasingly more complex.

'What we have is a *who:* a white male, Liam Holden, 18, also attended Parklands High School. He has just given a "no comment" interview. Won't say a damned thing,' said DC Briggs. 'Tough-looking little thing, he is. Fast too. I wouldn't have caught him without backup.'

Walker was constructing an evidence board on the wall at the front of the room as he always did on any potential homicide case. So far, he had pictures of Charlotte Porter, Mohammad Ali Hussein, a snapshot of CCTV footage of a red Ford Focus, 2011 model, and a photo of the Pike Tower. He'd arranged it so that Charlotte's picture was next to the Pike Tower, in the centre, with Mo and the car off to one side, with Mo connected to the car with some red string held with Blu Tack—an adhesive tack which had also been used to fix the pictures to the wall—and the car was also connected to Charlotte with more string.

'I think we could do with a tech upgrade in here, sir,' said DC Briggs. 'It's hardly *Minority Report*, is it?'

'Focus, please, Detective,' said Walker, not getting the reference. He wasn't big on pop culture—had never had the time for it. 'This is the serious part. And it's how I've always done things. If it ain't broken…'

DC Briggs held out another picture for Walker to take. It was a mugshot of Liam Holden.

'This is him,' she said. 'A witness from the Majestic Coffee Lounge has him getting out of a small red car and letting Mo inside, around eight to eight-thirty, just after Mo hurriedly left the café.'

The only other person in the room, DI Hogarth, was, as usual, sitting in front of his laptop computer, busily tapping away on it. He'd been overweight the last time Walker had worked with him on the Alan Smith case—a case that would last long in the memory—and it seemed he'd somehow got even larger in the interim.

'I rang the café,' he said. 'They only have a camera pointing at the cash register, which is no big surprise. Nothing external. And unfortunately, I couldn't get anything decent from anything else nearby too. It seems they found something of a dark spot, although that was probably more than likely fortuitous rather than planned, I'd say. I do have the car driving past on one of Barclays's cameras, but again, side view and no registration plate.'

'Never mind. We'll get it. So…' said Walker, musing on it.

'This Liam was already in the car. They picked Mo up around eight, eight-thirty. Then Charlotte got in at 8:37pm, and they arrived at the Stump Lane Store at 8:42, got some booze, and then left again at 8:46. And then we lose them. But Charlotte turns up dead at the Pike Tower in the morning, after what looked like some kind of party gone wrong. We have our timeline, the car, the place, and two possible witnesses who may or may not have been involved or present.'

'But Mo claims he was dropped off near his home before they went to the Pike, and Liam won't say anything at all,' said DC Briggs. 'We need more. We need that car reg.'

'Did you manage to track down this Wilko character?' asked Walker, looking at DC Briggs. 'And find out what kind of car he drives, if he owns one? It's almost six. Zachery Statham should be here soon. I wanted to get them here together, remember?'

'I do,' said DC Briggs. 'Sorry. It's been a busy day. I got his address, tried calling, but nobody was home, and there was no car in the driveway either. DI Hogarth has contacted the DVLA, trying to see if there are any registered cars under that name. They're going to contact us soon to confirm.'

A notification bell chimed on DI Hogarth's computer. He tapped on it a couple more times, before saying, 'It's them. Got it.'

'Detective?' said Walker.

'The registration of one red Ford Focus, 2011 model, belonging to one Alex Wilkinson,' said DI Hogarth.

'A.K.A., *Wilko*,' said Walker. 'We've got him! Let's go back to his house, DC Briggs, wait for him there if we have to. And then we'll pick Mo back up too, get them all in here together. With any luck, one of them will squeal, dob on the rest, try to get off lightly. We've seen it before.'

'We have indeed, sir,' said DC Briggs. 'But I've got a feeling there might be more to this one than meets the eye.'

CHAPTER TWELVE

'This him?' asked Walker. They were parked up outside a less than attractive terraced property on Robin Road in the Leyland area of Moss Side.

'Nice place,' said DI Brigg. She meant that it wasn't. The place was a mess—an old, soiled mattress leaned against one of the properties, bits of graffiti was sprayed on the road and footpath and on one of the buildings, and various bits of junk and odd ends lay scattered about in several of the more poorly kept front yards, including someone's old shoe.

'Not everyone is lucky enough to be brought up in a grade 1 school catchment area,' said Walker.

'Yup. There's nothing *outstanding* about this. Requires improvement, at the very least,' said DC Briggs. Walker looked at her. He wouldn't have expected her to know anything much about schools and catchment areas, what with her not having children yet. He remembered it all well, though, from when his two kids were young. 'I'm an aunt,' she clarified. 'That's all my sister talks about.'

They got out of the car and approached the building they had down as the registered home of Alex Wilkinson.

'Still no red Ford Focus here,' said Walker. 'He must be out.'

'Well deduced, sir. Or he's ditched the car,' suggested DC

CHAPTER TWELVE

Briggs. 'Maybe thinking it contained evidence?'

Walker rubbed his chin. They needed more than circumstantial evidence. They needed something solid to go off, something more tangible. He knocked on the door, fist tight, three raps: *knock, knock, knock.* Then waited.

The door opened, a woman who looked to be in her early fifties opened it, hair a mess like a disused bird's nest, smelling of smoke—although Walker guessed she may have been quite a bit younger if she'd had a hard time of it.

'What is it?' she asked, abruptly. 'Hey, I don't need no Christian bull—'

'We're with the Lancashire Constabulary, madam,' said Walker, before she could go on and slam the door in their faces. I'm DCI Walker, and this is my colleague, DC Briggs.'

'Nice to meet you, ma'am,' said DC Briggs.

'Wish I could say the same. What's this about?' she asked. 'Has our Alex done something stupid again?'

'Is Alex home, Mrs Wilkinson?' asked Walker. 'We'd like to have a word with him. Several, in fact.'

'My name is Kathy Johnson,' said the woman. '*Wilkinson* was his arsehole dad's name. Haven't seen him for years, and a good thing too. Piece of shit. He left me right in it.'

'That's too bad, Mrs Johnson,' said Walker. 'Is your boy here?'

'No. He isn't. Not seen him for a bit,' she said, looking around at the street, probably checking to see if any neighbours were watching. They weren't, at least, not that Walker could see.

'And by "a bit", you mean? How long has it been since you've seen him, exactly?' asked Walker.

'Oh, he comes and goes, the little bugger. He does what he

wants, treats this place like a hostel. I should kick him out. He's old enough now. I was doing my own thing at his age,' said Kathy. 'Complete waste of space, he is.'

'We're going to need a rough time and date, I'm afraid,' said Walker. 'For our records. We need to know when you last saw him.'

'What the hell has he done now then?' asked Kathy. 'Is he in real trouble this time? They don't usually send detectives. This is serious, isn't it? That's it. I'm done with him. I've had enough. I saw him on Thursday I think, when the bin men were here. I remember 'cos I jokingly said there's always a bad stink wherever he turns up. He didn't think it was funny. No sense of humour that boy, just like his dad. Needs some discipline too. What day is it today?' Kathy rubbed her head, like she was hungover, or perhaps still on something. Her eyes were squinting, struggling with the light, pupils dilated.

'It's Sunday, Kathy,' said DC Briggs. 'You haven't seen your boy for three days?'

'Nope. Is that what it's been. Jeez. Time flies. Is that all then?' she asked, seeming relatively unconcerned given that her boy had been missing for several days and was being investigated by the Lancashire Constabulary.

'Your son drives a red Ford Focus, 2011 model, is that correct?' asked Walker.

'Yeah. Something like that. I think so. How did you know that? What is it, a hit and run?' asked Kathy. 'Is that what this is?'

'That will be all for now,' said Walker, handing Kathy one of his cards with his name and mobile number on. She took it, winked, and stuffed it in her bra. Walker tried to ignore that. 'Please call us immediately if you see or hear from him. This is a serious matter, Mrs Johnson. We need to speak with your son urgently.' Kathy nodded and closed the door.

Walker and DC Briggs walked back to the car, and DC Briggs put her hand on top of it before getting in, speaking to Walker over the car's roof.

'Not much love there, was there?' she said. 'No wonder the boy's going off the rails. I feel a bit sorry for him.'

'Well, just remember that poor girl, and what was done to her, and then see if you still feel sorry for him,' said Walker, reminding her of what kind of animal Alex might be.

'Unless it wasn't him,' said DC Briggs.

'Of course,' said Walker. 'Unless it wasn't him. Let's go try to pick up that boxer-cum-tyrant then, as the shopkeeper said—*Mohammad Ali Hussein*. We need to bring him back in—keep him for the full allowable duration this time. He blatantly lied to us, and it's time to find out why.'

CHAPTER THIRTEEN

Having left Ben, Mo headed back to his home, in the opposite direction to what Ben was going in. He didn't know why, exactly—call it *intuition*, or a lack of trust—but he turned around to see Ben not headed up the footpath as expected but taking a hard left into Chorley train station itself. Mo stopped in his tracks. If Ben legged it, then it would look even more suspicious than it already was. The police hadn't connected Ben to the case yet, but if they found out that one of Mo's friends had disappeared, then it would just dig them all in deeper. For now, as far as he knew, Ben and Wilko were out of it, and he intended to keep it that way for as long as possible.

'Ben!' he shouted, but his friend was too far up ahead to hear above the noise of the traffic, and he disappeared into the station building.

Mo ran to try to catch up, in case a train was already in, ready to leave. He'd never been very athletic, and his skinny, gangly frame struggled to make up the ground. If a train was waiting to leave, and Ben got on it and it left, he'd never catch up to him, not unless Ben wanted to be caught. 'Ben! Ben!' he continued to shout as he ran, panicking a bit, hoping that he might be heard. He made it to the station building and

CHAPTER THIRTEEN

got inside, but Ben wasn't there—he'd evidently already gone through to one of the platforms. He intended to leave and never come back. Mo knew it. He'd not managed to convince him to lie low and just get on with things as usual. It seemed he'd not got through to him at all.

'*Shit*,' said Mo to himself. Some other commuters were looking. They probably just thought he was late for his train; people were always running around at train stations. One was looking at a timetable on the wall, another was sitting, staring at Mo, before looking down at their phone.

The world seemed to stand still for a second, and Mo wondered whether this might be the last time he ever tasted freedom. Realisation hit him like a brick wall in the face, making him physically jolt. Although he already understood the enormity of the situation he found himself in, in an intellectual sense at least, the emotions of it had barely scratched the surface, struggling to break through into reality. But now they were about to do so in a major way, and it scared Mo. He was in a *lot* of trouble.

He ran out onto the nearest station platform—Platform 1—to find it empty. There was no one there. 'Shit, shit, shit!' What if Ben *had* just got on a train, and it had left while Mo was catching up? If he didn't answer his phone, he'd never be able to talk to him, and his parents would eventually call the police, and they'd say he'd gone to meet Mo if Ben had told them, or they'd name him as his best friend. Either way, the police would want to know what the hell was going on, as they'd only just had him in to talk about what happened to Charlotte Porter. They'd know something was up. They'd know Ben was involved, somehow.

He looked across to the other side of the station, and on the opposite platform stood Ben, just staring down at the tracks, as yet unaware of Mo's presence.

'Ben! Just... wait there,' said Mo, holding his palm out, motioning for Ben to stay put, but there was no reaction. He was comatose.

Mo headed for the underpass, the stepped subway that connected Platforms 1 and 2, the only platforms at the modest-sized Chorley train station. He legged it, jumping down several steps at a time, trying to make it to Ben before a train arrived. It didn't take long, but long enough for the smell of urine to seep into Mo's nose—some drunks or louts had obviously taken a leak down there. When he made it up onto Platform 2, Mo saw that a train was approaching on their side while Ben continued to stare down at the tracks, seemingly still unaware of Mo's presence, or disinterested, or deep in thought.

'Ben, what are you—?' said Mo. And then it hit him. Ben wasn't going to get on the train. He wasn't going to go on it at all. He planned to do the ultimate in running away: he was going to do himself in. '*Ben!*' screamed Mo, his emotions now getting the better of him. Ben was his best friend, the only real friend he had. It was bad enough that Charlotte was dead. He didn't know what he'd do if Ben left him. He felt like he was going mad, like the world he knew was a place he no longer recognised. Everything was upside down.

The train got closer, and Ben just stood there, the tips of his white New Balance trainers close to the edge of the platform, *too* close. Everything seemed to be happening in slow motion now, but at breakneck speed at the same time.

'Ben, no. Stop!' shouted Mo, as he continued to run, out of breath, his muscles seizing up, but getting within touching distance. He reached out to grab Ben just as the train came within a few metres of them, touched Ben's jacket with his fingertips, felt the smooth fabric of it. But before he could grab anything, get some purchase, Ben was no longer there.

CHAPTER FOURTEEN

Alex Wilkinson was sitting in his red Ford Focus, 2011 model, for what would be the last time. He'd had it for around two years—ever since he'd passed his driving test—and in that time, he'd grown to love it, probably more than anything else he owned in the world. He called it 'The Biohazard', due to it basically not being in the best shape, and tending to smell of petrol and oil, which often dripped down here and there, staining the driveway or whatever he was parked on. Despite its faults, though, it was his, and it had given him a sense of freedom and space to breathe; and he was grateful for that. He'd have long since gone mad without it, he thought, and he'd be sad to see it go. But go it must. He had other priorities right now.

He was parked at the Hunter's Hill quarry car park in Hill Dale near Wrightington, around a twenty-minute drive from his home in Moss Side, Leyland. Not that he felt like he had much of a home. He hardly went. He hated it there.

He'd been to this place before, more than once, knew of it as a good spot to have a smoke late at night, get baked. Not many people came here, especially late at night. It wasn't night-time right now, though. It was six in the evening—a time when most people would either be coming home from work or starting their evening meal. It figured, as the small car park was deserted, giving him the time and space he needed to do what he needed to do.

He'd rolled a joint and sparked it up, for old times' sake, putting the driver's window down to let the smoke out. He breathed it in, deep, burning his lungs, and then held it there for as long as he could, before letting it out again. He coughed and spluttered and took a drink from the half-empty can of Coca Cola he had in the cup holder. It did the trick. He felt calmer, more able to do what he had to; it stopped his mind from racing away from him, made him less manic.

His thoughts were pulled, kicking and screaming, towards his mother, as they often were, to what she'd done to him when he'd been little, what she was still doing to him, what she'd made him into. His anger bubbled. One time she'd made him drink *Fairy*—the washing up liquid they'd always used—as punishment for breaking the neighbour's window with a football. It was only a goddamned accident! He was just a boy. He'd tasted the vile stuff for days. It was horrible. It all came back to him whenever he smelled the stuff. And then there were the beatings, probably once every couple of weeks, for years. Another time she'd held his arm down and burned him with a hot iron. He rolled his sleeve up and felt the scar, lightly rubbing his fingertips over it, grimacing with the memory. That's when *he'd* started to come, of course—the Master—to watch, oversee, order it, laugh at it. Alex had only been little when he'd first appeared, had learned to live with the visits of this interloper, keep it a secret. He had to. He knew the torment would only get worse if he told anyone. The Master knew all about Alex's abuse, watched it, took part in it, even. Alex thought the mysterious stranger had come to help him at first, to save him, perhaps replace the father who'd upped and left when he'd been just a baby. But he was wrong; he was just a monster, there to enjoy his suffering, humiliate him.

He'd never told a soul about any of this—his torture, his suffering. He was ashamed of it. Embarrassed. If he'd have told his mates, they'd have just laughed at him for being such a pussy, for being bullied by a woman. Would probably have told him to just stand up for himself. But he'd been terrified of her for years, and despite him growing up and now becoming a young man, he was still scared of her, and of the mysterious stranger who seemed to appear every time she had a meltdown and turned violent. His mother simply had a hold over him he just couldn't break free of. She made him take pills every day to keep him docile and compliant, but they were becoming increasingly unrelenting, urging him to do terrible things, their demands becoming more extreme. They were experimenting on him. If he didn't do what they said, they promised to vivisect him, sell his body parts on the dark web, or lobotomise him, shut him up for good. They always knew where he was, using his phone to track his every move; and they were always in his head, even when they weren't.

'Bitch!' he said, taking another swig of coke, and then another drag of his reefer. He took a quarter bottle of McKendrick's Blended Scotch Whiskey out from his backpack, removed the cap, and poured a generous amount into the can of coke, giving it a mix by swashing it around a bit. He took a generous swig. And then another, finishing the can off.

When he was done with his joint too, he popped what was left in the can, then slowly got out of the car. He put the backpack on, and then opened the car boot. Inside was a lime green twenty-litre petrol fuel can, which he'd bought at B&Q

CHAPTER FOURTEEN

and filled up at the petrol station on the way over.

He unscrewed the lid from the petrol can and started to haphazardly splash fuel all over the car, and then inside of it too, on the front and back seats, and then finally in the boot as well. It pained him to do so, as he really did love that car. But it was time to say 'farewell'. He walked over to the main road to make sure no cars were coming, to make sure that no one was around. There wasn't. So, he walked back to the car and took out the cigarette lighter he had in his pocket. He put his thumb on the spark wheel, feeling its grooves.

'I should have torched your house too, mum, with you inside it,' he said, before throwing the lighter on the car. Flames *whooshed* and started to go up, quicker than he'd expected, so he took a step back. The fire warmed and illuminated him, and he stood there for a few seconds, hypnotised by it, before shaking his head and running off into the quarry, out of sight, before anyone came and saw.

CHAPTER FIFTEEN

'What is it now?' asked Walker. 'What's all this?'

They were on their way to Mohammad Ali Hussein's home again, passing by McDonald's near Chorley town centre, but there were emergency services everywhere—ambulances blazing past, police squad cars arriving, and then the fire service as well. Walker, who was in the driver's seat this time, pulled over to let some of them past.

'It's all happening today, isn't it, sir? Let me check, see what's going on,' said DC Briggs. She got on her two-way radio and pressed a button. It had been on silent mode so their investigations wouldn't be disturbed by the day-to-day chatter of officers on duty. They only really needed it for backup or emergencies. 'Does anyone know what's happening near the A6 close to McDonald's in Chorley? It seems like all hell has broken loose, over.'

She waited for a few seconds, enough time for Walker to get moving again, albeit cautiously. 'Got a jumper at the train station. Doesn't look good,' came a reply from a concerned sounding male. 'A real mess, apparently. Not looking forward to this. All available units to assist, if possible, over.'

'Roger that,' said DC Briggs.

CHAPTER FIFTEEN

They took a few seconds to take in the news. 'Good God. Must be one of those days,' said Walker. 'Not a good day for Chorley.'

'Shall we take a look?' asked DC Briggs. 'I mean, offer some help?'

Walker thought about it. 'No. We've got to focus on our own case. You know how crucial those first twenty-four to forty-eight are. We can't risk compromising it for a simple suicide case—if that's what it was. We can't get distracted.'

'Sure. Hey, *wait…*' said DC Briggs, suddenly sitting forward in her seat, looking at a pedestrian hurriedly passing by, her eyes widening. 'Isn't that—'

'Got it,' said Walker. He'd already seen who she was talking about, had locked on to them like a heat-seeking missile. It was the lad they'd been on their way to see—it was young Mo. Walker pulled over and took his seat belt off, before getting out of the car, not even closing the door properly. 'Hey, Mo. Hold up! We were just coming to see you. Mo!'

Mo saw them, looked like he might run for a second, but then his shoulders slumped forwards. He looked for all the world like he was going to cry.

'You don't understand. It wasn't me,' he said, as Walker approached, his lower lip starting to quiver. 'I didn't do anything.'

DC Briggs was out of the car now too. She held out a hand, urging him to stay put. 'It's okay, Mo. We just want to have another chat with you. There have been some developments, that's all.' Another ambulance whizzed by, siren on, lights flashing, and Mo looked at it, dumbfounded, like the world was ending. 'I'm gunna need you to get in the car now.'

Mo just stood still, paralysed, so Walker got even closer,

being careful not to scare him off. He didn't want to have to chase him if it could be avoided.

'Easy, Mo,' said Walker 'We're gunna figure this out.'

'I really didn't *do* anything,' said Mo. 'He was my friend.'

'Who was your friend?' Walker got close enough to grab his arm, got a good hold, and led him to the car. He was much bigger and stronger than Mo, who was just a scrawny kid. Mo watched as more emergency services whizzed past, shaking his head in some obvious distress.

'I can't believe this,' said Mo. 'It's unreal.'

'Come on. Get in,' said Walker, and Mo complied without resistance. Walker closed the door and got inside the car with DC Briggs.

They got moving without talking, Walker taking a right on the roundabout, back towards Chorley police station, away from the mayhem.

'Who was your friend, Mo?' asked Walker again, turning his head slightly, back towards Mo in the back seat, while still keeping his eyes on the road. 'Who were you talking about back there? Do you know something about the incident at the train station just now? Were you there? Did you see what happened?'

Mo clammed up, just gazing out of the window. Being a student with aspirations of being a lawyer himself, Walker knew he'd know enough about the British legal system to realise it wasn't a good idea to talk without legal counsel. He was being smart—probably—able to think, even in unusual circumstances—which was kind of impressive for a young lad. Either that or he'd withdrawn into himself, too disturbed to say anything. Walker glanced across to DC Briggs, raised his eyebrows, communicating that they had something, although he wasn't quite sure what, yet. She shook her head, ever so slightly, probably in disbelief a bit herself at everything that was suddenly happening. She wasn't as experienced as him, was still surprised by what people could do. But she wouldn't be, given enough time in the job. Even Walker, though, with all his years of experience, was still learning new things. He didn't know everything. He did know one thing, though: they weren't going to let Mo go so easily this time, not unless they were sure he was in the clear—and Walker was pretty sure he wasn't. Not completely, anyhow. He could sense it. Young Mo was too much at the centre of everything, the nexus point. Something was badly amiss with him, and Walker was damned well gunna find out what.

* * *

'DI Hogarth, what do we have?' asked Walker. They were back in the Incident Room at Chorley police station with Mohammad Ali Hussein and Liam Holden each safely locked up in individual holding cells, awaiting processing.

'We have Mohammad Ali Hussein on CTTV at Chorley train station, approaching the newly deceased there, just before he was killed by an oncoming train. And… well, it's not entirely clear from the footage whether Mo was trying to help, or if he pushed him,' said DI Hogarth. 'Here. Take a look for yourselves. It's inconclusive.'

Walker and DC Briggs stood over DI Hogarth, eagerly looking at the footage he had on his laptop computer. It was taken from a lofty angle—as most CCTV footage is—

showing the back of one Benjamin Jackson, stood at the edge of Platform 2. He'd been identified from a bank card in his wallet, something the attending officers had retrieved from his scattered remains.

On the video, Mo could be seen entering the platform, running towards Ben at speed, and then Ben falling onto the tracks just as contact was made between the two of them, a train almost instantaneously arriving just when and where Ben had fallen. It didn't look good for Mo, especially given his recent involvement in the Charlotte Porter case, and with him being an ongoing person of interest in that case. Now he was involved in two cases, if indeed they were separate, that was. It seemed too much of a coincidence that he was suddenly at the epicentre of everything, that people were dying all around him.

'Jesus,' said DC Briggs, jolting back as she watched the image. 'That's awful. I've never seen anything like it.'

'It is indeed. But I see what you mean, Detective,' said Walker, talking calmly to DI Hogarth, less affected, having seen it all before in his long career. It wasn't his first train fatality either. There were more than people might think—two to three hundred suicides on the train lines every year in the UK alone when Walker had last seen. So, the incident wasn't entirely unusual. It was the involvement of Mo, specifically, that was bothering Walker. If it hadn't been him, he could have more easily passed it off as a simple suicide case. But with his recent involvement in the Charlotte Porter case, this just added a few more question marks. 'You're right. It's hard to see whether he was trying to pull him back, or whether he was shoving him. Can you slow it down a tad?'

'Course,' said DI Hogarth. 'But, believe me, it doesn't help—

CHAPTER FIFTEEN

or I'd have already showed it to you like that.'

He did as asked and set the video in slow motion, but, as stated, seeing it like that only served to muddy the waters further. From this angle, it was impossible to see exactly what had happened with any degree of certainty.

'Have the parents of the deceased been informed yet?' asked Walker.

'Yes, they have,' said DI Hogarth. 'We have a Family Liaison Officer, DI Sally Keane, on site as we speak, offering them support. They say that the two boys, Ben and Mo, are the best of friends—have been for years. That Mo wouldn't do anything to hurt Ben.'

'I see. We saw Sally recently with the Charlotte Porter case as well. Did she mention any indications of depression or any previous suicide attempts from the deceased?' asked Walker. 'Any history with mental health services?'

'We don't have an official report in yet, but DI Keane did say that the parents knew nothing of any depression in Ben, although they did apparently say he'd been acting a little strange over the past couple of days, like something was on his mind,' said DI Hogarth. 'But he wouldn't tell them what—just kept passing it off as nothing.'

'Seems like too much of a coincidence to me,' said Walker. 'I'd say the two cases *are* likely connected—that Ben was also involved in the Charlotte Porter case, maybe felt guilty, couldn't live with whatever happened to her, something like that. I think he was with them, in that car, at least. Either that or he was threatening to come clean, so Mo pushed him.'

'Jesus. So, what's first then, Chief?' asked DC Briggs.

'Well, we definitely need more people on this now,' said Walker. 'We're not gunna be able to handle this workload all by ourselves. See if DI Riley is available from Skelmersdale, and maybe Detective Inspector Chris Lee as well. Both of them would be useful on this. They've worked well with us before, as you know.'

'Will do,' said DC Briggs. 'And then?'

Walker thought about it. There were becoming too many moving parts. He needed to prioritise. But while he was thinking, a permanent member of staff from Chorley knocked on the door and popped their head around it. He was male, skinny, and the paleness of his face and the dark bags around his eyes told Walker he was either overworked or not in the best health—possibly both.

'Excuse me. We've just had a call come in, sir. That vehicle you had an APB out on—it's been torched, left somewhere between Parbold and Wrightington,' the man said. 'I've been told there's not much left.'

'Christ! It is all happening all of a sudden, eh? It doesn't rain but it bloody pours. Thank you, officer. That will be all,' said Walker, and the man left.

Walker put his head in his hands for a second, trying to think. He needed Alex Wilkinson. He was the last piece of the puzzle; or, at least, Walker hoped he was. The case was getting more complex by the minute. The other two boys were now safely locked up, so he had to prioritise bringing Wilkinson in, for now—the owner and most likely the driver of the car that Charlotte Porter was last seen getting into.

'Right. You come with me,' he said to DC Briggs. 'You can talk to DIs Riley and Lee on the way. We're heading over to this torched car, see what we can find. DI Hogarth, you get any available officers scouring the area, see if they can find Alex Wilkinson. He's likely on foot, or on public transportation.

CHAPTER FIFTEEN

Send them photos so they can identify him. We need to catch up to him, and quick, before he slips out of the net completely. Things will be delayed significantly if he leaves the area, and that could put more young women at risk. So, make sure all the officers understand the urgency of it. Finding him, or not, could be the difference between life or death for someone out there—the case could depend on it.'

* * *

'Here it is,' said DC Briggs. 'Just on the left up here.'

They'd arrived at Hunter's Hill quarry car park in Hill Dale. There were two cars in the car park: one police squad car with a couple of officers stood nearby, and one burned out Ford Focus, hardly recognisable as red except for one small untouched part of the paintwork on the rear side that gave it away.

They got out of the car and approached the wreck.

'I take it this is it then,' said Walker, stating the obvious, just to get things moving. The most senior of the two officers, presumably, stepped forward, male, middle-aged, with a moustache of all things—thick and bushy.

'DCI Walker,' said the heavily moustached officer. 'I'm PC Norris. This is how we found it. A cyclist called it in, alerted us to its presence.'

The registration plate was badly damaged, but was still able to be read, *just*, by taking some information from the front plate, and some from the back. Walker took a look around the car, all the way.

'Verified as the car we're looking for, right?' said Walker, needing that confirmation.

'That's right, sir. We have a matching reg, and the description fits. This is the one,' said PC Norris.

'Any items found in it?' asked Walker.

'It's still hot to the touch,' said PC Norris, sighing, 'but the initial inspection from a distance tells us that there's not much. A burnt out can of pop, maybe. A tire pump. That's about it that we can see. Oh, and a petrol can, which is somewhat unusual. Most likely used to torch it.'

'Yeah. Probably filled it up at a petrol station,' said Walker. 'How long since this was reported, exactly?'

'Say, about two hours, sir. We have the details of the cyclist who called it in if needed,' said PC Norris. 'The Control Room Operator will have the time log, if required.'

'An approximation of roughly two hours is good enough for now, Constable,' said Walker. 'He'll be long gone now then, even if he was on foot.' He looked around, surveying the area. 'Probably went in here, down into the quarry, I'd say, rather than back out onto the main road. He would have wanted to keep out of sight as much as humanly possible. Anybody know where this quarry path comes out?'

The other officer with PC Norris coughed, getting their attention. He was short, stocky, looked strong for his age, which couldn't be much more than mid-twenties. 'Comes out the top of Hillside Avenue,' he said. 'A well to do little area. My grandparents used to live there, before they passed away and the land got sold off to a developer. Roberto Martinez used to live there too! He might do still, I'm not sure. I'm PC James Swarbrick, by the way.' He was enthusiastic, young, clearly as yet to be beaten down by the job and his life, probably a newbie.

'Martinez?' Walked said, not understanding the reference, realising he was supposed to know who that was, but didn't.

'He's Portugal's football manager now. Used to manage Wigan Athletic? And play for them. You haven't heard of him?' asked PC Swarbrick. 'He's pretty famous.'

'We've got officers over that way as we speak,' said PC Norris, seeming a bit embarrassed by his colleague's comments, and putting an end to it. 'And scouring the wider area. Rest assured; we'll do our very best to find him.'

Walker wasn't so confident that they would find him now—they were too late. 'Let's get over there then, DC Briggs, take a look for ourselves.' He looked at PCs Norris and Swarbrick. 'You stay here, get this tidied up and over to forensics. This may be tied to a recent homicide, maybe even a double one, so we need it analysed ASAP.'

'Understood,' said PC Norris, his expression serious.

'And officers, if you do find anything else, be sure to let me know immediately,' said Walker. 'It's important.'

'Will do,' said PC Norris. 'Roger that.'

CHAPTER SIXTEEN

Walker pulled up just in front of Hilldale Avenue in Parbold, which was just a short drive down from the Hunter's Hill quarry car park, that was located at the top of Bannister Lane. It was an upmarket, quiet little part of Parbold, and being there reminded him of the last big case he'd worked, the one just a short drive away in Rufford. He hoped this one would have a more satisfactory ending.

'This is it,' he said, getting out of the car, DC Briggs following. 'He would have come out here, and then...' He looked around. 'Well, he could literally be anywhere now.'

Someone came out of the end terraced property they were parked up in front of—a man, past middle age at least, refined looking, smartly dressed in a V-neck jumper and khaki-coloured chinos.

'Er, would you mind not parking there, actually,' the man said. 'It's just we have some guests coming soon, and one of them doesn't walk too well. She's getting on a bit, you see, and—'

'We'll be on our way very soon, sir,' said Walker. 'Actually, could I just ask you a couple of questions? I'm DCI Walker of the Lancashire Constabulary, and this is my colleague, DC

CHAPTER SIXTEEN

Briggs.' He flashed the man his ID card and he jolted upright, just a touch, straightening his back.

'Oh, yes. Sorry, officer. Detective, is it? What seems to be the problem?' said the man.

'We're looking for a young man, white, nineteen years old, possibly carrying a bag of some description, like a traveller. Have you seen anybody like that today?' asked Walker. 'Perhaps in the last couple of hours?'

'Actually, there was someone down here earlier,' said the man. 'Saw him from the living room'. Walker took out a photo of Alex Wilkinson, showed it to the man. 'Yes. I think that was him. Is he in trouble? Is there anything to be concerned about?'

'Which direction did you see him go in?' asked Walker, pressing on, knowing time was of the essence.

'Well... he was just stood there for a while, on this corner, and then a taxi pulled up and he got in. Went that way,' he said, pointing in the direction of Parbold Village.

Walker was already getting back in the car, ready to move, with DC Briggs mirroring his actions once more. 'Thank you, sir,' he said. 'That will be all.'

They left, sped off in the direction of the village, hoping Wilko might still be there. Walker was motoring all right, breaking the speed limit. He didn't want to lose him. He knew it might be their only or best chance.

'What's in the village?' asked Walker, before realising exactly what was there, but before he could say it, DC Briggs beat him to it.

'Train station!' she said. 'Damn it. He's getting on a sodding train!'

'And then he could go anywhere,' said Walker through

gritted teeth, still mashing the accelerator, hoping the trains were not on time.

* * *

The car park at Parbold train station was pretty full, but Walker never intended to properly park up anyway. He just left it there as close to the station as he could get, blocking a couple of parked cars. They wouldn't be happy if they got back and found it like that, but that wasn't Walker's main concern right now. He had to get up on that station.

He got out with DC Briggs and ran up towards the station at a gallop. They made it up to one of the platforms. There was no one there. On the other side was an elderly gentleman, sitting, waiting for a train.

'Excuse me. You seen any young men waiting here, getting on a train perhaps?' asked Walker.

'A young man?' said the man, seeming a bit hard of hearing.

'Yeah. Have you seen anyone, sir?' asked Walker.

The man shook his head. 'There was a train leaving for Manchester when I arrived, almost an hour ago. I just missed it. The next one should be 'ere soon.'

'Damn it,' muttered Walker. 'Thank you, sir,' he said, looking at DC Briggs, facing her, the wind suddenly whipping at them, blowing DC Briggs's hair all over the place. 'If he's gone to Manchester, finding him is gunna get a whole lot harder.'

They started walking back to the car, quietly assessing their options.

Now in the car park once more, they walked past a taxi,

one that had the door open, the driver sitting inside. They hadn't seen it on the way out, as they'd been in a hurry to get to the station. Walked motioned for DC Briggs to stop, and he approached the taxi and its driver.

'Excuse me,' said Walker. 'Could you step outside for a second, sir. I'm DCI Walker of the Lancashire Constabulary.'

The man slowly got out of the car with his hands in the air. He looked of South Asian origin, perhaps Pakistani or Indian.

'There's no need for that, sir. You aren't in any trouble,' said Walker.

The man put his greasy-looking hands back down. 'So sorry,' said the man, with a thick accent. He wasn't second generation—had perhaps only been here for a few years. 'I didn't mean to drop litter. It just fell down and blew away. I eat. Fish and chip. Delicious.'

'We're looking for a young boy who recently took a taxi ride near here. You didn't happen to pick him up, did you?' asked Walker.

'A *young boy?*' said the man. 'I just pick up young boy. You have picture?'

Walker showed him the photo of Alex Wilkinson.

'Yes. That him. Young boy. Paid in cash. Gave me ten pound. Went to train station. Got on. That way,' he said, pointing in the direction of the Manchester route.

'When?' asked Walker, a little more urgently.

'When?' said the man. 'I been eating a while. Before that I take nap.' He looked at his watch. 'Maybe... more than one hour. Maybe one hour fifteen minute.'

'One hour fifteen,' said Walker, trying to work out where the train might be now. DC Briggs was ahead of him though. She was busily tapping away on her mobile phone.'

'Fifty-nine minutes from Parbold to Manchester Victoria,' she said. 'He's already potentially in the city.'

'God... damn it,' said Walker.

'Sir? Am I in trouble,' asked the man.

Walker shook his head. 'Get his details and come back to the car ASAP,' said Walker to DC Briggs. 'We need to get back to Chorley, find out if those boys have any idea where Alex might be heading. He's properly on the run now. Looks guilty as sodding hell to me. Running for his bloomin' life it seems.'

CHAPTER SEVENTEEN

DCI Walker exited Interview Room 2 with DC Briggs, having just got 'no comment' interviews from both Mohammad Ali Hussein and Liam Holden. It wasn't completely unexpected, given that they both had legal counsel, and would likely have been strongly advised to play it that way, but that didn't mean Walker wasn't disappointed. Despite his many decades on the job, he was still a touch despondent, every single time. It just made their task that much harder.

'We'll try them again in a bit,' said Walker. 'Try to play them off against each other, perhaps. A lot has happened. We need to tidy this up, get organised. Have DIs Riley and Lee arrived yet?'

'I think Riley has,' said DC Briggs. I saw a car pulling in before with someone that looked like him getting out. Not sure about DI Lee.'

'Well, we'll start getting things together, have a meeting when they're all here,' said Walker. 'I need the little boys' room first. And then I'm gunna fix a drink. I'm parched. See you in the Incident Room in five. You want anything? Some caffeine? I need your brain synapses firing on all cylinders for this.'

'That's okay, sir,' said DC Briggs. 'My brain is just fine. But thanks for asking.'

***

With DIs Riley and Lee having now arrived, they joined Walker, DC Briggs, and DI Hogarth in the Incident Room, ready to go over what they had. It wasn't exactly a dream team—a skeleton crew at best—but it was all they were gunna be able to assemble for a case such as this, at present. Resources were at a premium.

It was important to organise at this point rather than having them all running around everywhere on wild goose chases. They needed to formulate a plan of action and follow up on any loose ends. That was how they were gunna get the best out of their modest-sized team. The case was growing, quickly, getting out of hand. Walker needed to get it under control. He wasn't too disappointed that the two new detectives hadn't arrived sooner, as it had given him a little time to get things prepared and together, get his ducks in a row.

'Okay. DIs Riley and Lee, thank you for coming here at such short notice. We'll get you up to speed in no time,' said Walker. 'Now...' He went to the front of the room, started to reorganise the evidence board he'd set up for the case. 'What we have then, is one deceased young girl, a *Charlotte Porter*, aged sixteen, looks to have been the victim of a sex attack, possibly raped—that is yet to be confirmed—and then killed either accidentally or intentionally up near the Pike Tower at Rivington.' The photograph of Charlotte was already on the wall, as was Mo's, and to that he added the mugshots of Alex Wilkinson, Benjamin Jackson, and Liam Holden. 'We have four boys who were possibly involved in this attack, one of which is on the run...' He pointed to Alex Wilkinson. 'One of whom is deceased—either suicide or pushed on the train tracks...' He pointed at Benjamin Jackson, before pointing at Mohammad Ali Hussein. 'By this guy: *Mohammad Ali Hussein*—his best friend, apparently. Seems like a nice lad, to be honest—but you never, ever know, do you?'

Walker picked up a pile of freshly printed pieces of A4 paper, containing a full report of the timeline and events so far, for each of the inspectors to refer to. He started to hand them out. 'I've put together a concise summary of events thus far. As you can see, a red Ford Focus, 2011 model, owned by Alex Wilkinson—the boy on the run—is known to have first picked up Mohammad Ali Hussein near the Majestic Coffee Lounge, while already carrying Liam Holden, another of the boys, and then we have Charlotte Porter also being picked up by the same car soon after. They then stopped at the Stump Lane Store to buy some alcohol, and then we have nothing... until Charlotte Porter is found dead near the Pike Tower the morning after. And on the same day, a few hours after Porter is found dead, Benjamin Jackson can be seen on CCTV at Chorley train station, either jumping of his own free will, or being pushed in front of a train by Mohammad Ali Hussein. It's a lot, I know. So, we're theorising that Benjamin Jackson may also have been in that car, or have been involved somehow in some other way, and has either been killed to stop him from reporting what happened, or he's committed suicide, maybe as a result of the guilt over whatever happened to Charlotte. Mohammad Ali Hussein and Liam Holden are currently being held, here at the station, and Alex Wilkinson is now on the run, having torched his car and likely any evidence that might have been in it. He's possibly in or around Manchester now, best guess. He's also been identified as being up at Rivington the day before the attack. We've got Forensics testing the clothes of the two boys in custody, although they probably changed and got rid of whatever they were wearing, if they have any sense, so not expecting much there.'

DI Riley cleared his throat, getting ready to speak. 'So... what we have here then... is an absolute freaking mess,' he said.

'That would be an adequate descriptive, Detective, yes,' said Walker, knowing they had a tough one on their hands. 'And it's our job to untangle that mess. Now, we already have more than a few actionable points to follow up on, witnesses that need interviewing and the like, to see if we can squeeze any more information out of them—particularly one taxi driver and one café owner. We do need to try to establish what these boys were wearing that night—scrutinise the CCTV footage again, ask the witnesses about their clothing, then check their wardrobes for any matches, bring it in for testing—you never know, we might just get something. Log that in the action book too. However, for now, I think we need to mobilise our limited resources to focus on capturing Alex Wilkinson, as he seems likely the key to this whole thing.'

'Agreed,' said DI Riley, looking around at his colleagues, who all nodded their approval.

'As the notes say, he was last seen at Parbold train station just before a train left heading to Manchester,' said Walker. 'So, we need to track him.'

'We can examine all CCTV footage of the stations between Parbold and Manchester,' said DI Riley, 'starting with Manchester, as that's the most obvious destination, unless he has some friends he can stay with somewhere in-between.'

CHAPTER SEVENTEEN

'DI Hogarth, can you manage that?' asked Walker, knowing damned well he could, but just wanting it confirmed and the actionable point allocated.

'I can indeed,' said DI Hogarth, tapping on the laptop in front of him.

'We also need to release a press statement ASAP,' said Walker. 'We have a possible sexual predator and murderer on the loose, or at least an accomplice to murder, and so people need to know so they can protect themselves,' said Walker. 'We can't release a mugshot of him, or his name at this point, as he may be innocent, and we don't want people taking the law into their own hands, hurting an innocent person. But what we can do is release a rough profile of him, so people—and young women in particular—can be more careful, at least be aware of the danger.'

'I think that's sensible, sir,' said DC Briggs. 'Under the circumstances.' As the only woman currently in the room, she was the only person there who could really empathise with the victim, and how powerless she might have felt. 'Although this is something that women need to be aware of all the time really, anyway, of course,' she added. 'I'm sure you're aware that one in four women have been the victim of a rape as an adult in the UK; one in *four*. That's over six million women.'

'Of course. You're right,' said Walker. 'Most women are probably already being as careful as they can. But I still feel we have a responsibility to release that statement.'

'I'm on it, sir,' said DI Lee. 'I'll inform the press, get them over here.'

'Good,' said Walker. 'Arrange it for 6pm. Then go through the other actionable points in the log-book with DI Riley.'

'And what do you want me to do, sir?' asked DC Briggs.

Walker thought about it. 'Let's take a train. We'll start at Parbold, get off at every stop between there and Manchester Victoria, talk to a few people, staff and the like, see what we can find. Someone must have seen him.'

'Really, sir?' asked DC Briggs. 'That might take a while. Shouldn't we just go by car?'

Walker shook his head. 'No. I want to see what he's seen, feel what he felt. I want to get inside his skin a bit. That's how we'll find him.'

'And what about Mohammad Ali Hussein and Liam Holden, sir?' asked DC Briggs. 'Shouldn't we talk to them again before we leave?'

Walker gave that a little more thought. He needed to get as much information as he could, and quick, before Alex potentially hurt anyone else, or slipped through their fingers for good. But he also didn't want to try too soon with those two boys, let them dig their heels in further. He wanted to give them time to think about things, to make them nervous and edgy—even more jittery than they already were. That was when people tended to make mistakes, to talk when they shouldn't.

'No. Let's give them a little more time to stew. Let's take a train ride, get back here for the press conference, and then talk to the boys again after that,' said Walker. 'You're alright for a late one today, aren't you?' He knew that she would be, but it was still polite to ask.

DC Briggs shrugged. 'Course, sir,' she said. 'As always.'

CHAPTER EIGHTEEN

After returning to Parbold train station, Walker and DC Briggs sat on a wooden bench on the platform that would take them to Manchester. The train was due any minute. They'd timed it well.

'He probably sat right here,' said Walker, seeing that they were on the only seat on the platform. 'He'd have been nervous, knowing someone could have found that burnt out old car any minute. He'd have been in a hurry too, hoping the train was on time, wanting to get away.' He was just talking out loud, sharing his thoughts with DC Briggs, trying to get in the boy's head.

'If he smokes, he probably needed a cigarette,' said DC Briggs, looking around on the floor, joining Walker in the speculation. There was an empty cigarette box, a pack of Benson & Hedges, with a couple of fag ends nearby smoked right down to the filters. 'Maybe those' she said, pointing.

Benson & Hedges—the cigarette brand his sister's killer had been smoking all those decades ago. He'd only recently found out the brand, with advances in forensic analysis now able to distinguish the particular ash made between one brand and another. It was a major breakthrough for his sister's cold case, and for criminal investigations in general. But since he'd found out, every time he'd seen the brand, it had taken him back to that—his very reason for following a career in policing in the first place. It was something that was always in the back of his mind, no matter what case he was working on.

'It's not really the kind of cigarette brand that the young people are using these days, is it?' he asked the much younger DC Briggs, not quite sure about what he was saying, not really being in touch with the youth anymore, he thought, being a man quickly sliding past middle age and into a whole new category. 'It's all e-cigarettes and vaping these days, isn't it? Strawberry and spearmint flavour and the like? All that nonsense.'

'Probably,' said DC Briggs. She was no young bunny anymore either in her thirties. Walker was clearly asking the wrong person. 'Do you want me to collect a sample, just in case?'

'Yes. Just in case we need a DNA match,' said Walker, still waiting on the results of the inspection of the body, half expecting it to return a foreign DNA sample if the girl was the victim of a sex attack, as it so appeared.

DC Briggs did as requested, bagged one of the smoked filters in a transparent evidence bag, sealed it up, and put it in her pocket just as the train was arriving.

'Here we are,' said Walker, not that DC Briggs wouldn't have seen or heard the train coming what with the racket it was making.

'And so it begins,' said DC Briggs. 'Let's see where our boy has got to, try to bring him in. Hopefully, he's not got too far.'

* * *

CHAPTER EIGHTEEN

Walker was on the phone again sitting next to DC Briggs on the train to Manchester, talking to DI Hogarth, trying to find out if he had anything yet—maybe some CCTV footage that might point them in the right direction, save them some valuable time. Walker knew that DI Hogarth could work quickly, but what he said surprised even him.

'You've already spoken to *all* of the Station Managers?' asked Walker, wanting confirmation. 'There's... like... twelve stations between Parbold and Manchester Victoria, isn't there?'

'Thirteen,' said DI Hogarth, dryly. 'And yes, I have. They've all checked their footage from that particular train, and there's nobody who matches the photograph I supplied of Alex Wilkinson. I double checked all the footage myself as well, got it forwarded to me. It didn't even take that long.'

'What about Manchester Victoria itself?' asked Walker. 'No positive ID there either?'

'No,' said DI Hogarth. 'But most commuters exited there, so it was crowded, more difficult to see. He could have been one of several of those passengers, but the footage wasn't good enough to be able to say one way or another, I'm afraid. The Manchester force said their facial recognition software isn't quite as good as what you see on the telly, and their AFR tech was halted some time ago.'

'AFR?' asked Walker.

'Sorry. *Automatic Facial Recognition* technology, sir. They used it at the Trafford Centre on every shopper that entered for six months. People didn't like it,' said DI Hogarth. 'No longer in use, so we can't go down that road.'

'But you can say he didn't get off at any of the other stations?' asked Walker. 'You manually checked?'

'That's correct. But Salford Crescent was also a little crowded, so not one hundred per cent on that one either. All the others are in the clear though. It's either Salford Crescent or Manchester he got off at.'

'Thanks,' said Walker. 'Anything else?'

'Yes. We have a report from the forensic examination of Charlotte Porter. We've got DNA from the semen and saliva of one male, and also the DNA from the saliva of one other male. So, it seems this may have been a double attack, at the very least,' said DI Hogarth.

Hearing this kind of thing crushed Walker's soul that little bit more every time. But he was hoping some good might come out of the results, somehow. That he could at least save someone else from the same fate.

'Okay,' said Walker. 'Get someone to go back to Alex Wilkinson's house with a search warrant. Get something we can get DNA off—a toothbrush, comb, or a used bottle of pop, something like that. If we can get a match, we have strong circumstantial evidence with that alone. At the very least, we can put him at the scene.'

'Will do, Chief,' said DI Hogarth. 'You gunna be back for six then, for the press conference?'

Walker looked at his watch. They still had several hours yet, but time was flying. They'd need to get a move on to be back in time.

'Yeah. We'll be there,' said Walker.

DI Hogarth paused, breathed into the phone, making it sound like a typhoon was whipping up. 'I'm ordering some food in—a pizza, some wings. You want anything?'

Walker looked at DC Briggs, put the phone on speaker. 'DI Hogarth is ordering food. You want some for when we get

CHAPTER EIGHTEEN

back?'

'Domino's,' said DI Hogarth, with a tone that seemed to be designed to tempt them into it. 'We could make a party of it, have a quick get together before cracking on. I'll ask DIs Riley and Lee too.'

'I'm in,' said DC Briggs. 'I'm famished already.'

'Alright then,' said Walker. 'Get us something... whatever. You decide what. But there won't be any parties, not until this case is all neatly wrapped up. We'll work through dinner on this one. There's too much to do.'

'Fair enough,' said DI Hogarth. 'I'll get on it.'

'Oh, and Detective,' said Walker.

'Yeah?'

'Get a DNA sample from the deceased Benjamin Jackson as well, will you? I have a feeling that the second DNA sample found on Charlotte Porter may be from him. And also do one for Liam Holden as well, so we have a full house? We already have a swab from Mohammad. Haven't the results come in for that one yet, to check for any match?'

'Not that I'm aware of. I'll chase it up. I'm on it,' said DI Hogarth. 'Over and out, Chief.'

'Well, at least we're getting *somewhere*,' said DC Briggs. 'And I don't mean closer to Manchester.'

'Yup. But we've still a long way to go yet before we can get a conviction for any of this. And first... we need motive, something beyond a few boys trying to have a good time with a girl. There seems to be more to it than that. I can feel it.'

'Yeah, me too,' said DC Briggs. 'I know exactly what you mean.'

CHAPTER NINETEEN

Alex wasn't sure where he was heading to yet. He just knew it had to be somewhere far away from here. The heat was most definitely on—more than at any other time in his life, by far—and he was gunna be Public Enemy Number One, he knew it. They should have got rid of the body. It was never gunna look like a drunken accident; never in a million years. They had experts in forensics these days. He'd seen the shows on TV—*Line of Duty*, the *CSI* franchise in America, *Luther*, *Criminal Minds*—he'd seen them all. But he had no choice. *They'd* told him to leave it there. He'd always thought those shows were purely fictional actually, until he'd researched it online after Charlotte died, found they actually did some of that stuff in the real world too. Who'd have thought? They could identify you from saliva these days—*goddamned saliva!* She'd been in his bloomin' car, for Christ's sake—that's why he'd had to torch it, *his* beautiful car, to get rid of any fingerprints or DNA, or anything else she might have left behind in there. God knows what. He'd thought about hoovering it, giving it a good clean up, but that probably wouldn't be enough. He wasn't even sure he knew how to use the damned thing—the Hoover—as he'd never properly tried it. Except that one time he'd used it to give

CHAPTER NINETEEN

himself a love bite, and then had experimented, unsuccessful, in giving himself head. It bloody hurt too. He'd only been thirteen at the time; was super horny and didn't know any better. And it seemed he'd not learned much since then. If he'd used the vacuum cleaner, that ridiculous-looking Henry Hoover with its stupid smug grin, his mum would want to know in what way he'd messed up again this time. She'd be furious. When he messed up, she inevitably wasn't happy. She really let him know about it. So, he'd asked *them* what to do about the car and the DNA, but they'd just laughed at him; one told him to go kill himself, one ordered him to go on a rape and murder spree, the voices in his head goading him until he just begged them to shut up. He was tired of it; so, so tired. But he had to do what the Master said. He knew what might happen if he disobeyed.

Having left Manchester Victoria station, he found himself just wandering around, in no particular direction, to begin with. Their voices had stopped for now, leaving him alone, as they often did, allowing him to take a breath. But he knew they'd be back soon enough; they always were. He'd been in an art gallery at one point—he wasn't sure which one—just gazing around at the works in there, his head empty, almost zombie-like. There was this one piece that just seemed to be a mess—paint randomly wiped and splattered onto a canvas by the artist in various dull colours onto a black background. It was called 'Futility'. It felt like his life.

He'd come up with the idea to try to leave the police a message without *them* knowing. He didn't want to turn himself in—the police might not believe him: that he'd been made to do what he did. And even if they did believe some of it, they'd just throw him in the nut house, probably, and that was even worse than prison as far as he was concerned. He wanted to get away, escape, once and for all, start a new life, with a new identity. He knew *they'd* never let him do that, though—his controllers. They'd never let him go. They always knew where he was, somehow. But he wanted the police, and everyone else, to know he wasn't a bad person, at least, that he just needed help, that it wasn't his fault, or his choice. It was out of his hands. He was just a pawn, ready to be sacrificed. In his mind, he was as much a victim as those girls were.

He couldn't believe what was happening; how his life had come to this. He'd never been the brightest, he knew that, had always struggled at school, got poor grades. He'd left school with only two GCSEs, not even passes—a grade 3 in art and a grade 2 in German, of all things, which wouldn't be much help in the real world, not unless he decided to make a go of being an artist in Munich or Berlin or whatnot. Art was one of his few real interests. It was the only thing that really made him feel calm—almost serene. But he'd have to be an anonymous street artist now, what with him likely being a marked man and all. This situation he was in was a whole other level of dumb: it made his exploits at school seem like genius compared to this.

But if any of those knob-heads dobbed him in, he'd kill them—he really would. They'd promised, and he expected people to keep their promises. His mother always did. When she said she was gunna do something—especially to him—she always followed through, and he had the scars to prove it.

He thought about going back to the train station, maybe going somewhere else—like Glasgow, or London, perhaps. Maybe he could make it across the channel, he thought,

CHAPTER NINETEEN

into mainland Europe, and from there he could literally go anywhere. He needed to leave this place for a while, keep tabs on what was happening from afar. And then, if the case was ever closed, ruled as an accident or whatever, he could come back, get on with his life; if his bloody mother ever let him, that was—if she would ever just *die*, of an overdose, or something. She'd been drinking and smoking and injecting herself with this and that ever since he'd been young—self medicating, self-soothing, self-regulating. Not that it had done much good. She had a wicked temper and it only got worse when she drank, most of the time. She was out of control—completely mad, violent. He wasn't totally sure he hadn't lost it himself too, come to that. It was all enough to make anyone go crazy.

He decided to head back to the train station, go somewhere else, hopefully throw the police off even more. He walked past a homeless man sitting on the pavement, the man's clothes grubby and torn, his face dirty, hair greasy, eyes defeated. He stank, even from a couple of metres away in an outdoor space. Alex thought if he stayed here, that's what he'd become—just another nameless disgusting smelly homeless guy, with no ID, no known address, and no history. He couldn't do that. He'd rather die.

He thought about calling his mum, or one of the boys, see if there'd been any developments. He was desperate to know what was going on, but he couldn't risk being tracked down somehow. Not now. He was getting paranoid, he knew, and the only reason he hadn't ditched his phone yet was because he needed it to navigate, and to get information from. He'd feel lost without it. He was a zoomer, a Gen-Z kid. He had no idea how people survived before Google and the Internet, where people used to get their information from. He wondered how long he might last out there, without the Internet. Not long, probably. He didn't know how to find or do anything without the good old World Wide Web. Plus, he had to properly destroy the phone, and he hadn't had the opportunity yet. There was evidence on there, data that he had to get rid of. He'd do it soon though, before he moved anywhere else.

He was just getting back to Victoria Station when he saw a man and a woman approaching. He didn't know why he stopped—maybe the way they were looking around checking everything, or their demeanour, and the belts they had on with accessories attached—but he thought they might be plain clothes police officers, looking for him. Or at least, they might be aware of a person of his description being on the run. So, he ducked into an alleyway before they saw him, crouched down behind some large communal bins. They walked past, right past, and continued up the street. 'Shit,' he whispered. He waited until they were completely gone before he came out again, and he headed in the opposite direction, continuing on toward the train station.

This was good though, as if they were tracking him, he'd just given them the slip—could catch another train and then their task of finding him would get a whole lot harder. Manchester was a major city with rail networks going all over the country. They'd never have the manpower to check every single station; at least, he didn't think they would. And if he stayed off the grid—well off it—he might have a chance of lying low for a while. He'd withdraw all the money he had, cover his face with his T-shirt while drawing the cash maybe, or pay someone else to do it, and then ditch his cards, destroy his phone too. He'd pay for everything with cash from now on, would never sign his real name if he stayed anywhere. He'd leave no trace behind of his existence, either digital or physical. He'd become a ghost. That was his plan, anyway.

By the time he got back to the station, Alex had a newfound positivity, that everything was going to be okay. They couldn't prove he'd done anything wrong. Not really. They had nothing. There were no CCTV cameras up on the Pike. Any evidence would be circumstantial. It wasn't illegal to have a party, have some fun—at least, not when he last checked. They'd be alright. People had accidents all the time. They just had to ride it out, stick together, not say anything. They'd only be screwed if one of them told.

He passed a Starbucks Coffee shop, and the TV caught his eye. He went inside for a second, got a bit closer. It was a Granada Reports news broadcast showing a mugshot of a young black boy, with the headline 'Fatality at Chorley Train Station: Boy, Seventeen, Dies on Impact'. Alex squinted his eyes, got a bit closer. It was him alright. His name was right there below the picture: *Benjamin Jackson: Deceased*.

'Oh, no,' said Alex. 'Ben? What have you done?'

It seemed that Ben had found his own way of escaping, something that Alex had not considered, not for a second—not yet anyhow. He was breathing heavily, his mind running wild, wondering whether Ben might have left something behind for the police to find—a letter of confession perhaps, telling them what had happened that night. He didn't want to think about it. He was breathing heavily, hyperventilating, his heart racing.

He ducked into the men's toilet and went over to a sink, splashed some cold water on his face. This was probably how he'd be washing from now on in the immediate future, he realised—in public restrooms—and his spirits sank further.

There was only one other guy in the restroom, who soon left, leaving Alex alone. He got out his mobile phone and checked his calls and texts—there was nothing new. Then, he wiped it, restored it to its factory settings, getting rid of all his data. It took a little time, but when it was complete, he put the phone on the tiled floor and started to stamp on it with the heel of his shoe, as hard as he could, again and again, until it was no longer usable. Then, he filled the sink up with water and stuck it in there as well, for good measure, before taking it back out, wrapping it in several disposable paper towels, and stuffing it in the garbage bin. *That should do it,* he thought. The police might have his mobile phone records by now, could probably track him with it. He should have got rid of it sooner. Stupid. He was gunna have to get smarter if he wasn't going to be caught. He'd have to grow up some. While he still had some hope he could outrun the police though, he knew he could never outrun *them*. He'd tried, and failed, many times; they always knew how to find him, somehow, wherever he went. They'd burrowed deep into his brain, knew his every move. Escaping them was going to require a different approach.

Alex walked out of the Starbuck's Coffee shop at Victoria Station feeling like a new man. He put his baseball cap low, over his eyes and face, and put his glasses on as well, so nobody would recognise him. He'd get all the cash he could, ditch his cards, and be on his way. They'd never find him. Not ever. But first, he had one last thing to do. Something he should have done before leaving but had wimped out. It was time to man up. It was time to do what he should have done years ago.

CHAPTER TWENTY

They'd been looking around the northern side of Manchester city centre for around two hours now, sticking within fairly close proximity to Victoria train station, trying to find out if anybody had seen Alex. Walker's heart had been pumping ever since he'd found Charlotte Porter's body, adrenaline kicking in and not letting up. But it was getting too strong now. He was getting heart palpitations, struggling to breathe. It was something that had been happening to him more and more since his illness—since being struck down with that rare recurrent form of meningitis that could strike again at any time. He thought it might be some kind of trauma-related symptom, something to do with heightened anxiety as a result of his health issues, and his sympathetic nervous system locking him into fight or flight mode for too long. Whatever it was, he needed to keep a handle on it, or he wouldn't be able to do his job properly. His doctor had given him some medication for it after a 24-hour heart rate monitor had ruled out any physical abnormalities—some Propranolol, beta blockers that helped to slow his heart down. He popped a couple of 20mg tablets in his mouth, swallowed them dry as he didn't have any drink. They'd kick in soon, he thought, from experience, settle things down a bit so he could think properly.

'You okay, sir?' asked DC Briggs, being unaware of his condition, along with the rest of the staff at the Lancashire Constabulary, and not knowing what he was taking.

'It's nothing,' said Walker. 'Just a headache. Some painkillers.'

DC Briggs shrugged it off, seemed to think no more of it.

They talked to several people on their way, mainly shopkeepers and street vendors—people who looked like they'd been there for a while, who might have seen Alex. None of them had. Wherever he was, it didn't look like they were gunna catch up to him anytime soon. It seemed that their little excursion would bear no fruit, except for one cigarette butt that could have been smoked by anyone.

DC Briggs looked at her watch. 'Time is ticking on. We still have to get back for that press conference, and you know how the trains are.' She meant they weren't reliable, and that they probably needed to head back soon.

Walker thought about it. It seemed they might be wasting their time here—time that could be better used elsewhere.

'Okay. Let's head back then,' said Walker.

DC Briggs nodded. 'Maybe we could grab a coffee and some snacks before we leave? I don't think I can wait for that pizza,' she said. 'I haven't eaten properly all day.'

'Sure. We can do that while we wait for the train,' said Walker. 'But be quick, mind.'

* * *

CHAPTER TWENTY

They entered the Starbuck's Coffee shop at Victoria station, the one they'd passed on the way out, but hadn't bothered to check as Walker had presumed Alex would be in a hurry, would have gone straight past it. However, now they were here, he figured he'd ask around while DC Briggs was making her order, give it one last shot.

'You're sure this is him?' asked Walker. He was talking to one of the staff members there, showing her a photograph of Alex—a young woman whose primary job, at the moment anyway, seemed to be cleaning up and wiping the tables.

'Yeah. Pretty sure. I have a good eye for faces. I'm a portrait photographer. He asked me where the toilet is, so I pointed him in the right direction,' she said. Walker looked around, trying to spot the lavatory. 'Over there,' she said, pointing.

'Thank you,' he said, before heading straight to the men's toilet, leaving DC Briggs at the counter.

He went in and there were a couple of guys in there, one urinating and one washing his hands. He cleared his throat to get their attention. 'Excuse me,' he said. 'DCI Walker of the Lancashire Constabulary. I need to search this room. I'm gunna need you out, just for a few minutes, as soon as you can.' The men quickly finished their business and exited the room.

Walker took a look around, inside the toilet cubicles, inside of the cisterns of each toilet, and then he started to root around in the rubbish bin. It was mostly used paper towels, some receipts, and one Snickers wrapper. But down there, near the bottom, was something heavier: one discarded mobile phone.

DC Briggs entered just as he pulled the phone out of the bin. 'Chief?' she said. 'One of the customers said there's some copper in the toilets who just kicked them out. You been making friends again?'

'Found this,' he said, holding the battered phone up for DC Briggs to see.

DC Briggs paused. 'You think it might be Alex's?' she asked.

'Well, since I just got a positive ID on him coming in here, I'd say so,' said Walker. 'In fact, I'd bet my life on it.'

Walker took out an evidence bag and carefully placed the phone into it, before putting the lot in his pocket.

'Maybe something to hide on there? Or he's scared of being tracked with it,' said DC Briggs.

'Or maybe he just doesn't want to be contacted,' said Walker. 'Either way, he's now digitally untraceable, unless he uses a bank card or has some other device, which is unlikely since he's ditched this.'

'So, our trip wasn't such a waste of time after all,' said DC Briggs, looking notably more upbeat about the whole thing.

'It seems so,' said Walker, also feeling pleased with himself. 'Let's go get that train, get back. Once that press release is issued, his face will be his main problem.'

'Sir? I thought you said we couldn't release his mugshot in case he was innocent, and someone hurts him?' said DC Briggs.

'Well, I've just had second thoughts, and that's a risk we're going to have to take,' said Walker. 'We need to bring him in. He's a danger to society. He's on the run, covering his tracks. Innocent men don't act like that. If we don't release the mugshot, then there's a danger that more innocent people might be hurt.'

'It's not easy this job, is it?' said DC Briggs.

'Look, we'll release his profile, and then we'll have people everywhere able to ID him. And as soon as we get anything, we'll be on him.'

'And if we don't?' asked DC Briggs. 'Get anything, I mean?'

'Then we'll come up with another plan,' said Walker. 'Now, you gunna use one of these troughs, Constable, or shall we be on our way?'

CHAPTER TWENTY-ONE

Walker and DC Briggs returned to Chorley police station and entered the Incident Room they'd set up, their base camp. Walker took out the phone he'd retrieved from the lavatory bin at Starbuck's Coffee at Victoria Station and put it on the desk in front of DI Hogarth; he was working on his laptop computer, as per.

'Oh. What's this?' he asked.

'Alex Wilkinson's phone, hopefully,' said Walker. 'Found it somewhere he'd been. Got a positive ID on him going into a Starbuck's Coffee bathroom. Found this in the bin there amongst all the paper towels.'

DI Hogarth glanced up at Walker. 'Been rooting around in bins again? That's quite the hobby you have, Chief,' he said, smiling.

'It's been badly damaged—probably on purpose. Looks like he's tried to destroy it. Think you can get anything from it?'

DI Hogarth inspected it, took a good look while it was still in the transparent evidence bag, examining it this way and that. 'There are many ways to destroy the data on a mobile phone for good—such as using powerful magnets, burning it, or grinding it to dust—but stamping on it or hitting it with a hammer is not one of them. This will prevent everyday

CHAPTER TWENTY-ONE

functionality, but it does not mean there'll be no data left to forensically retrieve. Some of it might be corrupted, but there should be plenty left,' he said. 'I'll see what I can get.'

Walker breathed a small sigh of relief. 'Good,' he said. 'It took all afternoon to get that, and little else. And I want confirmation that it *is* Alex's first. Check for prints too.'

'If it's his, it should be registered as such,' said DI Hogarth. 'But yes, I'll check for prints on it too, as a matter of course.'

DI Riley was also there, sitting at another desk, busily working his way through some paperwork, while DC Briggs sat near him, getting ready to write up her report of the past few hours.

'How's it going?' she asked.

He looked up, seeming like he'd been so engrossed in his work that he'd only really just realised they'd come in. He looked at DC Briggs first, and then Walker.

'Chief,' he said. 'A word, please.'

'What is it, DI Riley,' asked Walker. 'You got something too?'

'I'd say so,' said DI Riley. 'Quite a bit actually. We've had various forensic reports come in since you've been gone. The DNA samples found on Charlotte Porter's body were from Benjamin Jackson and Alex Wilkinson—the latter matching another sample we took from Alex's toothbrush. We have saliva from both on the body, and semen from Alex. He had sex with her. And there's more...' he went on, flipping a page on the report.

'What?' asked Walker, the suspense killing him.

'The autopsy revealed that Charlotte Porter had taken a blow to the stomach prior to her death, while there were also some...' He glanced up for a second, hesitating. 'And I quote, *genital injuries and tearing of the vagina*. Not pleasant reading but it is what it is. It seems she was sexually assaulted, at the very least. The cause of death is blunt force trauma to the head, most likely from a blow to the Pike Tower itself, as some of Charlotte's blood and skin was found on the stone building there,' said DI Riley. 'However, toxicology revealed that she was intoxicated, with both alcohol and marijuana being at high levels.'

'Then we have Alex Wilkinson for rape and assault, with Benjamin being implicated in this as well,' said Walker, 'which would explain why Alex is running, and Mohammad Ali Hussein and Liam Holden are not, and perhaps why Ben killed himself—probably a result of guilt or fear of being incarcerated.'

'But why wouldn't Mo and Liam talk if they weren't involved?' asked DC Briggs. 'Do you think they'd go to jail for their friends?'

Walker thought about it. 'I think they might go to jail *because* of their friends,' he said. 'Have you heard of "joint enterprise"?'

A light seemed to go off in DC Briggs's head. 'I have indeed. Covered it during my degree. Wait...' She opened up a laptop on her desk and tapped on the keys a few times. 'Here we are—joint enterprise. It says, *"Joint enterprise is a common law doctrine where an individual can be jointly convicted of the crime of another, if the court decides they foresaw that the other party was likely to commit that crime."* Mohammad Ali Hussein aspires to be a lawyer. He studies this stuff. Do you think that's why he won't talk? He's afraid to be convicted of murder under this common law doctrine?'

Walker looked at her, right in the eyes. 'Well... I'd say it's a distinct possibility, wouldn't you?'

DC Briggs opened her eyes, wide, and turned her mouth

down.

'Convictions of this type are more common amongst ethnic minorities too,' said Walker. 'For whatever reason, that would put Mo and Ben in a difficult position, especially if they were aware of this law, which it seems they both should have been, if Mo told his friend about it.'

'Okay,' said DC Briggs. 'So, this is getting clearer now. We have some boys picking a young girl up, looking to have some fun, have some drinks and a smoke, have their way with her. But she resists, and one, or two of them force her anyway. But she falls, or perhaps is pushed, in the struggle, and hits her head, which kills her. The boys panic, leave the body, tidy up the best they can, and hope it's ruled to be a drunken accident.'

DI Lee entered, looking a little flustered, his face red, a bit sweaty.

'Oh, sir, you're here,' he said. 'Thank God. I thought I was gunna have to do the bloody press conference myself. They said they're ready, that we have to start now.'

'At ease, DI Lee,' said Walker. 'I'm on it. We've just been going through some of the reports. Tell them I'll be down in five.'

DI Lee breathed a heavy sigh of relief. Clearly, he was not one for public speaking. 'Will do, Chief. Thank you.'

CHAPTER TWENTY-TWO

Walker faced a gathering of press inside a ground floor room they'd set up for just this purpose at Chorley police station. It was heavily raining now, so it seemed more practical to hold the conference inside on this occasion.

'Good evening, everyone,' said Walker, taking a seat at the front of the room, with DC Briggs sitting next to him—having not done anything like this since the last big case they'd worked on, the serial killer they'd apprehended from Rufford. It was a case he still thought about, one that had got into his very bones, kept him up at night. And now there was another one. 'I'll keep this as brief as possible. As you probably already know, a young girl was recently found deceased up at the Pike Tower in Rivington. She died of blunt force trauma to the head, but we've since been able to ascertain, through forensic techniques, that she was also raped and assaulted prior to her death. We believe that four young boys were either present or in close proximity during this attack, two of whom we currently have in custody, plus another one of whom recently died at the train station in Chorley—one Benjamin Jackson, possible suicide—and one more who we believe is on the run, last seen at Manchester Victoria train station. His name is

CHAPTER TWENTY-TWO

Alex Wilkinson, nineteen, from Chorley...' There was a flurry of activity as Walker said his name, with cameras flashing and journalists frantically scribbling notes in their various paper and digital notebooks. 'A photograph will be supplied of Mr Wilkinson. We are requesting that the general public come forward immediately if they see or speak to him, as we desperately need to have him in custody too, so no more people get hurt. And we urge caution, to not approach the suspect if possible, and to instead call us right away.' More cameras clicking.

'Have you charged the two boys in custody?' asked one of the journalists, a male, someone Walker hadn't seen before.

'Not yet,' said Walker. 'We're currently still building a case, which may prove them to be either innocent or guilty of being involved in the attack. It is, as yet, unclear. Now, if that is all... that's all we have to say at the present time.'

Another journalist, who'd been sitting in one of the chairs provided, stood up. 'Emma Thompson, Granada Reports,' she said. Walker knew exactly who she was. He'd been on a couple of dates with her, gone a little further than that, actually, before he'd told her he didn't want to see her anymore, that he wanted to try to give it another go with his wife. She hadn't been happy, probably rightly so. He may have led her on. 'If Alex Wilkinson has now made it to Manchester, he could travel to anywhere in the country, or beyond. What do you intend to do about this? Do you have the resources to conduct a nationwide manhunt? Or is there some degree of policing impotency now he's left the immediate area?'

Walker gulped, harder than he'd intended. She'd flustered him alright. She was talking about that time they'd got drunk and ended up in bed together, when Walker had trouble rising to the occasion because he'd been missing his wife. That's why she's used that word: *impotency*. He was sure of it.

'I can assure you we're doing everything we can to bring this crime to justice,' said Walker. It was a blanket statement he'd used before. They'd been taught to use such terminology so the general public and the press were appeased, so everyone was reassured they were doing their job and that everyone was protected from harm—when they really weren't that safe at all. 'Now, if that's all...' he said again, hoping to get away this time.

'Had the offenders been drinking or taking drugs at the time of the incident?' asked another journalist as Walker and DC Briggs were getting up to leave.

'We'll be in touch in due course,' said Walker, as more cameras flashed, and they got out of there. They made it out into the corridor and starting to climb the stairs to the Incident Room on the upper floor at Chorley police station, somewhere the journalists were, thankfully, not permitted to go.

'Hopefully that helps,' said DC Briggs. 'At least we have some eyes on the ground now.'

'Yes, we do,' said Walker. 'Now, let's talk to those two boys again, see if we can get anything more out of them. Hopefully, they've had some time to think and stew, and at least one of them is ready to talk. If not, then this one could drag on for a lot longer than we want it to.' He had a lot of experience with such cases by now, and knew if they couldn't find a quick resolution, then these things often dragged on for months or years, perhaps not ever finding the evidence they needed even after all that time—just like had been the case for his sister, which was now a cold case, almost frozen. But he hadn't given

CHAPTER TWENTY-TWO

up yet. He never would.

'Yes, Chief,' said DC Briggs. 'But maybe we can grab a bite of that pizza first?'

Walker had forgotten about DI Hogarth's order and sighed. He often forgot about taking care of himself when he was working a case. He didn't want to neglect DC Briggs though. He already felt protective of her, despite them only meeting less than a year ago. 'Okay, Detective Briggs. Let's refuel first. We can take a break for ten minutes. A little more time for those boys to marinate wouldn't be a bad thing, I suppose.'

CHAPTER TWENTY-THREE

Walker, DC Briggs, and DIs Hogarth and Lee were chowing down on some of the Domino's pizza and wings that DI Hogarth had ordered, their fingers all slick and greasy, mouths too busy to talk, when DI Riley walked into the Incident Room.

'How dare you enjoy yourselves without me!' said DI Riley, grinning.

'There's not much to smile about yet, Detective,' said Walker, munching on a ham and pineapple slice. 'We still have a lot of work to do. We're just taking five, that's all.'

'I thought you said ten?' said DC Briggs, or at least that's what Walker *thought* she said: her mouth was so full it was hard to tell.

'We've already been here for five minutes,' said Walker. 'And less talking means more eating.'

'Well, sorry to interrupt, but I have something,' said DI Riley. 'Liam Holden says he's ready to talk.'

Walker dropped his slice back onto the pizza box and wiped his mouth. 'Then why didn't you lead with that!' he said. 'We can eat later.'

DC Briggs reluctantly put her remaining piece of pizza back in the box too, rolling her eyes, before grabbing a napkin and

CHAPTER TWENTY-THREE

cleaning up, getting ready to leave.

'Well, it was good while it lasted,' she said.

'Okay. Let's go,' said Walker, looking at DC Briggs. 'It looks like we have another interview to do.'

* * *

Walker was sitting in Interview Room 1 with DC Briggs next to him and Liam Holden across the table. The audio recorder was already rolling, and they'd gone through the formalities.

'Liam, I understand you're ready to tell us some details about what happened up at Rivington Pike on the night Charlotte Porter died?' said Walker. 'Please could you take us through what happened, from start to finish, with as many details as you can remember.'

Liam's face was deathly pale. He was a tough-looking lad, but he knew he was in deep, right up to his neck, and he couldn't hide his fear of being locked up, possibly for life. It was all over him.

He nodded and struggled to swallow. 'It was just supposed to be a bit of fun,' he said. 'Nothing like that was supposed to happen.'

'So, what *did* happen then,' asked Walker. 'We need to know.'

Liam was short but stocky, muscular for his age—could probably hold his own in a fight. 'I can't name names, but we went up there just looking for a bit of fun, that's all. Charlotte decided to come with us—it was her choice. She wanted to have a good time as well. And she did. It was all good, to begin with. We 'ad a laugh.'

'Then what happened?' asked Walker. 'Because she was most certainly not *all good* by the end of the night. And she wasn't laughing. She's dead, Liam. Do you understand? Gone. Left there like a piece of garbage.'

Liam seemed highly irritable. 'I don't really know what happened,' he snapped. 'I left.'

'You *left*?' said Walker.

'Yeah. I wanted to go home early,' said Liam.

'And why would you do that?' asked Walker. 'When it was all such good fun?'

'I... I wasn't enjoying myself anymore,' said Liam.

Walker placed a photograph of the deceased Charlotte Porter on the table in front of him; she was lying on the ground next to the Pike Tower and her dress was clearly torn. Liam glanced at it, before looking away, seeming troubled by the image.

'Did you have anything to do with this?' asked Walker. 'Look at her dress. It's been torn to shreds.'

'Course not. I'm...' said Liam, backing up, not finishing what he was about to say.

'You're *what*?' asked Walker. 'Liam. You said you wanted to talk. What were you going to say?'

'Never mind,' said Liam.

DC Briggs sat forward. Her role was to intervene whenever she deemed necessary, to offer a less heavy-handed approach and some compassion, which they thought might help interviewees open up. And it often did. It was a well-practiced routine by now, and one that Walker and DC Briggs had become adept at.

'Liam,' she said, using her softest, most feminine tone. 'If you don't tell DCI Walker everything, then you're going to be

CHAPTER TWENTY-THREE

in a lot of trouble. If there's anything else, you should tell us now so we can help you.'

'You're looking at a life sentence, Liam,' said Walker. 'Unless there's evidence to the contrary that you did not contribute to beating, raping, and killing this poor girl.'

'Beating?' said Liam. '*Raping?* It's just a ripped dress, that's all. She probably did it herself on some brambles or something on the way over. Or she had too much of a good time with Alex, got a bit rough. People like it that way sometimes, you know. It's not all lights off and missionary position like in your day, is it?'

Walker took out a piece of A4 paper from the same file that the photograph had come from. This was a report from the coroner, detailing the results of Charlotte Porter's autopsy.

'The autopsy revealed that Charlotte Porter had taken a heavy blow to the stomach prior to her death by an object about the size of a human fist, with bruising that one would expect from being punched by a grown man. She also exhibited... vaginal tears, typical of either extremely rough or forced intercourse,' said Walker, his face glum, there being no need to act on this occasion as this kind of thing made his very soul ache. 'So, let me ask you, do you think she was having fun?'

Liam appeared surprised, although Walker had seen acting that good before. People could trick themselves into believing something else, and their face naturally followed.

'That's... We never...' said Liam, but he seemed unsure. 'I told you I don't know what happened. I left.'

'Yes, so you said. Mr Holden, unless you give us something to the contrary, we're building a strong case that you were in fact involved in the attack, rape, and subsequent murder of Charlotte Porter,' said Walker. 'In what is looking like a pre-planned group attack.'

'No. I'm gay!' Liam blurted out, now sweating. 'Alright? I'm bloody gay—a puff, a queer. That's why I couldn't have been involved in no lady rape. I've never told nobody. Not except that doctor I went to see about it. I couldn't have even got it up for her. That's why I had to leave, so the others didn't find out.'

Walker hadn't been expecting that, but it really was of little help to the case other than in providing a little context. Even if it could be verified by the doctor Liam was speaking of, it still wouldn't prove a thing.

'Why would you tell your doctor that you're gay?' asked Walker, wondering whether Liam might be HIV positive.

Liam sighed. 'I don't want to be gay,' he said. 'None of my friends are gay, I don't like gay things. I'm just... I wanted to see if the doc could do anything about it. Give me some medicine or hormone injections or something. He couldn't.'

'Look, Liam. Having a particular sexuality doesn't preclude you from being physically incapable of contributing to what was done to that girl,' said Walker. 'Unless you had another reason for being up there?' He didn't have any actual physical evidence that Liam had been to the Pike Tower yet—only that he'd been in the same car as Charlotte Porter and Mohammad Hussein, the one owned and registered by Alex Wilkinson. He'd been hoping Liam might implicate himself, and he already had by what he'd said. In that sense, the interview had already been a success. But Walker wanted more, to get everything he could while Liam was talking. He knew it might be the last time, that he could clam up again at any time.

Liam gave it some thought. 'Everyone's gunna know, aren't

CHAPTER TWENTY-THREE

they?' he said. 'That I'm gay.'

'Only if it has relevance to the case,' said Walker. 'Did you like one of those boys? Were you having a sexual relationship with one of them?'

'No,' said Liam.

'But you wanted to be?' asked Walker. Liam didn't reply, but his expression said that he did. 'Was it Alex Wilkinson? Were you in love with him?'

Liam stood up. 'I'm done,' he said. 'I should have listened to Mo. He told me not to say anything.'

'Sit down, Liam,' said Walker.

'I've had enough!' shouted Liam, pacing around a bit in the small space he was in.

'Liam, if you don't settle down, DCI Walker will need to restrain you, cuff your hands behind your back,' said DC Briggs. 'If you don't want to talk anymore, that's up to you. But we're just trying to help you out of this very difficult situation, and we can't do that unless you tell us everything.'

Liam took a breath and sat back down. 'I know you have Mo locked up here too. But where is Alex, and...'

He stopped, probably realising they might not have Ben's name yet. But they did, and Liam wouldn't know what had happened to him yet.

'Liam. Listen to me very carefully. Benjamin Jackson is dead,' said Walker, giving it time to settle.

'Dead?' said Liam. *'Dead?* What do you mean?' he asked, in disbelief.

'He fell in front of a train at Chorley train station this morning, was killed instantly on impact. We think he may have jumped or have been pushed, we're not sure yet,' said Walker. 'Can you confirm that he was with you at the Pike

Tower the night Charlotte Porter died?'

Liam stood up again, but without the pacing this time. 'Is this a trick? If it is, it's sick. I'm saying nothing. I've had enough.'

'Liam, Ben really is dead,' said DC Briggs.

Liam sat down again and put his head in his hands. 'Jesus,' he muttered.

'Was he there?' asked Walker.

Liam looked up, full of emotion, but managing to hold back any tears. 'I'm saying *nothing*,' he said.

Walker took out one more report. 'Look, I didn't want to have to do this,' he said. 'But we need to know.' Walker placed the report in front of Liam. It contained three photographs: the first of some human remains on a train line, the second a closer shot of a wallet nearby these remains, and the third a close up of the same wallet open, with the ID card of one Benjamin Jackson. Liam looked at it, his jaw clenching, eyes a little wider, as the truth and realisation hit.

'Okay, okay! Put it away!' he said. Walker did as asked and removed the report.

'We're sorry about your friend,' said DC Briggs. 'And for you having to see that. But we really do need to know if he was with you that night, so we can understand all of this.'

Liam shuffled in his seat. 'Yeah. He was with us,' he said. 'But he didn't hurt Charlotte. Ben wouldn't hurt a fly. He was a gentle sort. Never even seen him have a fight. He was...' Liam started to break down a little. He couldn't speak any more.

'Thank you, Liam. When you're ready, I need you to talk us through exactly what happened that night, everything you know, step by step. Can you do that?' asked Walker. 'Take

CHAPTER TWENTY-THREE

your time.'

Liam took a few seconds to get himself together. 'So... we picked Charlotte up at the bus stop.' His voice was shaky, full of emotion.

'And who is *we*? For clarity,' asked Walker.

'Me, Ben, Mo, and Alex,' said Liam. 'It was a bit of a tight squeeze in the car. We got some booze—Mo went in to get it by himself—and then we went up to the Pike. We got wasted, had some fun, played some music on our phones, and then at some point, Alex went off with Charlotte, behind the back of the Pike Tower. When he came back, he was buzzing his tits off, said she was well up for it, that I should go next. I panicked. I didn't think I could even get it up for a girl; they'd all know. I told him I didn't want his sloppy seconds, enough with the freaky shit, but he kept pushing, called me a pussy, a queer, said I was sad. I didn't know what to do, so I stormed off, told him to go, you know... stuff himself. He was being a total dick, trying to pressure me into doing something I didn't want to do, so I just got the hell out of there.'

'Then why did you run from DC Briggs and the other officers?' asked Walker. 'Why wouldn't you just talk earlier?'

'Because I didn't know how to get home, so I just waited by the car. Alex, Mo, and Ben eventually came, but without Charlotte. They were in a state. Alex said there'd been an accident, that Charlotte was dead—that she'd banged her head or something. We decided not to say anything to anyone, or we'd all be in big trouble. We all agreed: swore.'

'And that's everything?' asked Walker. 'If you really weren't there when Charlotte was hurt, if you co-operate, things won't be too bad for you. Is there anything else, Liam?'

'I can't believe Ben is dead too,' said Liam, beginning to

break down.

'Was it Ben that you liked, Liam?' asked Walker.

Liam nodded, now crying.

'Okay. You did good, Liam. You did the right thing. This will help your case. Take a little time to take in the news about Ben, and we'll get back to you when we figure this mess out,' said Walker. 'Unless you have anything more to add?'

Liam shook his head and put his head in his hands again. He needed some time, so Walker stood up, getting ready to leave him with DC Briggs for the time being. 'I'm sorry about your friend, Liam.' He looked at DC Briggs. 'Take him back to the holding cell, when he's ready, and meet me back in the Incident Room. I'll go over what we have, get ready for the next step.'

CHAPTER TWENTY-FOUR

She was perfect, they'd said—just like the others. None of the girls had dobbed him in for what he did. Not one. Nobody wanted to be publicly shamed or humiliated, wanted their worst secrets getting out in the open. It would somehow make it worse, he thought, if everyone knew, stop them from burying it, stop them from trying to forget. So, he'd been in the clear; until Charlotte, that was. That hadn't gone as planned. The game had now changed.

He'd seen this one at Manchester Victoria, had followed her via tram to Abraham Moss Metrolink, in the suburban area of Cheetham Hill just outside the city centre. It didn't take long, just a couple of stops. Once off the tram he'd followed her along a quiet grassy embankment lined with trees and bushes, and he'd dragged her, at knifepoint, behind one of those bushes. There was nobody else around. She was all alone with him. He had her. She was his.

'Keep still now,' he said, in a low tone, almost whispering. He'd already hit her in the stomach once, immobilised her, just like he had with the other girls. He didn't want to. But the voices he was hearing wouldn't accept anything less. They were out of control now. They wanted another kill. The last one, although an accident, had given them a taste for it, and they wanted more—demanded it. The girl tried to scream so he hit her again, even harder this time. He couldn't let anyone hear. It did the trick, took her breath away, making her unable to speak. 'This will go a lot easier if you stop struggling.'

He forced himself on her, had his way with her. This was the part he liked. It made him feel powerful—made him forget about everything—and of course he was a young man, and liked to have sex, even if it wasn't consensual. And it wasn't like he had any choice in the matter. When he was done, he heard his mother's voice again, and her confidant—that dark demon, the *Master*—telling him to finish her off. He knew they couldn't risk letting her go this time, like they had with the others. The police were already on to him. He might even be in the news. She could call them this time, as soon as he left, give a description of him and where he was. And then he'd be screwed. No. They didn't know where he was right now, and he intended to keep it that way. It wasn't like it was his fault. He was being instructed, *ordered*. He had no choice, or the pain would start all over again.

The girl had recovered a bit now, but she was whimpering, in shock at what had just happened. She looked about sixteen, but some were more mature than others. It seemed this one was not so grown up. *'Please. Let me go now. Please don't hurt me anymore. I won't tell. I won't say anything,'* she whispered, looking at Alex right in the eyes.

Alex pushed his glasses a bit further up his nose, as they'd got wonky during the exertion. 'No, you won't,' he said. His mother's voice was shouting at him now. *Do it, Alex. Do it now, or else!*

He grabbed a substantial piece of rubble that was nearby, held it in his hand.

No, not that. Strangle her this time. Squeeze until the bitch stops breathing!

'No, I can't…' said Alex, hesitating.

Do it now! You know what I can do to you.

'Who are you talking to?' said the girl, whimpering.

Alex dropped the rubble and placed both hands around the girl's neck. She tried to stop him but didn't have the strength. She was only small and skinny, just like all the others. He squeezed and squeezed, not enjoying this part one bit, feeling disgusted at the softness of her neck and the crunching of her windpipe, her expression also repugnant—eyes wide, bulging, going red. She was no longer pretty. She was repulsive, and her arms were flapping around like a wounded bird trying in vain to get away. In a word, it was *horrible*.

And then she stopped moving; her arms went limp, falling to the floor.

She was dead.

Good, said the Master. *That's good, Alex. Good boy.*

CHAPTER TWENTY-FIVE

'We have another one, Chief,' said DI Lee. 'A young girl found dead just outside of Manchester. Another blonde. Looks to have been assaulted and strangled—marks around her neck. You think it's our boy?'

Walker had only just got back to the Incident Room having interviewed Liam Holden, with DC Briggs now having caught up to him.

'Where at?' asked Walker.

'Abraham Moss Metrolink,' said DI Lee. 'It's got a direct connection to Manchester Victoria—just a couple of stops away.'

Walker banged his hand on the table. 'Damn it!' he shouted, exasperated, taking a breath, a moment to get himself together. 'There are gunna be more if we don't bloody find him soon. Get all available resources on this as a priority, urgently. Liaise with the Greater Manchester Police as well. Get everyone on it. Lock the area down before he gets away again. Collate all available CCTV records. Find him.'

'Will do,' said DI Lee, scrambling, looking through various papers, while DI Hogarth also tapped busily on his keyboard.

'Where's Riley?' asked Walker, feeling a bit annoyed that the

CHAPTER TWENTY-FIVE

young detective never seemed to be around when he needed him.

'He's already headed out there,' said DI Lee. 'Didn't want to disturb you while you were with Holden in case you were at a vital moment with him. Made the decision to get over there and make a start, with it being time-sensitive and all.'

Logically, Walker knew it was the right decision, but it still irked him that it wasn't he himself who was making all these calls. He liked to be in control as much as possible—didn't completely trust others to get the job done. Unfortunately, it wasn't a job that could be done alone. He needed his colleagues more than ever given his less-than-optimal health condition these days. It was a team game.

'I'm heading over there. DC Briggs, you can sit this one out since we already have Riley over there. See if you can locate Alex Wilkinson's mother, bring her in for a chat. Maybe she knows something. Maybe he's been in contact with her, and she's not told us, wanting to protect her boy. Either way, we need to talk to her,' said Walker.

'Got it,' said DC Briggs.

'So, DI Hogarth and myself shall stay here to orchestrate everything else? Get through the action book?' asked DI Lee.

Walker thought about it. 'Yes, that would suffice for now, Inspector. And let me know when the mother is here. I want to talk to her myself.'

* * *

What immediately struck Walker about the victim nearby

Abraham Moss Metrolink was the similarity in appearance to Charlotte Porter. She didn't just have the same build or general appearance. She was the spitting image—same hairstyle, height, weight, similar dress, and her face also had a remarkable likeness.

'Well, he certainly has a type,' said Walker. 'We need the media to detail this, so young girls with a similar look can be extra careful.' He was talking to DI Riley, who'd been at the scene for some time already.

'Noted,' said DI Riley.

'You find anything that might link the two cases yet, apart from the obvious?' He was talking about the torn dress, ripped in a similar way to the Charlotte Porter case, strap broken, the adjoining dress torn from right to left—meaning the offender was probably right-handed.

'Just the ripped dress, sir, but if the autopsy reveals any blows to the stomach, then that will tell us more, along with a match on any DNA, of course, if she was raped, which it looks like she was,' said DI Riley. 'What type of rapist do you think we have here anyway? I was considering a power assertive typology at first, but there seems to be a lack of consistency, with elements of anger retaliation and even sadism present.'

'It's not quite like in the undergraduate lectures, DI Riley,' said Walker. 'Out in the field, those nice, neat categories can become a little fuzzier.' Riley wasn't one of the more experienced DIs that Walker had worked with, and he hadn't long since completed his policing degree. But Walker thought the young DI might actually have a point. In the first murder, multiple typologies might have made more sense, as it looked like there were several possible offenders. But this time, it seemed Alex was acting on his own, yet the attack was still

CHAPTER TWENTY-FIVE

inconsistent with a single typology. 'But you have a point. It's almost as if more than one person has carried out this attack—same with the Charlotte Porter case too, which is why we were thinking more along the lines of a group attack. But given what we have here, that might not necessarily be the case. The rest of those boys could just have been at the wrong place at the wrong time. There's something else we're missing.'

Walker crouched down next to the body. Her blue eyes were still open, staring into space, devoid of soul or life. He lifted up her dress, already wearing latex gloves so as to not contaminate the scene.

'I didn't want to touch anything before you got here,' said DI Riley.

Walker nodded, appreciating his patience, while he carefully peeled back the dress. She wasn't wearing any panties and there was some bruising around the stomach area, especially toward one side where her hip bone was.

'Any underwear retrieved from the crime scene?' asked Walker. DI Riley shook his head. 'He likely took them, unless she wasn't wearing any to begin with, which seems unlikely. Same bruising around the stomach, like a blow has been made here. I think this is our guy. Get DNA samples to confirm. We need a match to be absolutely sure, and the sooner the better.' Walker put the dress back down, where it had been, and closed the girl's eyes using his thumb and index finger. 'We got an ID?'

DI Riley nodded. 'She had various cards with her name on: a *Sally Dawber*. Her purse had been discarded to one side. No cash in there though.'

'Right. Inform her family and get an FLO over there to help them through it. I'm going back to Chorley to talk to

Alex Wilkinson's mother. Maybe she knows something about where he might have gone. It's not much, but for now, I'm afraid it's all we have.'

CHAPTER TWENTY-SIX

DC Briggs knocked on the door of Kathy Johnson's house in Moss Side in Leyland for a second time. The door opened a tad, Kathy peering through the crack she'd made. 'You again?' she said. 'How many times? You've been twice already, looking through all our stuff last time. The boy barely lives here. Can't you just leave me alone?'

'I'm afraid not, Mrs Johnson. Your son Alex has been involved in a very serious crime, and we have reason to believe he may just have committed another,' said DC Briggs. 'We're going to have to bring you in to the station for further questioning.'

Kathy opened the door wider, huffed. 'You're arresting *me*?' she said. 'What the hell have I done? I don't know anything about Alex's—'

'I'm not arresting you, Mrs Johnson. But we do need you to help with our enquiries. And refusing to do so might be considered to be a perversion of the course of justice. So, I could arrest you if you refuse, although I'd prefer not to do that. This is an urgent matter, Mrs Johnson. I'm not asking,' said DC Briggs, putting her foot down on this occasion in the absence of DCI Walker, knowing that time was of the essence in this case if no more young girls were to be hurt.

'Sodding ridiculous,' said Kathy, not looking impressed one bit. 'I'll go get me bag.'

'You do that, Mrs Johnson,' said DC Briggs. 'Get everything you need. This might take a while.'

* * *

'Do you know how many times I've had to come down to the station for that bloody boy?' Kathy Johnson was sitting across from Walker and DC Briggs in Interview Room 2 at Chorley Police Station, with Walker having just returned from Abraham Moss. He looked through a file he had in front of him, detailing Alex Wilkinson's criminal record.

'Three,' he said. 'Three times. Twice for anti-social behaviour and threatening an officer, and once for stealing some vodka when he was just fifteen years old.'

'Well, it seems you know better than me then,' said Kathy. 'But too many. That boy is just like his father. *Just* like him.'

'And his father was…?' asked Walker, flipping through his papers, not finding anything detailing Alex's biological, or any other, father.

'Dominic Wilkinson,' said Kathy. 'Ditched us shortly after Alex was born. Bastard. Ran off with another woman. Never seen him since.' Considering this must have been almost two decades ago, going off Alex's age, Kathy still seemed significantly hurt by this, like it had only happened yesterday.

Walker scratched at his stubble. He wanted to dig deep into the psychology of Alex—get into his head, find out what made him tick, and what kind of trauma he might be carrying that fuelled his behaviour. 'And did his father have any history of criminality?'

'I don't know. Why don't you check? You seem to know everything else,' she said. She clearly deeply resented being taken down to the station, and Walker was just glad she was saying anything at all. They didn't always, especially if they had a son to protect. The mothering instinct was normally strong.

'We certainly will. I just wanted your take on it first,' said Walker. 'If you wouldn't mind.'

Kathy thought about it. 'I supposed he could be violent sometimes, especially when he'd had a drink. Knocked me about a few times. Said he was sorry and that he wouldn't do it again. But he did.'

'I see. I'm sorry to hear that, Mrs Johnson. Is there anything else?' asked Walker. 'Any other crimes you know of involving either Alex or his father?'

'I think Dom nicked some stuff sometimes. Came home with things he couldn't possibly have afforded. Brought home this posh watch one time—some old Rolex. Must have been worth a few bob. He didn't keep it for long though. Probably sold it,' said Kathy. 'Said it felt too heavy when he was wearing it.'

'I see,' said Walker.

'He was no saint,' said Kathy, underlining her assessment of her ex-partner. 'Good riddance, I say.'

'Mrs Johnson. Your son, Alex, has been involved in what we believe is not one, but two rapes and murders, committed against young women,' said Walker, never breaking eye contact, trying to gauge her reaction. 'Has your son ever demonstrated any proclivity towards violence, especially against members of the opposite sex, or those physically inferior to him?'

Kathy's reaction was difficult to gauge. It seemed she was in disbelief, couldn't comprehend that Alex might have actually done such things.

'My Alex would never do anything like that,' she said. 'He might be a bit naughty sometimes, but he isn't no rapist or murderer. He's soft. Soft in the head. You must have the wrong person.'

'Mrs Johnson, we have a DNA sample from a semen deposit found on the first victim, matched to Alex, we have CCTV footage of her getting into Alex's car just hours before her death—a car that has since been purposefully and deliberately destroyed—and Alex is nowhere to be found,' said Walker. 'And now we have a second victim with the same M.O., found just a short distance from where Alex was last seen. I know it's hard to accept, but it seems that your son has done these things, and now we must find him before he hurts anybody else. Can you help us do that?'

Kathy seemed to think about it, like she was considering the possibility, but then her expression changed, perhaps backing up, resisting the idea. 'So, he had sex with a girl. That's not a crime, is it? Good for him. It's about time. And then she had some kind of accident and he's panicked, ran off. I don't blame him. Your lot have been giving him a hard time since he was a young lad. He probably thinks you have it in for him.'

Walker looked at DC Briggs, who gave a slight but perceptible shake of the head, indicating that she also thought they weren't going to get much more out of Kathy Johnson.

'Kathy,' said DC Briggs, taking over, seeing if she might be able to get through to her. 'I can't pretend to be a mother,

CHAPTER TWENTY-SIX

and know how you're feeling, because I'm not. But I do have a nephew, and I'd just be a mess if he ever got involved in anything illegal. I'd defend him until the end though. *Except* if other people were in danger. Maybe your Alex is not well. Maybe he needs some help. To give him that help though, we first need to find him, or other young girls might also get hurt, or worse. You know this is the right thing to do.' She'd given it her best shot. Now it was up to Kathy.

'I'm sure he'll come to you when he's ready,' she said. 'He didn't do this. He's not responsible. I'm sure of it.'

It was a dead end. She wasn't going to give them anything, even if she did have any idea where he might be, which was unlikely.

'Okay. Thank you for your time, Mrs Johnson,' said Walker. 'If you've nothing else to say, we'll now need to search your home again to look for any further clues as to Alex's whereabouts. DC Briggs and I will personally escort you back to your house and conduct that search. We already have a search warrant. Now, is there anything else you can tell us?'

Kathy shook her head and looked away defiantly.

'Right. Let's go then,' said Walker, looking across to DC Briggs. 'And bring plenty of evidence bags, just in case.'

CHAPTER TWENTY-SEVEN

Alex's bedroom stank. It smelled like it hadn't been cleaned in months—years, maybe. Walker opened the bedroom's royal blue curtains and dust plumed out onto the black carpet. Then he opened the dark grey blind that lay behind the curtains and, after a bit of wriggling and pushing, cracked a window open, letting in some fresh air.

'It's rank in here, eh?' said Walker. DC Briggs was covering her mouth and nose with her hand, removing it and putting it back several times while she got used to the aroma. 'I don't know how people live like this?' she whispered as Kathy Johnson was downstairs having just driven her back, possibility listening.

Walker started to carefully look through some of Alex's things. The room was a mess, bed unmade, sheets stained, garbage here and there: some empty crisp packets on the floor, empty Coca Cola bottles dotted around, used tissues. They should have brought hazmat suits—it was an environmental disaster.

'Leave no stone unturned,' said Walker. 'We need something here.'

They got to work, wearing latex gloves and holding crime scene fingerprint brushes in case Alex had brought any items

CHAPTER TWENTY-SEVEN

back from any of his victims—perhaps even victims they didn't yet know about. There wasn't much of any note, just typical teenaged boy's things: some old footy mags, a base guitar and small amp, a keyring with the Heineken brand label on it.

Walker looked under the bed. It was littered with stuff. There were bits of junk and garbage under there, some odd items and old toys that appeared to be from his younger years. But there were also three boxes with lids on. He slid them out and opened one up.

Inside the box were some hardcore pornographic magazines. Walker flipped through one.

'Boys and girls are so different, aren't they?' said DC Briggs. 'I really don't know what you lads see in that stuff. It's horrid.'

'Yeah. You're probably right. It is pretty typical for a teenaged boy to have stuff like this though,' said Walker. 'Nothing unusual there. Although... I'd have thought the youngsters relied more on digital images these days. He must like the retro stuff. Or he found them and couldn't throw them away.'

'Or he's paranoid about a digital trail,' added DC Briggs.

Walker stopped on a page that featured a bisexual threesome, including some male homosexual acts. It seemed this page had been particularly well used, with the corner of it being dog-eared several times.

'Possibly likes both boys and girls,' said Walker. 'We'll make a note of that in case any male victims show up.'

He opened up the second box, which was filled with various old wires and electrical adaptors. The third box, however, was stuffed with pieces of A4 paper folded in two. He started to open some up. They were sketches, and violent ones at that, most with a common theme: a female being tortured in various creative ways—one being hanged, another on fire, one more being shot with a gun, and one wounded with an arrow. Some were also coloured in, with there being plenty of red used for blood. As he dug through the pictures, he found they became less mature and less skilful, suggesting that Alex had been drawing these for a number of years. But the themes were very consistent.

'Bag these,' said Walker. 'Evidence of violent fantasies involving women, with elements of sadism and torture. He wants to humiliate, to destroy these women. He's obsessed with it, has been for some time. Might even use them as masturbatory material.'

Inside of this same box also lay an old Swiss army knife, but it was all rusted up, the various tools not easily able to be pulled out. Walker inspected it while DC Briggs watched on, kneeling nearby.

'Maybe he got a new one?' she said. 'Perhaps a bigger knife, something more threatening. He might need something like that to more easily coerce those girls.'

Walker nodded. 'I think we're done here,' he said.

'None of this is gunna help us find him, is it Chief?' said DC Briggs.

'Probably not,' said Walker. 'But I have an idea. It's not much but... come on.'

* * *

Walker had posted undercover police officers at every station within three stops of Manchester Victoria, with instructions

CHAPTER TWENTY-SEVEN

to identify and arrest Alex Wilkinson. They'd needed to draw on every possible resource in order to be able to do this, but he'd managed it, *just*, calling in a few favours in the process. Working for three decades or so with the Lancashire Constabulary came with its benefits. Now all he needed was a positive ID, and for one of those officers to arrest him and bring him back. Easier said than done.

It seemed Alex was using public transportation to get around, namely trains and trams, so that was as good a place to start as any. With his last known location being at Abraham Moss, they focussed on and around this area, but Walker also knew he really could literally be anywhere by now, and that he'd probably got as far away from this Metrolink as possible—if he had any sense—having just killed another girl there. It had now been confirmed, via DNA matching, that Alex *had* also carried out this crime—and so this updating of the case to serial murder status had allowed more resources to be channelled their way. This was very much Walker's area of expertise, and so he knew all too well that if they didn't catch up to him soon, then another victim might well soon turn up.

Walker was back at Chorley station orchestrating the whole thing on his mobile phone—the two-way police radio was just no good at such distances, not what it was designed for. DI Hogarth had set the iPhone up for him so the line was open to all officers in the field, simultaneously. Any sniff of their guy and he'd be back out there himself, getting on his tail.

'PC Keen, anything?' asked Walker, doing the rounds.

'Negative,' said PC Keen. 'Will keep looking.'

'PC Khan, what do you have, over?' said Walker.

'A dodgy knee from going down the underpass stairs, but other than that nothing, over,' said PC Khan.

Walker put the mobile phone he was using back on the table in front of him, leaving the line open, and sighed. They'd get the media on it soon too, issue a warning to young girls in particular of the description of the first two victims. He'd set up a sit down in one of the discussion rooms with some of his most trusted and reliable media contacts. He needed some help on this one, and he wouldn't be shy in saying so. He knew not everyone watched the news, of course, and even when they did, not everyone listened. But it was the best he could do, for the time being.

He also had DI Hogarth sifting through the social media accounts of all those currently involved, including Liam Holden, Mohammad Ali Hussein, Charlotte Porter, Benjamin Jackson, and of course Alex Wilkinson himself. To add to that list there was now also the second victim, Sally Dawber—although no connection could currently be found between her and the others, so it did seem that this was an unplanned opportunity attack.

Although they knew Alex had ditched his phone, this did not mean that he hadn't got hold of another one or had some other kind of mobile device that could connect to the Internet, so they wanted to see if there was any online activity, or an attempt to contact any of his so-called friends in some other way. If he did, it might be possible to pin down his location from the wireless signal used. They were grasping at straws, Walker knew, but he was out there somewhere. They just needed a trail of breadcrumbs to follow. In recent years, Facebook in particular had become a key tool in police investigations, with suspects' accounts accessed to look at recent activity and connections with others. It was a whole new science, and Walker was beginning to feel out of touch,

CHAPTER TWENTY-SEVEN

wondering whether his days as a detective might be numbered.

'I might have something here,' said DI Hogarth, who was sitting in front of his laptop computer, as standard. 'A message posted on Mohammad Ali Hussein's Facebook page. *Remember what we agreed? – A.* It's from a recently created Facebook account, with the name "Kid A". Could be Alex. The same message is also posted on Benjamin Jackson's Facebook page. But nothing on Liam Holden's, probably because he has his account set to only allow friends to post on his timeline. 'And there's more...'

Walker moved in, getting close to DI Hogarth, looking over his shoulder at the computer screen. 'What is it?'

'Kid A has also been logging on to Charlotte Porter's account. He commented 'RIP' on one of the photos. So, whoever it is, they have a connection with at least three of those involved. And with it being signed "A"...' said DI Hogarth, throwing his hands in the air. But here's the best part.' He tapped on his computer once more, bringing up a map. 'He's been using the Wi-Fi signal from a Tesco's supermarket in Atherton. It's about a kilometre from the train station there, easily walkable.'

'Zoom in on that,' said Walker, so DI Hogarth did as requested, put it on satellite view.

'He's logged on twelve times in the past few hours. All from the same location,' said DI Hogarth.

'Well, it'd be suspicious for him to be hanging around inside Tesco for hours on end, keep coming back in just to use the Wi-Fi. Maybe he's found a place outside, close enough to use the signal, but somewhere relatively private,' said Walker.

'Let's take a look at the Street View then and see.' DI Hogarth virtually whizzed through the streets surrounding Tesco's supermarket in Atherton, before settling on an image and zooming in. 'There,' he said. 'On Tyldesley Road across from the Atherton Arms. Close enough to Tesco to possibly catch their Wi-Fi signal, but fairly private. He might have been sitting right there on that wall. Nice quiet spot—back-alley type thing leading out from the back of the store. Probably little used. I reckon he's been sitting there, best guess. Maybe he's found a place to rest up nearby too, get a little sleep and whatnot, eat some food. He's probably tired. He's been up to a lot in the last forty-eight hours.'

'Right. Let's get over there. We'll go by car, me and DC Briggs in one, and DIs Lee and Riley in another. Let's see if we can catch him at it,' said Walker. 'Can you alert us whenever Kid A is back online, using Tesco's Wi-Fi again?'

DI Hogarth smiled. 'Yes. Of course, I can. That's exactly what I'm here for.'

'That you are,' said Walker. 'That you are.'

CHAPTER TWENTY-EIGHT

Alex dug his second-hand iPad out from his backpack and turned it on. It was an old model, much chunkier than they are now—but all he could afford. It would do for now. At least he could log on to the Internet. Tesco's Wi-Fi signal had proven to be the most stable, so he'd stick by there for a bit, recharge. He thought about where he might go. Maybe he could disappear to the highlands of Scotland for a while, live off the land, scrounge for food out of some local bins. People chucked all kinds of things away. If food went past its sell-by date by just one day, people would just throw it out. It was madness. He'd survive, somehow—at least for a while, until the heat was off, until he'd had time to think, get a solid plan.

He wanted to know where his friends were, whether the police had spoken to them yet. Ben hadn't replied to his message. Mo neither. And Liam hadn't accepted his friend's request. They weren't that stupid though. They'd know it was him. So, he deduced from their non-response that either they didn't want to talk to him, or they couldn't.

'Where the hell are you?' he muttered. He was sitting on a small wall at the back of Tesco's, just close enough to be in range of their Wi-Fi signal. He dug his fingers into the soil of the barren flower bed that the wall was holding, felt the dirt. He knew he'd be a part of such dirt one day, just like those girls would be. He took his hand back out and wiped it on his jeans. 'You'd better not have said anything, put me in it. I'll bloody kill you.'

He Googled each of his friends' names next, trying to see if there was anything else, any news article about the case, perhaps, containing their names. One article came up containing Ben's full name, from a local newspaper called the Lancashire Telegraph. The headline read: 'Local Boy, Benjamin Jackson, Killed at Chorley Train Station'. Alex almost dropped the iPad, just about gripping on to it before it hit the ground.

'*Shit!*' he said. 'Ben?'

He got up, punched a wooden fence opposite him, and then again, several times, until the pain hit.

'God damn it,' he said. He went back to his iPad and scanned the article: *Probable suicide, but also elements of possible foul play that are being investigated by the local police.* Alex looked up and his rational brain started to wrestle back control. If Ben was dead, then at least that was one less witness. That was something. Who was he kidding? He'd left evidence everywhere. The police would catch up to him eventually. It was only a matter of time.

Alex put his iPad back in his backpack. He'd go back to that place he found, get a little more rest. They wouldn't find him there, in the woods, deep in the undergrowth. He'd be safe for a little while, at least. He had some water, and some snacks, and a little shelter if it rained. And it wasn't even that cold. He'd get his head down for a bit, try to process everything that had happened.

CHAPTER TWENTY-EIGHT

When he got up to leave, though, a girl walked past, and he heard his master's voice again. *Let's have another look at HER,* he said. *She might be another one. Hurry now. Go!*

Alex grabbed his backpack and got after her, his thoughts racing, frantic, fear folding in, suffocating him. He knew there'd be a world of pain with his name on if he didn't catch up. He didn't *want* to hurt anyone. Not really. But then he heard his mother's voice in his head too, as always, vibrating in his skull, taunting him, telling him he was filth, nothing, a loser, a coward. He hated her. He always imagined her eyes, her face, smelled her perfume, whenever he hurt someone. It spurred him on, allowed him to do what needed to be done. He was sorry to those girls—they didn't deserve it—but he really had no choice. It was out of his blood-stained hands.

CHAPTER TWENTY-NINE

Walker and DC Briggs were parked at the Atherton Arms, right across from the area they thought Alex might be using to connect to the Internet. DIs Riley and Lee were also parked up at the Tesco's car park, surveilling the front of the supermarket, in case Alex might go inside.

'I think we're too late,' said Walker, getting out of the car. He called DI Hogarth on his mobile and his colleague answered after two rings. 'He still online?'

'No, Chief. Logged off about fifteen minutes ago,' said the DI. 'Didn't post anything new though.'

'Shit.' Walker hung up. 'He's gone,' he said to DC Briggs, who'd now also got out of the car and closed the door. 'Let's take a look around.'

'Sir?' asked DC Briggs.

'He's logged on from this location several times in the past few hours. He must be lying low somewhere, close-by,' he said, gazing around. 'Maybe we can find him.'

DC Briggs nodded. 'What about DIs Riley and Lee?' she asked.

Walker got them on the two-way radio. 'Riley, Lee, he's not here. We're going to take a look around, see if we can find

CHAPTER TWENTY-NINE

anything. One of you stay out front, and the other bring the car around the back, park up at the Atherton Arms and keep watch from there, see if he returns.'

'Got it, Chief,' said DI Riley. 'Let us know if you need back-up.'

'Will do, over,' said Walker. 'Come on.'

* * *

'What's that?' said Walker. He'd spotted something while peering through a crack in a fence that allowed him to see in somebody's back garden. He got a bit closer, scrunched his eyes up to see better.

'What is it, Chief?' said DC Briggs, looking around the street, making sure they weren't getting any undue attention.

'Looks like a dirty old tent,' he said. 'In what is otherwise a very well-kept garden. You knock on the door, see if there's anyone in. I'll wait here, in case it's our boy and he runs.'

DC Briggs did as asked while Walker waited, trying to see if he could get a better view, pulling himself up on the fence and looking over. A couple of minutes later, DC Briggs came back.

'No answer,' she said. 'Must be out.'

Now it was Walker's turn to look up and down the street. When in plain clothes, it was better not to get any attention—it prevented having to explain things to the general public and show their ID badges. That only slowed things down. But luckily, there was nobody around.

'Give me a leg up,' he said. 'Hands together.'

DC Briggs looked unconvinced. 'Sir. I'm not sure I can—'

'Nonsense,' said Walker. 'Just take some of my weight, and I'll do the rest, pull myself up and over.'

It wasn't the highest of fences, but with Walker still not being in the best of shape, he wasn't totally confident he could manage it. DC Briggs did her best to hoist him up, and Walker did the rest, as promised, managing to get one foot on the top of the fence, and then get his leg over. It was the first time he'd managed that feat in quite some time.

He dropped down, into some bushes of the non-prickly variety, and got over to the tent. 'Hello. Is anybody there? Sorry to bother you. It's the police. There was no answer at the door.' He unzipped the tent, getting ready in case Alex was in there, immediately stepping back in the event he had a weapon.

There was nobody in there.

What was there, though, was a child's tea set and some teddy bears and other cuddly toys. It was a child's plaything. Alex wasn't here.

Walker was just about to leave the same way he'd entered when a man came out of the house, bleary eyed, like he'd just been sleeping.

'*Hey!* What the ff—'

'It's okay!' shouted Walker. 'I'm DCI Jonathan Walker of the Lancashire Constabulary. We're looking for a dangerous offender who's on the run and we thought he might be hiding out in here. Apologies.'

'Bollocks,' said the man. 'You wuz tryin' to rob us, weren't ya?' The man grabbed a loose brick from the garden, started to walk over, menacingly.

Walker held out his hand. 'Easy.' He removed the ID card

that was hanging around his neck on a lanyard, threw it over to the man. He didn't catch it, but the man stopped to pick it up, never taking his eyes off Walker. He scrutinised the card.

'Police Officer. Warrant number 193675. Jonathan Walker, Detective Chief Inspector,' he said, reading the card. 'Lancashire Constabulary.' He threw the ID card back and Walker caught it by the lanyard this time. 'You could have just knocked.'

'Er, we did, sir,' said Walker. 'No answer.'

'Oh. I guess I fell asleep,' said the man. 'Been working lates. Can I help you?'

'No. We'd better be on our way', said Walker, before taking a photograph of Alex Wilkinson from his pocket and getting closer to the man. 'I don't suppose you've seen this guy knocking around, have you?'

The man took a good look. 'This the guy—the fellow you're looking for?'

'Have you seen him?' asked Walker, a bit more urgently.

The man rubbed his stubble, which would soon be classed as a beard if he didn't attend to it. 'You know what... think I saw him hanging around near the bottom of... whatsit? Tyldesley Old Road. Was wearing a black baseball cap, I think, carrying a backpack. I remember cos he bumped into me by accident, didn't say sorry. Looked in a hurry. I thought he looked dodgy, like maybe a dealer. Is that why you're looking for him? He been dealing to the kids round 'ere? Getting them all messed up?'

'Tyldesley Old Road. What else is near there?' asked Walker.

'Oh. Nowt much. Just the stadium for Atherton Collieries,' said the man. Walker looked at him, not quite sure what he was talking about. 'They're a football team,' explained the man.

'Not a very good one, mind. In the Northern Premier League. That sounds better than it actually is. They're a non-league side. Amateur.'

Walker sighed, thinking this information would probably be of no use. 'Anything else?' he asked.

'Er, well... there's Chanters Brook,' said the man. 'A little brook with some trees and a bit of grass here and there. Not much greenery close to here, but that's survived somehow.'

That sounded a little more promising to Walker—somewhere Alex might conceivably be drawn to for some respite.

'Can I exit from your front door this time?' said Walker. 'Almost put my back out climbing over the fence.'

'Course,' said the man. 'No problem.'

* * *

Walker and DC Briggs eventually found their way over to the wooded area that the man had described, less than a kilometre from the Tesco supermarket—the area called Chanters Brook. It was public, derelict land that offered some possible privacy. But it was a fairly large area with dense undergrowth and plenty of trees, so even if Alex was there, he still wouldn't be easy to find.

'Let's take a good look around in here,' said Walker. 'If I was on the run, hiding, this might be just the kind of place I'd be drawn toward to get some rest. It's not much, I know. But it's all we have for now, unless he goes back to that supermarket. Try not to get scratched up too much, DC, and watch out for any nettles.'

'Oh, Chief, I didn't know you cared!' said DC Briggs, smiling. She was having him on. She knew damned well that he cared about her. They'd only been working together for six months, but in that time, Walker had grown fond of DC Briggs. They'd even had lunch together a time or two while off duty. She was becoming like family—not that he saw much of his real family these days. He saw more of her. Much more. He thought they might even become proper friends, over time.

'Just stay behind me,' said Walker. 'Just in case.' He wasn't talking about the nettles now. He was concerned that Alex could be in there, might attack them.

They cautiously entered the wooden area, with Walker leading and DC Briggs taking up the rear, as instructed. It was dense, in part, and slow going, with them having to duck down below various branches and climb over bits of foliage, brambles, and random bits of trash. They were getting scratched up and muddy, despite being careful, and they were both increasingly irate with the bugs and bites, which were incessant.

'Stop,' whispered Walker, after some time struggling, putting his hand in the air, signalling for DC Briggs to stop moving, just in case she'd not heard him properly. He'd seen something. It wasn't much—looked like some old asbestos corrugated roofing sheets piled up here and there within a large bush that had grown over and around the detritus over time. Two of the rectangular sheets were placed together, though, creating a tent-like structure, with pieces also placed at the two ends, covering the void. It couldn't have ended up like that by accident. It was too structured. Someone had obviously arranged it like that.

There were also a few bits of trash next to the strewn-about sheets, and there was a gap into the bush that allowed access in and out. Walker rocked his head, indicating that he was going to head inside, and for DC Briggs to follow. He got his baton out, ready for action, should he need it, gripped it tightly.

'Is anybody there?' asked Walker. There was no reply. 'Hello? This is DCI Walker of the Lancashire Constabulary. If there's someone there, I need you to come out. I need to talk to you.'

Still nothing.

'Sir,' said DC Briggs, pointing to some trash on the floor. It was the wrapper from a loaf of bread with the Tesco brand on it.

Walker got on his two-way radio. 'We're on the north side of Chanters Brook. We may have found something. Stand by for back-up, over,' he said. There was no reply. *'Riley!'* The radio crackled into life.

'Understood,' said DI Riley. 'Standing by.'

Walker got close enough to the corrugated sheets that had been placed together, stepping over one that was on the floor in front of the structure.

'I'm coming in,' he said. 'We're armed, but we won't hurt you if you remain calm.'

Walker was just about to remove the corrugated sheet that was blocking the entrance to the tent-like structure, when it exploded out into his face, battering him and making blood spray from his nose. He fell backwards on his arse, right into some nettles, and Alex kicked and pulled the rest of the corrugated sheets down and started quickly moving in the opposite direction, through the bush. DC Briggs got after him before Walker could get back up.

CHAPTER TWENTY-NINE

'Constable!' shouted Walker.

He got up and followed, but Alex was quick—quicker than the both of them—and he seemed to know where he was going and how to get out better than them. He obviously had a well-studied route and lost them, slipping through the dense undergrowth and foliage while they struggled and kept getting stuck on brambles and branches. It was futile. They'd have to go back around, find another way through.

'Damn it!' said Walker, getting back on his two-way radio. 'DIs Riley, Lee, suspect heading north from Chanters Brook, coming out of the woods. 'I repeat, our suspect is heading north from Chanters Brook, coming out of the woods, over.'

'Roger that, Chief. We're on it,' said DI Riley. 'He armed?'

'Unknown,' said Walker. 'But definitely dangerous. He gave us the slip. We're still in the woods, but in pursuit, over.'

'Chief, wait,' said DC Briggs. She was backtracking. She'd seen something over towards another pile of corrugated sheets. Walker followed.

'We have to get in pursuit!' said Walker. 'Go around, somehow. What is it, Constable?'

And then he saw it. The arm of a girl, fingernails painted.

'There's someone here,' said DC Briggs.

Underneath a couple of the pieces of old corrugated roofing sheets was a young woman—blonde, hair tied back, looked just like Charlotte.

DC Briggs and Walker worked together to carefully remove the roofing sheets from her body, lifting them and throwing them to one side. Then they both got down on their knees, next to the woman.

'What about Alex?' said DC Briggs. 'Shouldn't one of us follow?'

Walker nodded, and was just about to get up, when the woman stirred. She was still alive. He got on his mobile phone.

'This is DCI Walker. We need paramedics on the north side of Chanters Brook in Atherton, immediately. We have another victim, still alive this time. Requires immediate medical assistance,' said Walker. 'The offender is confirmed as Alex Wilkinson. We have officers in pursuit, but we need all available resources ASAP, to lock this area down. Suspect is extremely dangerous. Get the choppers or drones over if possible. We need to find this kid.'

Walker hung up, satisfied that the officer on the end of the line understood the urgency of the situation.

The young woman was regaining consciousness now, opening her eyes.

'It's okay,' said DC Briggs. 'We're police officers. You've been hurt. We're here to help.'

They helped the woman sit up and she held her stomach.

'He hit me,' she said, her voice hoarse. 'In the stomach. I thought he was going to kill me.'

Walker looked at DC Briggs but said nothing, them both knowing that the woman had just had a close escape—that Alex probably *was* going to kill her, or thought he had already.

'But...' said the woman, seeming confused.

'But what?' said Walker.

'He seemed sorry. Seemed, conflicted. Said he had to. Said he had no choice, that *they* were telling him to do it,' she said.

Walker looked at DC Briggs again, knowing the situation had just become a whole lot more complicated. If Alex had mental health issues, there was no telling what he could do. Walker knew Alex was at an age where the onset of disorders like schizophrenia could begin, and that schizophrenia in particular had a high rate of experiential auditory hallucinations—which might indicate that Alex was hearing voices that weren't there. Of course, these experiences could be episodic, Walker thought, and Alex might have been together enough in the aftermath of Charlotte's death to get the others on board for covering for him, if the hallucinations had stopped. Either that, or someone was actually coercing him to do the things he was doing. But that seemed less likely.

'Don't worry, help will be here soon,' said Walker. 'We're going to get you somewhere safe. What was Alex wearing? Can you remember?' Walker and DC Briggs had both seen Alex running away, but it had all happened so quickly, and he wanted a third opinion, to make sure they nailed down what he had on the best they could. He knew it could be important.

The young woman focussed, trying to give it some thought. 'He had a baseball cap on, black I think, with some writing on it. And glasses, a hoodie, like a dark red-ish colour, and jeans.'

'That's great,' said Walker. It matched what he'd remembered, and some, and DC Briggs nodded, confirmed she was in agreement. 'Well done.'

DC Briggs held the woman's hand. She was cold, her dress ripped, her expression one of disbelief—but she was alive. 'Hold on, luv,' she said. 'We've got you.'

CHAPTER THIRTY

Walker and DC Briggs arrived at the Royal Bolton hospital, having followed the young female victim they'd found —a Kimberly Bowen—and the ambulance that had taken her. They had officers on the ground, one police helicopter, and a drone out looking for Alex in the area where they'd found her, as requested by Walker. There was little more they could do themselves for now with regard to the search. Walker knew he'd have had no chance chasing a nineteen-year-old on foot by himself, not with him having a head start, and he hadn't wanted DC Briggs to pursue alone—the boy was too dangerous. Since DIs Lee and Riley were close by, it was better to let the other officers deal with it, have himself and DC Briggs focus on the victim.

They needed to get as much information from her as they could. She was the first victim that had been found alive. They needed to see if they could get any clues as to Alex's state of mind, his likely behaviours, and where he might be heading. If they didn't find him soon, it might turn out to be the best chance they had, for now—so it was an insurance policy in the eventuality of Alex escaping again. While they had all available resources desperately trying to lock down Atherton and the surrounding area so Alex couldn't get any further, it

CHAPTER THIRTY

wasn't an easy task; there were so many ways in and out. They had to concede that Alex may have got away from them again, despite being so close.

DC Briggs helped Kimberly to sit up in the hospital bed she'd been given—one in a private room, for now, while she was being assessed—giving her a hot cup of coffee which she immediately cradled, despite having a blanket around her.

'Is there anybody you'd like us to contact for you, Kimberly?' asked Walker. He still had some tissue stuffed up his nose to stop the bleeding from when he'd been hit, and he pulled it out, now satisfied that the bleeding had stopped. 'For support, I mean.'

She shook her head. 'Not right now. I need some time to process this myself first. And you can call me *Kim*.'

Walker sat down, next to Kim, bedside, gently rubbing his nose, with DC Briggs sitting on the opposite side on another movable chair.

'Are you feeling okay, Kim?' asked DC Briggs. 'Are you well enough to talk to us?'

Kim nodded. 'I mean, I'm not *okay*, okay, but yeah, I can talk to you. It helps actually. Helps me to process things. Is *he* okay to talk?' she asked, looking at Walker, who didn't look in the best shape either. It was worse than it looked, really; he had blood stains all down his white shirt and tie where he'd had the nosebleed, and he scratched at his arm where he'd fallen in the nettles.

'I'm fine, thank you. Look, Kim, this young man who attacked you: he's very dangerous. You had a lucky escape. He's already killed two young women that we know of, and possibly more,' Walker said, giving it a few seconds to settle. 'That's why we so desperately need your help, so this doesn't happen again. We believe your attacker may be mentally unwell, unstable.'

Kim appeared to be in shock, but then relief seemed to wash over her, perhaps realising what a lucky escape she'd had.

'He strangled me,' she said, rubbing her neck, her voice still rough. 'I thought I was a goner.'

Walker guessed that Alex thought the same, which was why he'd hidden her under those corrugated roofing sheets. He was going to leave her there like some trash, and he even had the arrogance to get some rest first. He'd now strangled his last two victims, but the first one—Charlotte Porter—had probably been pushed and died from a blow to the back of the head, most likely from hitting the Pike Tower. Walker wondered why the discrepancy between the first and proceeding attacks—what had changed? Perhaps his mental illness had progressed, or maybe the first victim *was* an accident, and this pushed him over the edge, causing a mental breakdown and the onset of something like schizophrenia, making him hear voices telling him to do these awful things. Or, he was already hallucinating, somehow managing to keep things under wraps, and Charlotte's death was an accident and this tipped him further over the edge, supercharging his delusions, making him turn violent.

'Well, you're going to be okay,' said DC Briggs, offering some support to Kim. 'It's all over now. You're safe.' She was just trying to make her feel better. They both knew that Kim would never truly feel safe ever again. She was a victim now, and nothing would ever change that. It was a part of her history.

'Kim, can you tell us anything else about your attacker? Anything he said to you, or any items he had with him?' asked

CHAPTER THIRTY

Walker. 'I'm sorry. I know you've been through a lot, but—'

'He had a knife,' said Kim. 'I didn't know that at first, of course. He didn't pull it on me right away. When I first saw him, he was crossing the road and our eyes met and he smiled at me, and I smiled back. I don't know why. I guess I thought he was cute. We were going the same way, walking at about the same speed, and he asked if I wanted to get past. I said it was alright, asked where he was going, just making small talk. He said he was going where his destiny allowed. I kind of liked that. Most boys just wanna chat you up, get in your pants, but he seemed different, sweet, even. I thought he might ask me out on a date if I played my cards right. But when we got over near the woods, in a quiet little area, he flipped, turned a knife on me, told me to get in there. I didn't know what to do. I wanted to run, but I froze. I was terrified. I just did what he said, and he marched me into those woods.' Kim started to get upset, crying a little. DC Briggs gave her a comforting rub of the arm.

'Okay. Let's back up a little bit', said Walker. 'While you were walking together, what did you talk about? Tell me everything you remember.'

Kim took a breath, got herself together, sipped on her coffee and then blew on it—it was still too hot.

'I don't know really. My brain's scrambled. I think we talked about music a bit. He said he liked alt-rock, was into Joy Division and Oasis. My dad never stops going on about those old Manchester bands. I heard nothing else growing up and grew to like that kind of music myself too, so we connected with that. But he seemed nervous somehow, like he was just going through the motions. I thought he was just on edge because he liked me. I guess I was wrong…'

'Okay. What else?' asked Walker. What she'd said wasn't going to be enough. He needed more.

'He asked if I came from a good family, which I thought was nice—nobody has ever asked me that before—and what plans I had for the future. He was wearing a backpack, so I asked him if he was travelling or going to study or something. He said he wasn't sure yet. That he just had to get away for a bit,' said Kim.

'And do you? Have a good family, I mean,' asked Walker.

She nodded, slowly. 'Yes. They're the best,' said Kim, getting a bit choked up again, before getting it back under control. 'And I told him as much. I don't understand. He seemed so nice at first. Why did he do that to me?'

'Back in the woods there, you said he seemed "conflicted", that you were under the impression he was being coerced to do what he did, that someone was telling him what to do. Was he talking to himself, at all, like he was having a conversation with another person?' asked Walker.

Kim nodded. 'Yeah. He was talking back to some voice in his head. He was frigging nuts.'

'Do you know what schizophrenia is, Kim?' asked Walker.

'It means you're mental, doesn't it?' she said.

'It means that the man who attacked you may need to access a mental health facility, and that he may have been hearing voices in his head telling him to do these awful things,' said Walker. 'It sounds like he's hallucinating. We'll do our very best to catch this young man, and rest assured he'll either end up in a high security mental health facility, or a prison, for a very long time,' said Walker.

'You have to get him,' said Kim. 'You just have to.'

'I personally won't rest until he's found, dead or alive,' said

CHAPTER THIRTY

Walker. 'You have my word on that.'

Kim nodded. 'Thank you,' was all she said, her eyes glazing over, staring into a distance that wasn't there. She needed some time to rest now. She looked spent.

Walker and DC Briggs got up and left the hospital room that Kim was in and closed the door.

DC Briggs took a deep breath. 'Well, that was heavy,' she said. 'Poor girl.' Walker thought there was a sadness in DC Brigg's eyes that went beyond the case, that there was something personal about it. He figured she might tell him about it one day, when she was ready, if they remained friends. But now was not the time.

'If the lad's hearing bloody voices, there's no telling what he could do next—although he does seem to be sticking to this pattern for now of attacking the same type of young woman, and in a similar way,' said Walker. 'His mother said his dad left for another woman. Perhaps Alex sees these women as femme fatales, as dangerous young vixens, just like the woman who broke his family up. Maybe he even saw a picture of her, this woman, and he's targeting young women who look just like she did. It might be useful to try to get a picture of that woman his dad left with, for comparison.'

'I suppose it's possible,' said DC Briggs. 'But all of this is not helping us find him, is it?'

'Not exactly. But it is helping us get into that boy's mixed-up head, which could aid in finding him,' said Walker. 'Maybe he's going to see his father—Dominic Wilkinson. Let's start there. Find him, see if Alex has been in touch recently.'

DC Briggs got on her phone immediately. 'DI Hogarth. Yes. We need an address, right now. It's Dominic Wilkinson, Alex's father. Yes. We're going to need to see him.'

***

'This is him—Dominic Wilkinson,' said DC Briggs. They'd come to Mesnes Street in Wigan to an estate agent called Northwood. Dominic Wilkinson was apparently the branch manager—not exactly the kind of rough down-and-out that Walker and DC Briggs had expected given the social standing of his previous partner. He'd obviously gone up in the world.

'Mr Wilkinson,' said Walker. 'I'm DCI Walker of the Lancashire Constabulary. Is there somewhere private we could talk.'

'Yes, of course. I've been expecting you. One of your colleagues informed me. What's this all about?' asked Dominic. He was polite, well-groomed, professional—nothing like Alex's mother, who was coarse, notably lower class, and extremely rough around the edges.

They went through to a private room at the back of the office and sat down at a desk, Dominic on one side, and Walker and DC Briggs on the other, door closed.

'We have reason to believe that you fathered a child named Alex Wilkinson. He's nineteen now,' said Walker. 'Is that correct?'

Dominic looked a little shook up and took a long breath, looking concerned. 'Not heard that name in a while. Nineteen, eh? Already. Is he in trouble?'

'I'd say so,' said Walker. 'And a lot of it. We're trying to locate his whereabouts. You wouldn't have been in contact with him or his mother recently, would you?'

Dominic shook his head. 'Haven't seen them since he was a baby. Never heard anything. I lost touch with his mother,

CHAPTER THIRTY

Kathy—although she hounded me for a while, kind of. That's why I moved away from Leyland. I'm over in Standish now. It's nicer there.'

'Mr Wilkinson, it's very important that we find Alex. He's been hurting people', said Walker. 'Two people are dead. We have reason to believe he might be mentally unstable.'

'Oh, my God. That's... That's awful. What have you done, Alex?' Dominic took a moment, his emotions running away with him—a mixture of something like guilt, regret, and longing, Walker thought, by the looks of it. 'I always worried he might go off the rails. But I didn't think it would be anything like this,' he said. 'Can't say I'm surprised he's a mess though, brought up by her. She was feral—a druggie, a real alcoholic. She even drank cough medicine; anything she could get her hands on really. Had daddy issues. I'm surprised the boy even made it through the pregnancy. She was using all the way through. It was an accident, you see—the pregnancy. She was only twenty-three when the test came back positive, and I was just a year older. I never intended to stay with her. I couldn't. It was just supposed to be a bit of fun and I got trapped. I met someone else eventually and... that was that. I'm still married to her. We have three kids together, a good life.'

'I see,' said Walker, calculating that Kathy would now be around forty-three years old based on Alex being nineteen, a little bit younger than he'd first thought, based on her appearance. 'Do you know if there's any history of mental illness in the family, on either side?'

Dominic thought about it. 'Kathy's brother—Alex's uncle—was a bit odd. I think there was something wrong with him. I'm not sure what, exactly. And Kathy also started to see a counsellor just before she stopped hounding me,' said Dominic. 'Rams-something, it was called—Ramsford, or Ramsey Counselling. Maybe Ramsdale Counsellors? Over in Chorley. She told me about it, said she was getting some help, that she was gunna try and let go of me, when things started to get weird, I mean. She was turning up at my door in the middle of the night, wasted, stuff like that. I was just glad when it was over. I'm sorry I can't be of more help. Like I said, I haven't seen either of them in almost twenty years.'

Walker nodded. 'Just one more thing. Could we get a photo of your wife, for our investigation?'

'My wife?' said Dominic. 'Why do you need—'

'We need information about everyone connected to the boy,' said Walker. 'If you wouldn't mind.'

Dominic took out his wallet and opened it up to reveal a family photo, including the face of his wife. She was plump but healthy looking with permed brown hair and glasses—nothing like the appearance of the victims found.

Walker took out his mobile phone and set it up to take a photo. 'May I?' he asked, and Dominic nodded his complaisance before Walker took the snap.

He and DC Briggs stood up. 'Thank you for your time, Mr Wilkinson. If you hear from Alex, or his mother, or anything at all pertaining to the whereabouts of Alex, then please get in touch with us.' Walker handed Dominic a card with his mobile number on it. 'Like I said, it's very important.'

'Will do,' said Dominic. 'And please... don't hurt him. It's not his fault. I should have... I should have been there, somehow. Done something.'

'We'll do everything we can to bring him in peacefully,' said Walker. 'We'll do our best.'

CHAPTER THIRTY

* * *

'*Suspect heading east down Cumberland Avenue!*' It was an officer from the police helicopter. 'Matches the description provided. All units. I repeat, *all* units!'

Walker and DC Briggs had already returned to Atherton, having been informed of a possible sighting. They'd tracked the suspect covertly at first, trying to wait until he was away from people, so he couldn't hurt anybody else.

'He's running,' said the officer in the chopper. 'He's on to us. He's spooked. Heading east. Move in. I repeat move in and prepare for arrest.'

Walker put his foot down on the accelerator, engine squealing, got to the east side of Cumberland Avenue ready to block off any escape. He stopped the car and got out, DC Briggs following, saw the suspect heading toward them, stopping, looking around in a panic. He started running back in the opposite direction and Walker got after him. There were more officers moving in from the other side, but Walker motioned for them to stop. He wanted to bring Alex in himself. He had him. He was cornered.

Walker caught up to him as he was slowing down, trying to find a way out. He tried to get into someone's back garden, but Walker grabbed him with ease, pulled him to the ground.

'It was just a bit of goddamned weed, for God's sake!' said the young man. 'I won't do it again, okay? I just wanted to try it.'

Walker got off him. It wasn't Alex. He had a black baseball cap on, and a hoodie, and he looked a bit like him—but it wasn't him. He'd got away again. Walker got on his two-way radio.

'All units stand down,' he said. 'This is not our man. I repeat, this is not Alex Wilkinson.'

DC Briggs caught up to them, huffing and puffing. 'Sir?' she said.

'It's not him,' said Walker. 'He got away.'

Walker rubbed his forehead, ironing out some stress. It was never easy. Not ever.

CHAPTER THIRTY-ONE

Walker arrived at the office of Doctor Alfred Johansen at *Johansen Counselling and Psychotherapy Services* on Avondale Road North in Southport. It was easy enough to find and had its own modest-sized car park at the front of the detached Edwardian building that looked like a large house, but which had now been reappropriated for various businesses. He'd got a message from Dr Johansen saying he'd seen some disturbing news on TV about one of his past clients—an Alex Wilkinson—and that he may have some useful information for the case he could disclose under such circumstances, information pertaining to Alex's mental health history. With Alex still on the loose, having got away again, Walker needed something, anything, to get back on his tracks. He needed to get inside his head.

He hadn't waited long to go through to Dr Johansen's office, and the secretary had made him comfortable in the waiting room, providing him with a cup of water, while the doctor finished up with a client.

'Detective Walker,' said Dr Johansen. 'Thank you for coming over here at such short notice. I'm not sure I could have got away from the office today. I have several more clients to see yet.'

'That's quite alright, Doctor. You have important work to do too—lives to save, and all that,' said Walker, feeling a bit windswept. It was getting gusty out. He'd left DC Briggs in the car this time, letting her take a break, eat a sandwich that she'd bought at the petrol station on the way over—ham and cheese with some red onion. It had smelled good, and Walker wished he'd got one for himself now too. He hadn't any appetite when she'd gone in, but he had now, suddenly. He'd just have to suck it up, get something later.

Dr Johansen nodded. 'You're too kind. Please, come in and sit down.'

They both took a seat, Dr Johansen in a comfortable leather chair, and Walker on a fabric sofa that clients could obviously use to lie down on if they wished.

Walker pulled out a notepad and a pen, ready to take some notes if required. 'So... you said that Alex Wilkinson was a past client of yours?' he said. 'We believe that Alex may have had a psychotic break of some kind, has killed two women that we know of, almost murdered a third. She survived, somehow. We got there just in time. But Alex got away. We need any information you might have that could help us find him, or to determine what kind of state of mind he might be in right now. Any insights about his behaviour from a trained psychologist such as yourself would be much appreciated at this juncture.'

'Yes. I was very sorry to hear that. We have confidentiality agreements in place, of course. But when a client threatens the lives of others, we are able to breach those agreements,' said Dr Johansen, pushing Alex Wilkinson's file over for Walker to see. He had a slow and precise style of speech that Walker liked, which probably helped in opening up clients too. It was easy to listen to, although he did have a slight accent that

CHAPTER THIRTY-ONE

Walker couldn't quite place—probably Scandinavian, judging by his surname. 'I first held sessions with Alex a couple of years ago. He was initially diagnosed with depression, but also demonstrated some of the early warning signs of a bipolar disorder. I was concerned about an acute manic episode occurring—a psychotic break, as it were. He was unstable and potentially volatile, but I've since stopped doing the pro bono work, unfortunately, as I don't have the time anymore. So, I stopped seeing him a while ago. I sent a referral in to the NHS, but you know what they're like. I'd be surprised if he made it through the system without a strong willingness to do so—which he didn't. I think his mother made him come here. She said his behaviour was out of control, was concerned about him harming himself or others. It seems her concerns were justified. I felt his condition could be controlled through a combination of medication and therapy, and I set him on that course.'

'I see,' said Walker, looking through the report he'd been handed. 'Just a moment'. It read:

After several sessions with Alex, it has been determined that in addition to suffering from depression, he's also begun to construct fantasies that he may be having trouble distinguishing from reality. During one session, he arrived in an extremely agitated state and demonstrated possible delusions of persecution—accusing his mother of controlling and punishing him. He felt like everyone was out to get him. During the weeks spent with him, there was a notable general decline in his mental well-being. If these manic episodes increase in frequency and intensity and become more acute, leading to more obvious delusions and hallucinations, then anti-psychotic medication could be prescribed. At present, mood stabilisers and anti-anxiety medications are recommended over anti-depressants that could exacerbate his condition.

DIAGNOSIS: Depression with indications of possible bipolar II disorder developing.

40mg of citalopram has been prescribed to begin with, with mood stabilisers to be added if further manic episodes occur. Clozapine is also recommended if outright psychosis develops and proliferates, and clear and obvious delusions and/or hallucinations occur. GP to follow up every three months unless conditions worsen or there is an adverse reaction to the medication.

At the end of the report, it was signed with his name: Dr D. Johansen.

There were several follow up reports attached, single sheets, with nothing much noted other than that Alex had some minor side-effects from the 40mg of citalopram during the first two weeks of ingestion—some diarrhoea, anxiety, and general indigestion—with it noted that all of this is not unusual while the body gets used to the medication. The patient had been signed off after one year of use, with a plan to continue using the medication and to reduce intake over the next year until it could be stopped completely. The case had subsequently been handed over to Alex's GP on a permanent basis.

'And you have no idea where Alex might be right now. He hasn't been in touch?' asked Walker.

'No. I'm afraid not,' said Dr Johansen.

'The victim who survived—she said Alex seemed to be talking to someone, having a conversation with someone who wasn't there. I have limited knowledge of mental health disorders, but I was thinking *schizophrenia*: delusions and auditory hallucinations? Does that sound possible?'

CHAPTER THIRTY-ONE

'That is just one possibility,' said Dr Johansen. 'Like the report says, he showed some of the early warning signs of a psychotic break via possible delusion of persecution, paranoia, agitation, and mania, and really needed closer clinical monitoring. He had also noted in one of our sessions that he was drinking and smoking cannabis to try to feel better. This is not unusual behaviour for someone who is depressed. It's a form of self-medication. However, a high THC product could have exacerbated a tendency toward these hypomanic states due to its psychoactive effects. The initial issue could have just been depression. Furthermore, it might also be the case that Alex's biology and environment could make him more susceptible to such drug-induced psychosis than the average casual user, so that's something to consider too. From what I could tell from our discussions, his mother seemed to be the main focus of his anger, along with his father leaving them when he was very young. I believed he should have been assessed for a bipolar II disorder, and watched in case it developed into bipolar I, with more intense episodes of mania. Unfortunately, he left my caseload before we could get to that stage. I'm only sorry that I couldn't be the one to do that. My time is limited, and there are so many clients to see, so many problems in the world.'

Walker paused, waiting to see if there might be more.

'I've had some financial issues as well, you see,' Dr Johansen went on. 'I enjoyed doing the pro bono work very much, but I needed to make more money, for my family. I'm married—two kids, and a dog. I had to let it go, focus on the paying clients.'

'I understand,' said Walker, while mulling over an idea. 'Been there, done that. Having said that, Dr Johansen, would you be interested in working with us, on a short-term basis—on the case, I mean. Your insights into his psychology might be vital. We'd pay you for the work, of course.'

Dr Johansen gave it some thought and flipped through a diary on his desk. 'Well, I have a couple of hours at the end of every day,' he said. 'My practice is only licensed to be open until five. So, I'm free about 5pm until 7pm. I could do that? I could use the extra money, actually. After that I really have to get home. We prioritise eating together as a family every day. We feel it's important.' Walker wished that he'd made such prioritises with his own family. Maybe then he wouldn't have lost them, he thought. But it was too late now.

'That sounds great,' said Walker, just pleased to be able to get a little more help with the case. 'Could you put together a psychological profile of Alex first, detail his most likely drivers of behaviour, that kind of thing.'

'Well, it was a while ago now, so I don't remember every detail of the case. However, with the permission of clients, I tend to record my sessions. I like to review whenever possible. My secretary transcribes the session and stores it digitally, in a password protected folder, and then I delete the recording to free up space on my hard drive. Alex did give his permission to record, I remember that much, because he kept leaning in toward the device when speaking at first. I'll provide copies of the transcripts for you, along with a copy of this report as well. We should be able to draw up a fairly robust psychological profile from all of that data, once I've reviewed it.'

'Great. And when that's done, could we meet at Chorley Police station, for a meeting, at 6pm tomorrow?' asked Walker. 'Is that doable?'

Dr Johansen appeared to make some calculations in his head.

CHAPTER THIRTY-ONE

'Yes. I can do that,' he said. 'Glad to be of help. Shall I see you out?'

'No. That won't be necessary, Doctor,' said Walker. 'I'll find my own way out. See you tomorrow then.'

* * *

'What do we have, Chief?' asked DC Briggs while she was just finishing off the last crusts of her sandwich in the car, licking her fingers, making Walker even hungrier than he had been.

'A Dr Johansen, a psychologist who's done a few sessions with Alex in the past. He concurs that Alex may have experienced a psychotic break of some sort that is driving his behaviour. He's going to work with us on this for a while, provide a psychological profile. It might help us find him.'

DC Briggs scrunched up the packaging from her now consumed sandwich and stuffed it in the plastic bag she'd got it with, tied it off ready for throwing away. 'Fantastic,' she said. 'Thanks for the break, Chief. I feel like a new woman. Kind of. So... where to now?' It was her in the driver's seat this time, giving Walker a well-earned break.

'I think it might be worth having another chat with Mohammad Ali Hussein,' he said. 'That boy knows something, and I think I can get it out of him somehow. He's holding back. Maybe he's scared of something, or *someone*. I don't know. But whatever it is, we need to find out, and quick; otherwise, some other poor girl is gunna fall victim to this psycho, and she may not be as lucky as the last—if you can call it luck, that is.'

CHAPTER THIRTY-TWO

'You know I can't talk to you without my lawyer,' said Mo. Walker had him in an interview room, alone this time. He felt he could unnerve the boy better without DC Briggs, make him come unstuck somehow.

'This is just an informal chat, for now, Mo,' said Walker. He hadn't put the audio recording device on yet. He'd not begun an official interview. He just wanted to talk to Mo, try to squeeze anything else out of him, as he'd clammed up the last time as soon as his lawyer had got involved. If he got the boy talking properly, though, then he'd turn the device on.

'Well, I've said all I've got to say already,' said Mo, folding his arms, tightly, like he was trying to keep all the words he wanted to say locked firmly inside his belly.

'What are you scared of, Mo?' asked Walker. 'You're just making yourself look guilty by not saying anything. You know that, right? Like you were a part of this, somehow. Like you all planned to kill that poor girl—or gang rape her, and it went wrong, somehow, with all the booze and drugs you boys were taking. Is that what happened?'

'I never planned *anything!*' snapped Mo, sitting forward for a second, then instantly retreating back, looking surprised he'd said anything. 'I'm sorry but… it wasn't like that.'

CHAPTER THIRTY-TWO

Walker knew he had him now. He'd broken his silence. And once it was broken, it was always easier to break it again. That was the hardest part.

'Look, Mo. Alex has killed another young woman, and he's attacked one more, who we presume he thought was dead too, but she made it, somehow. You need to tell us everything you know now, so nobody else dies,' said Walker. 'Alex is dangerous.' Mo seemed like a good boy at heart, and Walker was drawing on that, hoping he'd do the right thing.

'*What?* You're sure?' said Mo. 'That it was Alex, I mean. He's my friend. He wouldn't...'

'Yes. We're sure. I saw him myself at the last victim, but he got away. Left his DNA all over all three victims, and we have a match on the toothbrush from his home. It's definitely him. He wasn't even that careful. It's almost like a part of him wants to be caught. The question is, do you want to go down as an accomplice, or are you going to cooperate and help us find him, stop more people from dying?'

Walker let that hang for a second, hoping Mo would cave.

'I can't,' he said. 'You don't understand. I just can't.'

'You can, Mo. You just *won't*,' said Walker. 'Why won't you tell us what happened? Are you scared that Alex would hurt you too? Was he ever violent towards you?'

Mo shook his head. 'No. I mean, yes—he did sometimes get a bit rough. But nothing extreme. Nothing like that. That's not what I'm scared of.'

'Then what?' asked Walker. 'What *are* you scared of? Do you think that by not saying anything, you have a better chance of getting out of this?'

Mo gave it some thought. He was sweating, tired looking. He was burned out from the intense stress and worry of the past couple of days. He sighed.

'Have you heard of a law called "joint enterprise"?' asked Walker. 'You study law, right? Or you aspire to. Have you heard of this?' He was taking a shot, betting that this might be his reason for clamming up.

Mo reacted, flinched a little at the words, but said nothing.

'It's a common law principle,' Walker went on. 'It's a bit of an antiquated, outdated law, I'll give you that, but it means you can be found guilty of Charlotte's death even if you weren't the person who actually killed her. It means you can, technically, go to prison for life, just for being there, in certain circumstances.'

Mo started to sob—not the wet kind, but the dry, struggling-to-catch-your-breath sort, like babies do when they've been crying for too long and can't calm down. It wasn't the reaction Walker had been looking for. He wanted him to spill the beans, tell them what happened.

'Look, we're not gunna bang you up just for being there, not unless you did something really wrong. So, you need to tell us what happened,' said Walker. 'If you were just at the wrong place at the wrong time, if you did nothing wrong, you just need to tell us. We're not interested in putting an innocent kid behind bars just because of the colour of his skin. We're not like that. But if you refuse to cooperate, we'll have to assume that you *did* do something wrong and contribute to Charlotte's death in some way. Plus, whatever happens, if you don't help us, you'll have to live with the guilt of not stopping the next girl's death for the rest of your life, whether you're behind bars or not.'

Walker guessed that Mo would also know, as he did, that minority ethnic people were much more likely to be sentenced under the joint enterprise law than their white counterparts, which meant that Mo and Ben had been particularly vulnerable to such an outcome. Ben might have also known this, having talked to Mo, and may have panicked, or have not been able to live with what happened to Charlotte, or a combination of the two. Either way, he'd wanted a way out, and he'd found one.

Mo opened his mouth to speak, but then closed it again, nothing coming out.

'So... that's why you can't admit to being there,' said Walker. 'That's smart, Mo. *If* there was no evidence of you being there. But there's evidence everywhere. We're still processing it all. I'm sure there'll be something to tie you to the scene.'

Mo nodded, but then shrugged his shoulders, as if to say that was the best he could do, and Walker had to agree that he was probably right. He was stuck between a rock and a hard place, in a real predicament with no easy answers.

'Mo. We have you getting into Alex's car, we have you buying the alcohol that the victim had been drinking, and we have nothing to show that you came home early, like you claim,' said Walker. 'And we also have you at the train station, making physical contact with your friend, Ben, just as he was hit by an oncoming train,' said Walker. 'I think it's time to start talking. Think of those girls. Think how many more might die if you don't help us.'

Mo got super stressed looking with that, started hyperventilating, shuffling around. '*Alright!*' he said, shouting, finally exploding after holding himself together pretty well under the circumstances. 'Alright. I'll tell you everything I know. Just... don't let him hurt anyone else. Okay? Don't let him do that to anyone else.' He was properly crying now, tears rolling down his young face.

'We'll do our best, Mo. Just help us. Give me something,' said Walker, waiting, giving the boy time. He took a breath, prepared himself, while Walker now turned on the recording device and noted the particulars, ready to take Mo's statement.

'Okay. So... I went to study at The Majestic Coffee Lounge, just like I said. But after a while, my old school friend texted me—Liam. Said they, him and Alex, were up for some fun. Asked me to join them. I'd got through a lot of work in a short time, so I figured, *why not?* I could go for an hour or two. My mother would never know. Or, at least, that's what I thought. I deserved it. They were already close by, and I got in Alex's car. We picked Ben up next, and then we saw Charlotte at the bus stop, and Alex convinced her to join us for a bit too. It was all good. Everyone was excited. It was fun. We got some booze at the Stump Lane Store, as you already know, and I paid for it, and then we headed over to Rivington.'

'And then?' asked Walker.

'And then we drove up the hill on some back roads. We made it all the way to the Pike, where the tower is. It was exciting. We partied, got drunk, smoked a little weed.' He glanced up at Walker. 'I don't usually do that, but... it seemed like the right time. Everyone was having fun, Charlotte included.'

'So, what went wrong?' asked Walker.

'I thought I might have a chance with Charlotte. I've always liked her. But... she went off with Alex, behind the Pike Tower. I was gutted,' said Mo. 'They were there for a while. We were all wasted at that point—except for Alex, I think, who was driving and mainly just smoked weed. He was there with her a while, so I drank more, trying not to think about what was happening.'

CHAPTER THIRTY-TWO

'And then?' asked Walker, urging Mo on, knowing this was probably his best chance to corroborate what Liam had stated about that night.

'Alex came back, eventually, without Charlotte. Said she was wasted. Up for anything. Said he'd... he said he'd *banged* her, was how he put it. Then he started to tease us, saying we were all virgins, that we should all have a go. Said she wanted it. He started laying into Liam, saying he was frigid, or gay, having a real go at him. But Liam said he didn't want to go where Alex had been, or something to that effect, said it was all getting a bit freaky for him, and he stormed off, really pissed off at Alex's goading. Ben was next in the firing line. Alex really started to become animated, shouting "Ben! Ben! Ben!" Said he'd tell everyone he was gay if he didn't do it. Said that Charlotte was gagging for it, and all that. I didn't know what to think at that stage, what was going on, even. I was drunk out of my mind. Everything was spinning. I felt sick. Ben went to Charlotte, but when he came back, he said something was wrong. That they'd kissed, but then she'd fallen unconscious. That she wasn't moving or breathing. Said he couldn't see properly in the dark, so he'd used the torch on his phone as he felt like her head was wet. And it was. It was blood! He freaked the hell out. We all did when we saw. We panicked. Ben wanted to call 999, I think, but Alex stopped him, took his phone. Took all our phones. Said we had to calm down, to think. Said he was the only sober one, so we should leave the decision-making to him. He explained that it might look like we'd killed her, that we'd get in big trouble. And since she was already dead, we all agreed to leave her there, let the police think it was an accident—which it was. At least, I thought it was. I don't remember everything so clearly. It's all a bit of a blur, because of the drinks, and the…'

'The drugs,' said Walker. 'So, you just left her there, even though she might have been alive. You left her there to die'.

'We were *really* drunk,' said Mo. 'At least me and Ben were. I'm not sure about Liam. We found him waiting for us by the car, and we explained what happened, got him on board with the plan, just did what we thought best.'

'Best for yourselves,' said Walker.

'Yes,' conceded Mo. 'I'm really sorry.'

'Well, I don't think that will be any consolation to Charlotte's parents,' said Walker. 'They're beside themselves.'

Mo started to cry. 'Everything just went bad so quickly,' he said. 'One moment everything was okay, the next… My life… all our lives were turned upside down. It's like a storm just blew in and destroyed everything.'

Walker knew how that felt. It brought him back to *his* youth—he hadn't been much younger than Mo when his sister had disappeared and died. He knew the scars wouldn't heal quickly, that they'd last and be scratched at all through his adult life, occasionally getting raw and bleeding again.

'Can you tell me anything else, Mo? Anything that might give us a lead as to where Alex might be? Where he might be heading to?' asked Walker.

'I have no idea,' said Mo. He looked Walker. 'I really haven't.'

'What was he wearing, that night?' asked Walker. He was thinking about how they might need those clothes, retrieve evidence from them—blood and DNA from Charlotte—but he also wanted to get a general sense of Alex's clothing style, in case he kept changing up.

'Er… I think he had a hoodie on. He usually wears one of those. A black one, I think, or dark blue. And some jeans,

CHAPTER THIRTY-TWO

Adidas trainers, white, which he loves, and some glasses—black rim. He started wearing those a bit ago. And a baseball cap. I think it said "Confrontation" on the front.'

Walker wrote it all down. 'Thank you, Mo. You've been a great help. I'll do everything I can to help you from here on in. As there's no duty to rescue law in the United Kingdom, if Charlotte's death is found to be an accident, then you'll have nothing to worry about on that front.' Walker didn't always agree with the law, thought people should be made more responsible for others, but that didn't change anything. The boy hadn't broken any laws by leaving her there like that. 'There is the issue of you supplying alcohol to a minor, though, which may have contributed to the circumstances of her death. However, given that you've been cooperating with us and assisting in stopping any further crimes being committed, I'll make recommendations to the CPS on your behalf, try to get you off with a slap on the wrist. Does that sound okay? Now, there's also the incident with Ben. We need to understand what happened there as well. Can you tell us about that?'

Mo tightened up again, visibly vibrating. 'He jumped,' he said. 'I tried to grab him, but he jumped.' He started to break down, even more so than before. 'He was my... f-f-f-friend. And now he's dead, just like Charlotte. I should have stopped him.'

Walker put a hand on Mo's arm, but Mo pulled back, like he'd just been burned with a hot iron.

'It's gunna be okay,' said Walker. 'We're going to get you some help. In the meantime, if you can think of anything else, just call one of the station officers, and they'll get a message to me.'

Mo nodded. 'Okay,' he said, but he was anything but.

CHAPTER THIRTY-THREE

Alex got off the bus in Moss Side, near his home in Leyland, and went the rest of the way on foot. He was going home. To his mother.

He'd managed to grow a little facial hair, the early stages of a beard, and he'd changed his clothes since the weather had grown a little warmer. His hoodie was now stuffed inside his backpack, and he wore only a T-shirt—an Arctic Monkey's one with the logo and wavy line motif—blue jeans, black-rimmed glasses, and a grey beanie hat. He wanted to try to look different, in case anyone saw him, and he kept his head down while he walked, way down.

He rounded the corner to his estate, quickening his pace, should any neighbours spot him. Everyone would probably be looking for him. He knew that. He'd shave his head when he got home. Wear a cap that covered his face better, wear some sports clothes—try to look like someone who was off to the gym. But he had to deal with his mum first. She'd be there, waiting for him.

He got to the front door and inserted the key. The door opened. And there were no police there—staking out the place—at least, none that he could see. They weren't expecting him to come home. It was the last thing they were all thinking

CHAPTER THIRTY-THREE

he'd do. That was why it was so brilliant.

His mum was right there, sitting in her chair as usual, watching TV. At least, the TV was on, volume high, as it always was. But her head was back. She was asleep. A cigarette still burned in the ashtray, the ash still attached, snaking away from the filter and what was left of the tobacco and paper wrapping. Judging by the amount of ash burned and unflicked, she'd been out a good few minutes—something he'd learned over many years of observations.

Alex walked up, behind her, feet soft, featherlike. He grabbed an iPhone charging wire that was on the floor, unused, not even plugged in. Then he removed the USB connection from the plug, so he held only the wire, gently putting the plug back on the floor.

Now you're gunna get what's coming to you, he thought. *Fucking bitch. Always controlling me. I'm gunna put an end to this, once and for all.*

He wrapped the wire around his fingers on both hands, pulled it tight. It was strong.

It's your fault all those girls are dead. Always telling me what to do—making my life a living hell.

He stepped closer, ready to do what needed to be done.

Come on Alex, you can do this. Just do it. She has to die.

He got the wire around his mother's neck and pulled, hard.

CHAPTER THIRTY-FOUR

Walker was going through some paperwork on his desk, trying to make sense of the Charlotte Porter case and the subsequent attacks by Alex Wilkinson. Already a few days in now, the case was very quickly slipping away from him. He knew if he didn't catch him soon that Alex could be on the run for months—years even. There was a sense that their window of opportunity to catch him had already closed, and it vexed Walker. It always did. But this kind of attacker, preying on young, defenceless women, sat particularly badly with him, and he wondered whether he could have done anything more to facilitate a different outcome.

There had been numerous items in the logbook for his team to follow up on, and DIs Riley, Lee, and Hogarth had done a great job in following up on these leads and loose ends while himself and DC Briggs had been investigating what he felt were the key aspects of the crime. Most of these more mundane items had been dealt with satisfactorily, with their reports detailing what they'd found. But there were still one or two loose ends that bothered Walker. He put his pencil in his mouth, bit into it a touch, causing an indentation in the wood. It was a habit he'd had at school that he'd never really got rid of.

'Something wrong, Chief?' asked DC Briggs, who was writing her latest report for the case, ready for filing.

'No optician,' said Walker.

'What?' asked DC Briggs.

'Alex Wilkinson has been reported as wearing glasses, but there's no record of him from any optician in the area.'

DC Briggs smiled. 'Some of the kids these days wear specs as a fashion statement,' she said. Walker frowned. In his day, anyone who wore glasses would be ridiculed, called a *geek* or *specky four-eyes* or some other disparaging name. They'd never wear them willingly, if they didn't really need them to see. 'I know. Times have changed, haven't they? You can pick them up at the supermarket now, or on Amazon—ones with clear lenses. Or you can even buy some off-the-shelf with the lenses already in, without even taking an eye test. It just takes a bit of trial and error.'

'I see,' said Walker. 'It might be useful to know if his are for fashion or functionality though. And... apart from that, it seems he's already withdrawn all the money he had while he was in Manchester, so he's using cash only now, meaning we're not gunna be able to track him with any card purchases.'

'Yes, sir,' said DC Briggs. 'I saw the footage at the cash machine myself. He got somebody else to withdraw it for him. Or he had his card stolen. We have no idea who that person was. Probably just some passer-by. He looked rough, like a homeless man.'

'If this boy is delusional, with grandiose ideas, maybe accompanied with auditory or visual hallucinations as well if his condition has progressed, then you know he could do just about anything. He may be extremely paranoid. He may feel like he has no choice but to do the things that he's doing if his mind has turned against him. Who knows what story his mind has concocted,' said Walker. He'd worked on cases where the offender had mental health issues before. These weren't easy, especially since the offender was also a victim too—a victim of poor health, and quite often the victim of some kind of underlying psychological trauma themselves. Walker understood such delusions only too well. When he'd been in hospital with his first bout of meningitis, intense cranial pressure had caused him to hallucinate. He'd been convinced he was on some alien planet, being experimented on at some scientific facility, and everyone he saw had the same cloned face—that of one particular male nurse. It was terrifying, so he had a good idea how Alex might be feeling. If he was having some kind of psychotic break, and was hallucinating like he had been, he felt sorry for him. What he'd done would ruin his life, just as much as the lives of those young women.

'So, where do you think we should go from here with it, Chief,' asked DC Briggs. 'It's not like he's gunna just come to us, turn himself in, is it? We can't just wait until he attacks somebody else.'

'But it seems as though there's a high chance that he will attack again,' he said. 'We just don't know when or where.' Walker started to manically flip through some of the papers on his desk. He'd got the phone records from O2, Alex's mobile phone network provider, for the phone he'd retrieved from that bin at Starbuck's Coffee at Manchester Victoria train station. DI Hogarth had managed to get the location history of Alex's phone, to see where he'd been before discarding it.

'What is it?' asked DC Briggs. 'What do you have?'

'I'm not sure yet...' said Walker. 'Wait.'

CHAPTER THIRTY-FOUR

Walker clicked his fingers in the air, getting DI Hogarth's attention, who was sitting at the other side of the room, reading something on his laptop.

'You need me?' asked DI Hogarth.

'These mobile phone records of Alex Wilkinson,' said Walker. 'Can you plot this data onto a map, to show these various location points?'

'Of course,' said DI Hogarth. 'Give me a minute.'

'What are you thinking, Chief?' asked DC Briggs. 'We already checked out most of those locations. We couldn't find anything. They were all public areas, outdoors. He'd just been walking around.'

'But *why* would he walk around like that, aimlessly, in Manchester city centre, for several hours, before going right back to the train station, where he'd started, where we could find him? It doesn't make sense,' said Walker. 'What was he doing?'

'Well... you said he might be delusional. Perhaps he thought he was being chased?' said DC Briggs.

'He was being chased—by *us*,' said Walker. 'But if you're being chased, people tend to try to get some distance, not go around in circles like he has, and then end up at the same spot you started. What if he was trying to send us a message, somehow?'

'A message?' said DC Briggs.

'I've got something,' said DI Hogarth. 'This is interesting. Printing it out for you now.' The printer nearby Walker suddenly kicked into life, the wireless connection to DI Hogarth's laptop computer doing its job.

Walker stood up and grabbed the paper, had a good look at it. His eyes went wide.

'Chief. What is it?' asked DC Briggs.

'You're not gunna believe this,' said Walker.

DI Hogarth was smiling, nodding his head.

'Alex Wilkinson did leave a message for us. It's not perfect, but by tracking his activity, and joining the dots… It says *HELP*. Quite clearly. Alex wanted us, or someone, to help him.'

CHAPTER THIRTY-FIVE

'Chief, we've had a sighting,' said DC Briggs. She'd just answered a phone call in the incident room. 'Someone's called in, anonymously, said they've seen Alex, saw the posters around and the reports on TV saying he's wanted in connection with a series of violent crimes. Said they knew Alex. I've got a street name. You're not going to believe this!'

'He's back, isn't he?' said Walker. If someone had seen him, and knew him, it stood to reason that it would most likely be someone local.

'Yeah. Back in Leyland. How did you know?' said DC Briggs, with some urgency, eyes wide, not quite believing it. They'd chased him all over Manchester, and now he was back.

'Let's go!' said Walker, standing up, grabbing his belongings in hurry. 'Hogarth, you hearing this? Call the boy's mother. She might be in danger. We need to warn her. And tell her to keep him at the house if he turns up, if she can. We'll get over there as quick as we can. Send a couple of squad cars too. We can't let him get away this time. We've got him.'

'Will do,' said DI Hogarth, who rarely demonstrated any urgency, just like now, somehow managing to stay calm even in the most pressing circumstances. He always got the job done though, and Walker trusted him. 'I'll call DIs Riley and Lee too, get them to join you, just in case things get out of hand.'

Walker and DC Briggs exited, ran down the flight of stairs—Walking jumping one or two steps at the bottom of each flight for speed—out to the front desk where the main exit was located. But something was going on there, something that instantly stopped them in their tracks. 'What the—'

It was Alex. He was holding a shotgun. DIs Riley and Lee were already there too having probably just returned, hands on heads, crouched down on the floor alongside the two female members of staff who'd been manning the front desk, plus one male PC, and one rough-looking civilian, doing the same—a guy who'd likely been arrested or brought in for questioning in connection with some other crime. Alex saw them and his eyes went a little wider.

'Stop!' he shouted. 'Get down on the floor with the others.'

'What the hell, fella?' said the civilian guy on the floor, slurring his words a little, sounding either drunk or stoned, or both. 'Are you nuts? This is a frickin' police station. What do you think you're doing? You're gunna get us both killed.'

'Put the gun down, Alex,' said Walker, starting to slowly get down on the floor, holding out his hand, palm up, urging him to stop.

'Just get down!' shouted Alex. He was manic, out of control, and with him holding a shotgun, Walker was nervous. They needed to talk him down, deescalate. 'You don't understand,' said Alex, looking like he might cry. 'I have no choice. Just get down on the floor with them, will you? Please.'

Walker and DC Briggs got down nearby the others, but Alex stopped them before they could fully crouch down. 'Wait,' he said. 'Not her. Send the woman over to me.' He meant DC Briggs. He wanted *DC Briggs*.

Alex's hands were trembling like an Alzheimer's patient, and his contorted expression suggested to Walker that he really didn't want to do what he was doing. This was confirmed when Alex's jeans started to go dark around the groin area, getting wet, and bright yellow urine started to pool on the white polished porcelain tiled floor near the bottom of his pant-leg. He'd wet himself. He was absolutely terrified. He was just a boy, after all, still in his teens.

'*Okay!*' Alex shouted, hysterically, seemingly to nobody in particular. '*I'm doing it! Just... give me a minute, damn it.*' He looked at Walker. 'Send her over, now.'

Walker eyed Alex. 'We want to help you,' he said. 'But first, I'm gunna need you to calm down, make sure that thing doesn't go off. Where'd you get it from, Alex?' He was trying to distract him, get a dialogue going. 'That's a nice piece.' There were plenty of farmlands between Rivington and Chorley; Walker guessed he'd burgled a farmhouse, nicked it.

'Nowhere. Just... They say to send her over!' said Alex. He looked scared. 'I have to do what they say, or they'll hurt me.'

'Who is *they*, Alex? Nobody is going to hurt you, not if you let us help you,' said Walker. 'We can help get rid of those voices you're hearing; help you feel better.'

'But you'll put me in prison,' said Alex. 'Or some nut-house. I'd rather die.'

Alex was distracted now, the shotgun he was holding losing tension, slowly lowering it while he was talking, taking it off target. DI Lee, who was nearest to Alex, saw this, took the chance, against protocol, against Walker's micro shake of the head—who'd noticed him start to move—and lunged at Alex.

He wasn't quick enough though. The gun went off, blasting him in the shoulder, making him stagger back and fall to the floor.

'I told you all to get down!' shouted Alex, pacing around now, ruffling his hair, then pointing the gun back at them. It was a two-barrel shotgun: only one cartridge left.

DI Lee was sitting, at least, having the presence of mind to put pressure on the wound with his hand.

'You okay there, Inspector?' asked Walker.

'Just a nick,' said DI Lee, although it clearly wasn't. 'Sorry, sir.'

'Shup up!' said Alex. 'Just… stop talking. I want someone to get all the car keys now and put them in a bowl or something.' Everyone hesitated. *'Right now!'*

One of the female members of staff who'd been manning the front desk slowly stood up, getting consent from Alex with eye contact alone as she did so, obviously not wanting to spook him further. She started to hurriedly get together all the keys from the various squad and unmarked pool cars—some of which were safely inside a locked draw, which she opened with a key that hung around her neck, and others that were in the pockets of the various detectives and officers, who reluctantly handed them over. Then she put all the keys in a plastic bag, and carefully handed it over to Alex. He peered inside and then grabbed the bag, before hooking it on one of his wrists by stretching the plastic of the handle and pulling it over his hand.

'Now the girl,' he said.

'Woman,' said Walker. 'DC Briggs is a thirty-one-year-old woman. And she's not your type, Alex. Trust me.'

'She's not our type,' said Alex, talking to himself again. 'She doesn't fit the profile. Let's leave her here.' There were a few seconds of silence while everyone waited to see what Alex would do next. His eyes rolled upwards, like he was listening to something, or someone. 'Fine, I'll do it,' he said. 'Hand her over now, please.'

Walker paused, knowing this was a vital moment in the exchange. 'Come on, Alex. You clearly don't want to do this. If you want us to co-operate, you have to help us understand.' They needed to defuse his hostility, deescalate the situation by keeping him calm, stick to procedure when emotions were running high, using it as a beacon to follow when things got tough. DI Lee knew this too, of course, and had gone against protocol; almost fatally. Walker wouldn't take any more chances.

'You wouldn't understand,' said Alex. He was manic, his eyes darted around, here and there, sweating. 'Because I don't understand it myself. I'm not mad, like you think. It's my mother. She's telling me what to do, her and that demon. They're instructing me right now. You don't know what they're capable of. I've no choice. They made me come here, to up the stakes, to humiliate and kill a pig, they said—a female one—to feel the power for myself. The woman, *now!*'

'No can do,' said Walker.

'No,' said Alex. 'I can't.' He shook his head, pointed the weapon at the PC on the floor, and seeming reluctant, pulled the trigger. It shot him in the neck, blood spurting everywhere.

'No!' shouted Walker.

Alex quickly pulled some more cartridges from his pocket before anyone could react, reloaded the gun. He'd obviously practiced. 'The woman,' he said again, almost crying now.

'Alex,' said Walker, almost begging now. 'Please.'

Alex shook his head again and DI Riley rushed at him, probably realising that he was going to shoot someone else anyway. He did. The shot hit Riley around the stomach this time. It was turning into a bloodbath. Riley sat down, holding his belly, putting pressure on the wound like DI Lee was with his. The PC was just lying there, unresponsive, one of the female desk staff, the one closest to him, putting pressure on that wound, her hands covered in blood.

DC Briggs slowly got up, shakily, took a step forward. 'It's okay, Alex. We just want to help you,' she said, somehow managing to maintain that soothing tone she had, which she always used when interviewing suspects. 'You don't want to do this. You're a good boy, aren't you? Things have just got tough. We think you might not be well. The voices you're hearing, they're not real, are they?' They were all close enough to him to see that he wasn't wearing any earpieces, so nobody was instructing him that way. But he was ramped up, in a state of mania, and Walker knew that hallucinations and delusions could easily accompany such a state. He'd believe what he was telling them. They had to tread carefully, talk him down somehow, give him what he wanted. 'We can give you the help you need, nobody else needs to get hurt,' DC Briggs went on. 'I'll come with you, if that's what you want.' She was sacrificing herself, making sure nobody else got hurt.

'You,' said Alex, going over to the civilian and giving him a gentle kick. 'Get out of here.'

The man who'd been brought to the station slowly got up, looked at Alex, nodded, and then ran out of the station, laughing hysterically.

Alex then grabbed DC Briggs, went behind her, and shoved the shotgun under her chin, using her as a human shield.

CHAPTER THIRTY-FIVE

'If anyone follows me, she's dead. Do you understand?' said Alex. 'I'll shoot her while she drives. 'Dead, you got that?' They all nodded their understanding, not knowing what else to do.

And then he left, backing up out the door with DC Briggs in front of him, her eyes wide, full of fear.

CHAPTER THIRTY-SIX

Walker stood up, readying himself, trying to figure the best course of action. A couple of uniformed officers cautiously entered from upstairs—a male and a female—shocked at what they were seeing: one male PC on the floor, bleeding out from the neck, likely dead, DI Riley also badly injured, crouched down on the floor holding his stomach area, bleeding out, his white shirt now saturated with the stuff, DI Lee similarly injured, lying down, holding his shoulder, semi-conscious now, eyes rolling back, and two female officers who were also on the floor doing their best to support their badly injured colleagues.

'What the hell happened?' asked the male PC who'd just entered. 'Get some medics down here,' he said to his partner. 'Now! I'll get after them.'

'No!' said Walker.

'Sir?' asked the PC.

'You don't understand,' said Walker. 'He's got a gun. If we follow, he'll kill DC Briggs. He took her, threatened to do her in if we trail him. And, anyway, we need help here.'

'They've taken DC Briggs?' said the PC, while his partner was busy on the phone, calling the emergency services. 'Oh, my god. I used to work with her, before she became a detective.

CHAPTER THIRTY-SIX

We have to do something.'

Walker got over to DI Riley, helped him put some more pressure on the wound just above his stomach. 'You okay?' he asked.

'Just a little tummy ache, sir,' said DI Riley, grimacing, playing it down. At least he still had some humour. That was good. He was lucid.

'What's your name, Constable,' Walker asked the male PC who'd entered, who was just stood there, doing nothing, probably a little paralysed with the shock of it all. Walker recognised his face, but the man's name eluded him.

He seemed to visibly snap out of it. 'It's PC Grigg, sir. Barry Grigg.'

'Barry, you need to help check that PC over there, see if he's still alive. If he is, you need to get as much pressure on that wound as possible, slow down the bleeding,' said Walker. He didn't hold much hope for the PC down, who'd already lost a lot of blood, but he had to double check. The female desk staff were trying, but with three injured, they didn't seem to know who to prioritise, and the one who was on the PC appeared to have given up hope and had since moved on to helping DI Lee, who was slowly passing out. PC Grigg nodded and got moving. Walker would have checked him first, but DI Riley was nearer, and he also sensed that the PC was gone.

PC Grigg's partner was a little more on it. 'Paramedics on the way. Plenty of them. I'm PC Karen Morris, by the way.' She started to move over to DI Lee as well.

'Pleased to meet you PC Morris,' said Walker, in the chaos. 'How's he doing?'

'I'm fine, Chief,' murmured DI Lee, demonstrating that he was still with them, despite his eyes being almost closed. 'Just a little scratch.' It seemed that his wound was the least serious of the three, at least, unless he was playing it down too.

Walker now had a decision to make. If he followed DC Briggs and Alex, he ran the risk of him killing her, just as he'd threatened. But if he didn't pursue them, and DC Briggs needed him, she could die anyway. He had to somehow follow without being seen.

'You got any car keys?' asked Walker.

'PC Grigg,' said PC Morris. '*Barry!* You got car keys?'

'Yeah. In my pocket,' he said. He looked shaken; his hands now also covered in blood. 'There's nothing here.' He tried the man's pulse. 'He's gone.' He put his hand in his pocket and pulled out some car keys. Walker held out his hand, urging him to throw them, and he did—fairly accurately too in the circumstances. Walker caught them with one hand.

'You need backup?' asked PC Morris.

'No,' said Walker. 'Don't let anyone else follow. He can't see anyone tailing him or he'll kill her. You got that? I'll stay in close contact. You understand? Nobody follows.'

'Yes, sir,' said PC Morris. 'Got it.'

Walker made it to the exit a little sluggishly, the bright light blinding him; he still had some light sensitivity issues from his latest bout of illness, popped his sunglasses on so he could see better. One of the pool cars was speeding past so he closed the door over, got back inside a touch, so no one could see him, peering through the crack. He could just about see DC Briggs in the driver's seat. Alex was in the back seat, behind her, sitting forward, gun near her neck.

'*Shit,*' said Walker. He let the car go and then exited properly, hurriedly headed towards the car park. The car key he'd been given was for one of the squad cars—he located which one

CHAPTER THIRTY-SIX

easily enough by pressing the key fob and making the car bleep. He'd stand out like a sore thumb in that, a clearly marked police car. He'd have to use it to commandeer a civilian car. Not exactly protocol, but needs must. That was the only way he could follow without being seen. He got moving, tires screeching, out onto the main street, and quickly blocked off the road with his car, the oncoming traffic coming to a halt. Then he got out—leaving the door open—ran to the nearest car and flashed his police ID Badge.

'Detective Chief Inspector Jonathan Walker. I'm sorry. I need your car for urgent police business. It's an emergency. You'll be reimbursed if any damage is caused. Call the station in a few hours,' he said. He knew he had no legal authority to commandeer a motor vehicle, of course, but he was banking on the owner not knowing that, hoped they'd seen too much American crime telly, thought real life was like the movies. It was a gamble, but he had to try.

The couple in the car just looked at him, dumbfounded, so he banged on the bonnet to shake them out of it, speed things along. Every second was vital. 'Get out of the car, *now!*' he said, and the people started to reluctantly move, mouths open, eyes wide.

'You can't just...' said the man who'd been driving. 'How do we know you're—'

'You'll be reimbursed,' said Walker. 'Someone's life is in danger. *Keys!*'

The man reluctantly gave Walker his keys.

'You don't even have a uniform on,' said the man.

Walker had what he needed and got in the car and turned it around, quickly got moving in the direction that DC Briggs and Alex had gone, adjusting the rear-view mirror a bit so he could see properly, a necessity due to him being a bit taller than the car owner. It was an automatic vehicle, an ice-blue MINI hatch with sports stripes down the bonnet. But that wasn't a bad thing: it would garner less attention from Alex, at least, with it being far away from the type of unmarked pool car detectives usually drove.

Walker stepped on the accelerator, speeding, overtaking cars here and there to catch up, some of them beeping their horns, thinking he was just some mad driver in a hurry. When he got within viewing distance of the pool car Alex had taken—a red Audi A6—Walker slowed down, trying to remain inconspicuous, acting more like any other car driver. DC Briggs was sticking to the speed limit. Alex must have told her to drive sensibly so as to not draw any attention too. That was also good though. If it became a car chase, Alex would know he was being followed, and then DC Briggs would be in danger—at least, a more immediate danger than she already was. Plus, he wasn't sure the 61 reg MINI, circa 2012, would be much good in a chase.

For someone who seemed to be under extreme stress and pressure, Walker noted that Alex certainly was thinking clearly and making some smart decisions that were aiding his escape. The question was: *where was he taking her?* He seemed to have some sort of a plan but coming to the station to get another victim made no sense. He was just making things more difficult for himself. It was irrational. Then again, someone experiencing a psychotic break would behave in ways that made no sense to others. It would only make sense to him, in the end, and feed whatever twisted narrative his mind was concocting.

Walker was worried about DC Briggs though—more than

CHAPTER THIRTY-SIX

worried. They'd become close over the past few months; probably closer than any other policing partner he'd had in his three-decade-long career. They'd become almost like family, in a way, but he realised this might not help the situation, might cause him to make emotional rather than rational decisions, which was rarely helpful. He needed to remain calm, think clearly—but it wasn't easy. He had to find out where they were heading first, and he trusted DC Briggs to keep Alex as calm as possible. She had a talent for it, a soothing tone and a way about her that dissipated people's negative emotions—as much as they could be, anyway. People liked her, Walker included. He was just beginning to realise how much.

The car turned off and entered an old industrial estate. Walker knew of it. Some young louts hung around there sometimes, and druggies and dealers. There were several old, dilapidated buildings that had been declared hazardous, and folks were not supposed to enter the land, but people still did. He watched the car drive in all the way while staying there, near the entrance; and when the car disappeared completely, he parked up and got out, ready to follow more covertly on foot.

Walker made sure to stay close to the buildings as he moved, out of sight, and finally peered around a corner to see the pool car parked out front, DC Briggs and Alex no longer there. They must have gone inside, so Walker got his baton out, ready to use if necessary, if he got a chance, if he got close enough. He couldn't let Alex see him though—not yet. He'd vowed to murder DC Briggs if anyone followed, and Walker got the feeling he'd follow through on his word. But the chances were he was gunna do that anyway sooner or later—try to kill her—so Walker had to do something, had to act fast.

He cautiously entered the building through an old loading bay door, up a ramp, got inside. There wasn't much light in there, but enough to see. It was wrecked, detritus littered everywhere—bits of garbage, beer cans and bottles and shards of broken glass, chunks of rubble and pieces of bricks. Walker navigated through it, never taking his eyes off where he was going for more than a second, occasionally looking down as he stepped through or over something.

'Detective Walker.' It was Alex. He was stood on a gantry, up above, holding DC Briggs from behind, gun to her throat. 'We told you not to follow'.

Shit. Walker put his baton on the floor, it being of no use now, and slowly put his hands in the air.

'I just want to talk, Alex,' he said.

'I'm gunna have to shoot her now, let her fall,' said Alex. 'That's on you.'

'Wait!' said Walker, holding his hand out. He'd messed up, didn't expect them to be above him, thought he could follow in the shadows. 'Just wait, will you? You only have one cartridge left, right?' Walker was guessing, hoping he didn't have more, taking a shot. Alex fished in his pocket while continuing to hold the gun, pointed at DC Briggs, with the other hand. He didn't pull any more cartridges out. He was empty handed. 'If you only have one shot left, and you use it on DC Briggs, how are you going to get away, Alex?'

Alex hesitated, but his eyes were no longer on Walker. He was looking beyond him.

'What are *you* doing here?' said Alex. Walker turned around, expecting to see nothing—thinking Alex might be having visual hallucinations as well as auditory ones. But that wasn't the case. It was Dr Johansen. He was stood right behind Walker.

'It's okay, Alex. You can put the knife down now,' said Dr Johansen, calmly. Alex looked conflicted. Perhaps he trusted his former counsellor. 'I'm here to help. I've been assisting Detective Walker. We were scheduled to meet at the station at 6pm, but I saw you, Alex, when I was sitting in my car in the car park, holding this poor woman at gun point. Then I saw DCI Walker following, so I too followed him, just in case I might be needed, in case I could help. I just want to help you, Alex. I'm sorry. I should never should have stopped seeing you.'

Walker shook his head. The doc shouldn't have followed. He'd just put himself in danger. But since he was here, Walker thought perhaps if anyone could get through to Alex, he could. Dr Johansen would have talked to him at length during their therapy sessions, likely got to know Alex intimately. He might be able to reason with him, make him understand he was hallucinating, get him to see that nobody was out to get him.

'You've got to help me,' said Alex, but he was looking at Walker now. He looked terrified, like he was being tortured by his own inner version of hell.

'That's what we're here to do, Alex,' said Walker. 'We just want to help, to stop more people from getting hurt.'

'He's the devil,' said Alex, pointing at Dr Johansen with his free hand. 'He did this. He's a monster. He gave me drugs... it messed with my mind.'

'Alex,' said Dr Johansen. 'We've talked about this. About how you project your fears onto others, about how you want to make others feel the same pain as you do. But it doesn't help in the long term. It will only make you feel worse. Have you been taking your medication?'

'*There's nothing wrong with me!*' shouted Alex, but he sounded like a mad man, hysterical. 'You've mutilated me, rotted my mind with this, shit…' He took out a bottle of pills from his pocket, squeezed the cap off with one hand, and let them spill everywhere, dropping down like blobs of green rain, bouncing off the floor. 'No more!'

'You have to let her go now,' said Dr Johansen. 'Listen to us. Let her go.'

Alex looked like he was about to shoot DC Briggs, or push her and just let her fall. His eyes went wider and he tensed his arm, moved it slightly, looking like he was ready to fire.

'Please,' said DC Briggs. 'Please don't do this, Alex.'

Alex let her go, pushed her to one side and then put the gun barrel in his mouth and fired—the blast reverberating around the building—his body folding forward to tumble from the gantry, landing with a sickening *thud* on the cold, hard concrete below.

CHAPTER THIRTY-SEVEN

DC Briggs leaned up against the MINI that Walker had commandeered and since drove nearer the building, a blanket around her that one of the paramedics had given her. She was shaking—probably more from the terror of what had just happened rather than any cold itself, although it was chilly out. Walker stood with her, rubbing her arm, trying to offer some support, help her deal with what had just happened.

'You're alright,' he said, but he wasn't sure if he was telling her or reassuring himself. Probably a bit of both. He thought he'd lost her. For a second, he'd thought Alex was going to shoot her in the head and let *her* fall, before he'd done it to himself. Walker was still shaken up. 'You did a great job, Detective.'

'I couldn't do anything,' she said. 'I froze. He had me, real tight. Any wrong move and... I just froze.'

'It's okay. Happens to the best of us,' said Walker. 'It's not quite like in the movies, is it? This is real life bollocks. Not quite as glamorous this gig. Shit your pants stuff, this.'

'The others? Riley and Lee?' asked DC Briggs, probably suddenly remembering what had happened back at the station.

'I think they're gunna be okay,' said Walker, doing his best to reassure her. 'Not sure about the PC though.'

Dr Johansen approached them, having just seen Alex get zipped up into a body bag and loaded onto a gurney. He'd just said his goodbyes to Alex—who'd died instantly on impact, or something like that—had a moment with him.

'He was a troubled boy,' said Dr Johansen. 'But I never thought he'd do anything like this. He'd obviously stopped taking his medication. All the same, his condition had progressed unusually quickly. This is not the norm.'

'Well, we'll need a formal statement from you in due course, Doctor. In the meantime, go home, get some rest. We all need a little time to recover from this,' said Walker.

Dr Johansen nodded, and got on his way, going back to his car. Before he left, though, he turned back to Walker. 'I'm sorry how this turned out, Detective,' he said. 'It didn't go as I'd hoped. I just wanted to be here in case I could do anything.' Walker nodded his appreciation, before turning his attention back to DC Briggs, and the Doctor left. In the end, if Dr Johansen hadn't followed, DC Briggs could have been dead now. He'd have to thank him properly one day. But now wasn't the right moment.

'Let's get you home too, Detective,' said Walker.

DC Briggs started to cry, the shock of it all finally pouring out. 'I'm sorry... I'm a mess. Can you stay with me for a bit, at home? I don't want my sister worrying about this. She has enough to deal with, and she already agonises about my job enough as it is. I don't want her to know about this—not yet anyhow.'

'Course I will, Shel,' said Walker, dropping the formalities, which he sometimes did if they were outside of work. 'Come on. Let these lot do their jobs.' A whole team of paramedics, police officers, and forensic investigators had arrived by now, and were busily going about their business. 'You get in the car. I'll just be a minute. I want to take one last look around, make sure we've not missed anything, get this wrapped up the best we can.' He knew he was a workaholic at times, was guilty of overdoing things—his broken marriage was testament to that—but there had been one or two occasions in the past when such an approach had yielded dividends, and in a big way, so he'd kept the habit, just in case.

DC Briggs already knew this, of course—his habits and quirks—accepted it without question and got in the car's passenger seat. Walker gently closed the door after her, before re-entering the building that Alex had just killed himself in. There were still pills scattered all over the floor and Walker bent down, picked one up, took a good look. It was small, round, and green with 'M' engraved on one side and 'C11' on the other. It looked harmless enough, like little breath fresheners. He located the tub that the pills had come in and took a look: Clozapine – 100mg. It was the anti-psychotic drug commonly used to treat schizophrenia. Walker also noticed something else among the dirt and bits of rubble, which was now partially stained with Alex's blood. It was the pair of glasses Alex had been wearing, the one's with the black frames and clear lenses—lenses that were now cracked and broken. He carefully picked them up, took a look. At first glance, they looked like the run-of-the-mill standard cheap specs that one might pick up off the shelf at the local supermarket or something, but on closer inspection, Walker saw there were some little controls on the underside of the arms and a small charging point. He'd never seen anything like that before. He wondered what Alex did with them, and how they worked, exactly, whether they might have had any role to play in what had just happened. He thought they were probably just some kind of music player, stored those MP3s or whatnot, but he'd have to follow up, find out for sure. He carefully put them on himself for a second, but there was nothing, so he removed them and popped them into a plastic transparent evidence bag, along with the pill and container, and put the lot into his pocket.

He took a breath, relieved that no more young women were going to be hurt by Alex, but also sad that a mentally ill young man had just passed. The general public wouldn't give him too much sympathy though. The media would have a field day with it. But Walker wasn't going to be too down about what happened. It was probably for the best. Alex would have continued to have a difficult life. If he'd got better at all, he would likely have been tortured by what happened—if he'd had any conscience at all, which it seemed he did—and if he'd not got better... well, he would no doubt have been perpetually tortured by the voices in his head.

Walker took the glasses out of his pocket again, took a good look at them, felt an idea churning.

'*Voices*,' he said, in almost a whisper.

Walker got back to the car—the MINI that DC Briggs was now sitting in, still huddled up in the blanket in the passenger seat—and got in.

'A MINI?' said DC Briggs. 'Is this your style? You could have got something a bit better—a bit *roomier*.'

It was good. She still had a sense of humour, even in such circumstances. It would serve her well in her psychological recovery. She was gravitating toward something more normal.

CHAPTER THIRTY-SEVEN

'It was the sports stripes,' said Walker. 'I can't resist some good old sports stripes. Plus, it was the first car that stopped.' He didn't always respond like this, so affably, but he wanted DC Briggs to feel something commonplace, some light banter and repartee. It was an approach he'd used many times before and to good effect. He knew once she was alone, she'd be going over everything in her head, everything that happened, trying to figure out if she could have done anything better, whether Alex might still be alive if she'd made a different choice. But he also knew she'd never find the answer she was looking for: he knew because he'd been there himself, many times.

'You find anything?' asked DC Briggs.

'Maybe,' said Walker, starting the car up. 'I'll show you later. Let's get some rest first. You need it.'

'I'm fine,' she said. Walker looked at her, and her eyes met his. She was resilient, a fighter. She just needed to get over the initial shock. 'What did you get?'

Walker took out the plastic evidence bag containing the glasses, the pill, and the pill container. 'He was taking Clozapine, an anti-psychotic, and a heavy dose at that. And he was wearing these. They look like some sort of electronic device—maybe an MP3 player?' He handed the bag to her. 'See the controls on the underside of the arm. We were wrong. It wasn't so much a fashion statement after all, or a correction of his vision.'

DC Briggs looked at them and frowned, her forehead wrinkling up, wrinkles that Walker had never noticed before. 'You know… I've never used these things before—*smart glasses* I think they're called—never even seen any in real life, but I'm pretty sure you can take calls on them, hear with bone-conducting technology or something. It might even be possible to send and receive video too. Technology is moving so fast now.'

'Sounds a little sci-fi to me,' said Walker. 'A bit futuristic. The boy didn't seem to have much money.'

'Oh, we're already there, sir,' said DC Briggs. 'In the future, I mean. This kind of technology is already well used, and it's probably not that expensive for some of the more budget models, or second-hand ones on eBay. You really should study these things more, keep up with the times, Chief. We both should.'

'Oh, that's what I have DI Hogarth for,' said Walker, referring to the member of his team who was an expert in all things computer related. 'So, what are you suggesting, detective?' asked Walker, but he had a good idea what she was about to say, and just wanted it confirmed.

'I'm saying... someone may have been communicating with him on these things,' said DC Briggs. 'At least before he'd thrown his mobile phone away, that is.'

'So, you would need a phone to connect these things to?' ask Walker.

'I think so. It likely has a Bluetooth connection,' said DC Briggs, probably realising Walker didn't have a clue what that was from his blank expression. 'It's a short-wave wireless connection, a bit like the Internet, used to connect two or more devices. The glasses would link to a phone, which can then be used to connect to the Internet or a mobile phone network and talk to people.'

'I see,' said Walker. 'So, if he had a second phone?'

'I think we should let this one go, Chief,' said DC Briggs. 'It's over. We got the killer. Job done. I know it leaves a bad taste, but it is what it is. All the kids are wearing these gadgets

CHAPTER THIRTY-SEVEN

these days. If he had a second phone, forensics would have recovered it from the body by now. Let's go home, eh? You can follow it up if you like in the next few days, of course, just to be sure—I would too—but it's probably nothing.'

Walker thought about it, almost did as she asked, but something was niggling at him. 'Just humour me, for a few more seconds?'

DC Briggs let out a long breath. 'Okay. Then, theoretically, he could have been listening to someone, someone who might have been giving instructions to him,' said DC Briggs. '*Theoretically*. But unlikely. I'm pretty sure he'd need a mobile phone or a stable Internet connection to connect the device.'

Walker had assumed that Alex had been hallucinating, had been hearing voices coming from his own head. He'd also thought the case was finished, all tied up, but he wasn't sure now, had a funny feeling. He opened the car door, engine still running. 'Let me check the body, see if they've missed anything, before they take him away.'

DC Briggs nodded, resigned to the fact, put her head back on the car seat, taking in some deep breaths while Walker headed back out. The paramedics were loading the gurney onto the ambulance now, so Walker quickened his step, getting closer.

'Stop!' he said, holding his hand out, signally for them to halt what they were doing. The paramedics did as asked, setting the gurney down in the ambulance, but leaving the back doors open. 'I need to check the body again before it's taken away.'

One of the forensic investigators approached, a male donned in a white oversuit and hood. 'Is there a problem, Detective?' The man was pale, had a wispy moustache and round glasses, probably still in his twenties, perhaps fresh from doing graduate work.

'I need to double check the body for myself, make sure he didn't have anything on him,' said Walker.

'Fine. But I've already checked myself,' said the investigator. 'We have to bag any items before the body is taken away. I'm one of the SOCOs. There wasn't much. Just a bit of money, some gum, and a wallet to hold the money. That's about it.'

The Scene of Crime Officer seemed to know what he was doing, despite his young-looking age. Walker wondered whether he might be older than he appeared, had one of those boyish faces.

'No mobile phone then?' asked Walker.

'No. Nothing like that,' said the SOCO.

Walker got up into the ambulance, unzipped the body bag, started going through Alex's various pockets, anywhere he might hide a phone, frisking him. There was nothing, just like the SOCO had said. 'Okay. That will be all then,' said Walker, getting back down from the ambulance, and making his way back to the car. He got in and closed the door.

'Anything?' asked DC Briggs.

'Nothing,' said Walker. 'Must have forgot he was wearing the glasses then when he ditched the phone. Or he liked wearing them or was using them as a disguise.'

'I guess,' said DC Briggs. 'Can we go home now?'

Walker closed the door of the MINI, feeling dissatisfied with the outcome, and headed towards the home of DC Briggs.

* * *

Walker was sitting next to DC Briggs, who was now tucked

CHAPTER THIRTY-SEVEN

up in her double bed at home. He'd never actually been inside her place before, never mind her bedroom. It was nice, homely, clean-smelling and tidy—the exact opposite of his malodourous place.

'Nice digs,' he said, trying to make small talk, feeling a little uncomfortable in his policing partner's small bedroom, not quite sure what to say. Plus, his mind was still on the case. Something was still bothering him, niggling away. It still felt unfinished.

'What is it, Chief? You thinking about those damned glasses again?' asked DC Briggs, sipping on a cup of tea that Walker had made her. 'Not bad,' she said. 'Plenty of milk, just how I like it.'

Walker smiled. 'I've seen your hot milk with a dab of tea before.'

'So...?' she pressed.

'I'm not sure. I think I'll go talk to the mother. Something just isn't sitting right with me on this,' said Walker. 'Something about that boy's expression when he was at the station. And *urinating*? He was absolutely terrified.'

'Well... hallucinating can be scary, can't it? Didn't you experience something like that, when you were ill?' she asked.

Walker had indeed. He'd mentioned it to her before. But the idea that someone might have been talking to him through those glasses, instructing him, forcing him to do what he did, just wouldn't shake loose. If there was a possibility, even a miniscule one, he had to at least explore it, get to a point where it could be ruled out. 'Yeah,' said Walker, referring to his hallucinations. 'I did. At the hospital. And I didn't wet myself.'

'But he was just a young boy,' said DC Briggs. 'You have to

let go. It's over, Chief. Everyone who was involved in the Charlotte Porter case is either dead or in a holding cell. So, nobody could have called him even if he did have a second phone—which he didn't.'

Walker gave it some more thought. 'Yeah. You're probably right.' He took a breath, tried to turn off. 'I just got off the phone to the station when I was making your tea. It seems Riley and Lee are gunna be fine. Riley was especially lucky, just missed his organs somehow. They just need some healing time. They're being carefully monitored at the hospital.'

'That's great,' said DC Briggs. 'And the others?'

'All fine except for the PC. He didn't make it, I'm afraid,' said Walker. 'Did you know him?'

'Not really,' said DC Briggs, visibly shaken. 'But we'll have to do something for his family anyway.'

Walker nodded in agreement. 'Look, are you alright if I go now? I still want to talk to the mother, get things wrapped up properly. It's a loose end. And I don't like loose ends.'

DC Briggs sighed. 'You need to get some rest too. Don't you ever learn? You have to start taking care of yourself better, Jon, or find someone who will. You're gunna make yourself ill again if you carry on.' She cared about him too, and it didn't go unappreciated.

'Oh, is that an offer?' said Walker, trying to make light of it, suddenly wishing he'd said nothing before what he said even finished coming out of his mouth. 'Sorry, I... sorry. It was just a joke. I didn't mean...'

DC Briggs looked at him in a way she hadn't before. 'It's okay', she said, pausing like she was considering something. 'But since I have you all vulnerable, why don't you finally tell me what you're so damned sad about all the time. Even when

CHAPTER THIRTY-SEVEN

you make a joke, there's still some dark desperation deep in your eyes. What on Earth happened to you? Why *did* you get into policing? You once told me some copper put the idea in your head after you went off the rails as a kid. Is that all it was?'

Walker shook his head, resigned to telling her what really happened. She deserved to know. She'd been a good partner— a good *friend*. He always intended to tell her when the time was right, and that time seemed to be now. 'My sister was murdered when I was a teenager. Her killer was never found.' Saying it out loud made him feel a little lighter, made him feel closer to her too.

Shelly put her head down. 'Well, that trumps my trauma,' she said, smiling a pained smile.

'Did something happen to you too? Is that why you joined the force?' asked Walker.

Shelly took a deep breath. 'My... My sister was also attacked,' she said. 'Sexually, I mean. She's alive and well now, but it shook us at the time, turned our lives upside down.'

Walker wanted to comfort her, leaned forward for a hug, but pulled out at the last moment, rubbed her on the arm instead. 'We all have our crosses to bear,' he said. 'Some are just heavier than others.'

Shelly sighed, emotion seeming to ripple throughout her body.

'I guess this case was particularly difficult for you then?' said Walker. 'Sorry, I didn't realise.'

'You too. It did bring a few things back, didn't it?' she said, before visibly shrugging it off, which seemed to Walker to signal an end to the topic. 'Go see the mother then, and when you're done go home and get some rest. I'll call you in a couple of hours, make sure you do.'

Walker nodded. 'Yes, boss,' he said, sarcastically. 'I just want to see how she reacts, that's all, as she didn't seem to want anything to do with Alex the last time we spoke. And I want to see if she knows anything about those glasses, and what he used them for. I'll ask the other two boys about them as well, Liam and Mo, see if they know anything. We'll have to hold on to them for now, try to rule out any involvement in the Porter case.'

'Look, I'm *sure* all the kids use devices like those glasses these days,' said DC Briggs. 'He was just ill, clinically diagnosed. *Let... it... go.*'

Walker stood up. 'I'll talk to you later then. Take it easy.'

Shelly nodded and grabbed the remote to the TV and turned it on. 'Oh, and lock the door on your way out, will you?' she said, with a serious expression on her face.

'Course,' said Walker, knowing how vulnerable she might be feeling after what had just happened. 'I was going to anyway.'

CHAPTER THIRTY-EIGHT

Walker knocked on the door of Kathy Johnson's house, Alex's mum, and waited. He'd been told there was a Family Liaison Officer with her, a DC called Cheryl Broadbent who'd come by from Leyland Police Station. Like all FLOs, she'd been specially trained to work with bereaved families, to assist in situations like this. DC Broadbent opened the door.

'DCI Walker?' she said.

'Yes. I believe you're DC Broadbent, the FLO assigned to the case?' said Walker. 'How is she?'

'She... conflicted. I think she's still angry with her son. She'll be okay for now. I think I'll come back tomorrow, check on her again,' said DC Broadbent.

'She okay for a little chat then?' asked Walker.

'Yeah. I think so. But she's... you'll see. She's resilient enough. Old school. She may break down at some point, but I don't think that time will be just yet,' said DC Broadbent. 'She might still be in denial. There's nothing much more I can do for now. I'll be on my way.'

DC Broadbent left, leaving Walker to enter.

'Mrs Johnson,' said Walker, as he entered. 'It's DCI Walker again. We met already. May I come in?' There was no answer.

'Mrs Johnson? I'm coming in. Please don't be alarmed. I'm here to help.'

Walker went into the living room to find Kathy Johnson sitting in an armchair stoically watching the TV, smoking a cigarette like nothing had happened. The curtains were drawn, and with no window open, the room was stale and thick with smoke.

'Mrs Johnson, can I sit with you?' asked Walker. 'Just for a few minutes?'

Kathy shoved what was left of the ciggy she was smoking into an ashtray on a coffee table in front of her. 'It's like Piccadilly Circus in here today,' she said.

Walker sat down. 'Have you been there?' he asked, looking for an opening, a way into the conversation, wondering whether she might have been there with her boy.

'What?' said Kathy.

'Piccadilly Circus? In London? Have you been?' asked Walker. He was just trying to break the ice, get her thinking about something else.

'No. I haven't sodding been,' she said. 'It's a bloody saying, isn't it? What kind of a question is that? Are you the one who was with my boy? When he…'

'Yes. I was with Alex in his last few moments. I'm so sorry for your loss, Mrs Johnson,' said Walker. He noticed a line across her neck as she bent forward to get another cigarette. He'd not seen it at first as she was wearing a high neckline, probably to try to hide it.

'It's probably for the best,' she said, lighting the cigarette and puffing more smoke everywhere. 'Was always trouble, that boy. Never gave me a moment's peace.' She pulled up her jumper a little higher, covering the mark across her neck.

CHAPTER THIRTY-EIGHT

'He was a troubled soul, always, getting in fights and the like, getting in trouble with you lot. At least he'll finally be able to rest now.'

Something had happened to her to make that mark, that much was clear. It was fresh, red raw. Either she'd tried to kill herself as well, or...

'Mrs Johnson. Has Alex been here?' asked Walker. 'Before he... did what he did. He came back to Leyland. We thought he might be coming here.'

'Has he *been* here? Well, of course he's been here. He bloody lives here. You're not too smart for a detective, are you?' said Kathy.

She knew what he was talking about. She was being purposefully evasive. 'You know what I mean, Mrs Johnson. Did Alex come here, recently? Today? Did he hurt you? Or have you hurt yourself?' Kathy raised an eyebrow, demanding more. 'Your neck?' Walker clarified.

'It's none of your sodding business is what it is!' she snapped. 'My boy just died. What is wrong with you?' She turned the TV up, even louder than before, making conversation difficult, signalling an end to their talk.

'There's just one more thing, Mrs Johnson,' said Walker at a volume to compete with the TV, getting the glasses out that Alex had been wearing. 'Alex's glasses. Do you know anything about these?' He popped them on the table in front of her.

'Them's the glasses he wore, that's all. Some kind of fashion statement. Got 'em himself, somehow. Don't know where he got his money from,' said Kathy. 'Probably stole 'em. You can see yourself out.'

Walker stood up, realising he wasn't going to get much more out of her for now. 'I'll be in touch then, Mrs Johnson,' said

Walker, and he left the living room, heading back into the hallway, towards the front door. But when he got to the door, he hesitated, his fingers twitching by his side, his nose wrinkling up. He looked up the stairs and sighed. As much as he wanted it to be over, it wasn't just yet. There were too many loose ends that needed tying up. He wanted to have a quick look around, one last time, check things out, see if they'd missed anything during the previous search. The search warrant they had wouldn't expire for three months, so there was no issue in looking, but he wanted to do it quietly, without Mrs Johnson being there, distracting him.

He slowly crept up the stairs to try to avoid her attention—with them creaking and moaning here and there as he put his weight on—hearing the TV blazing from the next room, fairly certain that he'd probably have a few minutes at least as she'd just lit another cigarette. He didn't want her following, getting all animated, or having a complete meltdown. She'd just lost her son, after all. He'd already seen Alex's room, but there were two more bedrooms. He gently pushed the door to one of the rooms, its hinge squeaking a tad. It was small, something like a junk room, with bits and bobs piled up everywhere. Then he went over to the remaining door and opened that. This was clearly the main bedroom. It was bit bigger than the rest and contained a double bed. He stepped inside. There was a machine set up, pointing at the wall opposite the bed's headboard. He pressed a button on it that looked like a power switch, and it came on, buzzing, illuminating the wall with a blue rectangle and a menu. It was a projector. Walker pressed a down arrow on the projector, flipping through the menu, until he came to a setting called 'Connect to a Bluetooth Device'. *Bluetooth.* That's what DC Briggs had said, about Alex's smart

CHAPTER THIRTY-EIGHT

glasses. He didn't like coincidences like that. Not one bit. Although most devices probably had that function these days. But he didn't like *this*. He turned the device off again, took a quick look around the room: there were two drinking glasses on the bedside table, what looked like flute-shaped champagne glasses, and there was an empty bottle of something in the bin, alongside some used tissues and two condom wrappers. It looked like someone had been having a little party. It stank of it. Most worryingly, there was what looked like a blonde wig on the floor next to a crumpled dress—the very same look that Alex's victim's had.

Walker turned to see Kathy stood in the doorway, an angry expression on her face. He hadn't heard her coming.

'What do you think you're doing?' she asked. 'This is *my* bedroom.'

'I'm sorry,' said Walker. 'I needed the bathroom. Got a little lost. Just wondered what this thing was.' He pointed at the projector, knowing damned well what it was. 'Our search warrant is valid for a period of three months. What is this?'

'It's a projector. I watch films on it. What of it?' asked Kathy.

'Had some company?' asked Walker.

Kathy let out an exasperated breath. 'What is this?' she asked. 'My son has just killed himself. So, I had a little company. So what? Leave me alone.'

Walker sensed he should leave now, but he couldn't let it go. 'Mrs Johnson, your son was wearing smart glasses. I believe they could connect to a device like this, either directly, or through another mobile device, like a phone; or even two phones.'

'So? I don't know anything about that. I just watch films. My friend puts them on a USB stick for me,' she said.

'May I ask who has been here with you,' he said, nodding at the champagne glasses.

'I'm not a friggin' nun. I sometimes have men over, to sleep. It's not a crime, is it?' she said.

'No, it's not,' said Walker. 'But we're investigating the death of your son, and the deaths of the girls that he killed, so we're going to have to look at everything, including this. We're going to need to know who was here, what they did, and we'll have to get forensics in here to get some samples and the like. We don't want to leave any stone unturned.'

Kathy stepped back, just outside the room, and closed the door. A key jangled and the door *locked.*

'Mrs Johnson!' shouted Walker, getting over to the door, trying the handle: it turned, but the door wouldn't budge. 'Mrs Johnson! Open this door, *now!* Think what you're doing. You'll be in a lot of trouble for this.' There was no response. He could hear her running down the stairs. Then there was some banging around, maybe the back door opening. He went to the window, which was on the front side of the house. There was nobody around.

'Mrs Johnson! Get up here and open this door!' shouted Walker, as loudly as he could. He'd had enough with this family. He barged the bedroom door with his shoulder, but it was solid. Detectives like him seemed to whack open such doors with great regularity on the telly, but in real life, it was much more difficult. He hit it a few times, kicking it, barging it, over and over. A tiny crack opened up between the frame and the door, but it wasn't much. *'Kath-eeee!'*

He could smell something now. He knew that smell—smelled like a barbecue, or at least, the smell of a barbecue before any food gets cooked. It was the lighter fluid that

CHAPTER THIRTY-EIGHT

people use to get the coals going. And there was smoke already starting to seep under the door.

'Shit!' said Walker. She was burning the bloody place down, with him in it. He got on his two-way radio and pressed a button. 'All units to Robin Road, Leyland, Moss Side, number 28, immediately. Bring the fire services. I'm locked in the bedroom of a burning building. Repeat, this is DCI Walker, and I'm locked in the bedroom of a burning building at 28 Robin Road, over.'

'Roger that,' came the response. 'We're on it. Hold tight, detective, over.'

Walker took a look out the window again, wondered whether he might be able to climb down a drainpipe. There were none near the bedroom, and the ground outside was concrete paving flags, so jumping would be problematic too. Still, at least he wouldn't die. He could jump from the first floor, probably break a leg, get a few injuries, but he'd survive, at least—*probably*. He thought about having another go at opening the bedroom door, but that would only let more smoke into the room, cause more problems, and he might not be able to get down the stairs anyway if it was already on fire. He'd just sit tight, wait for the fire engines to arrive. Kathy Johnson had probably already got away by now. He needed to live to fight another day, find out what the hell had gone on here, what role she had to play in all this, why she was doing what she was doing. Clearly, there was more to it than he and DC Briggs had thought just a little while earlier, and he intended to find out what.

'*I'm sorry!*' shouted Kathy, and fire started to lick under the bedroom door now: the wood was burning.

'Kathy!' said Walker. 'Let me out!'

The smoke was starting to make him cough. He should have stuffed something under the door, filled the gap—but even if he had, that too would be burning, making it worse.

He went to the window again, opened it as wide as it would go, and looked down.

He was going to have to jump.

CHAPTER THIRTY-NINE

Walker stood with a fire blanket around him, looking up at the burning building of number 28, Robin Road. The Fire Service was currently dealing with it while Walker was being checked over by some paramedics—a male and a female in matching green uniforms. He was fine. The firefighters had turned up before he'd summoned the courage to jump, before the bedroom had really started to burn as well. They'd got him out through the window just in time.

DC Briggs rolled up, got out of her car without even parking properly, but managing to bump up onto a footpath, so as to not block any of the emergency services. She ran over, wearing some jeans, slippers, and the long T-shirt she'd gone to bed in. She'd obviously come in a hurry.

'Chief! You okay?' she shouted while she was still running.

'I'm fine,' he said, sipping on some of the water one of the paramedics had given him in a clear plastic cup. 'I thought I told you to get some rest.'

'What happened?' she asked, now face-to-face, breathing heavily. 'Hogarth told me. She try to kill herself?'

'She locked me in the bedroom, then set the bloody place on fire,' said Walker.

'In the bedroom? What were you doing in the—'

'I was taking a look around,' said Walker. 'She wasn't being very cooperative.'

The male paramedic put a stethoscope on Walker's chest. 'Take a deep breath,' he said, so Walker did. 'Bit scratchy, but you'll be fine in a couple of days,' he said, before removing the tool. He checked Walker's hands and lower arms, probably for any burns. There were none. 'Try to take it easy until then.' Walker nodded and the man got on with something else.

'You think she got away?' asked DC Briggs.

'Not sure yet,' said Walker. 'She might still be in there for all I know.'

They waited while the Fire Service did their jobs, with none of the police being allowed inside while they went about their business. DI Hogarth was also there, taking a good look around the perimeter of the building. He didn't do much field work these days, of course, what with his increasingly cumbersome frame—preferred desk work—but he occasionally managed it when they were short staffed, like now. A few police officers were out and about assisting too, scouring the area, trying to find the whereabouts of Kathy Johnson.

'Looks like we've both had a bit of a scare today then,' said DC Briggs. 'It never rains but it pours, eh?'

Walker took a few more deep breaths, trying to clear his lungs, coughing a bit more.

'Don't worry, it won't be like this every day,' he said to the much more inexperienced DC Briggs. She smiled a pained smile, having already had one or two days like this already.

A couple of the firefighters suddenly emerged from the building, one of them carrying a body—a female one: it was

CHAPTER THIRTY-NINE

Mrs Johnson. He set her down on the floor, carefully, while the paramedics mobilised, got ready to work on her. She was badly burned and wasn't moving. The paramedics tried to revive her for several minutes, without success.

The firefighter who'd carried Kathy out came over to Walker and DC Briggs, removed his helmet and breathing apparatus, putting them under his arm.

'Hi there. Are you the DCI who called this in?' he asked.

'Yes. I'm DCI Walker,' said Walker.

'This woman didn't die from the fire, although she almost certainly would have at this stage if she was still in there,' he said.

'What do you mean?' asked Walker.

'I mean she hung herself before the fire got to her. It's not uncommon for people to try to kill themselves when they can't escape a fire—find a preferable way of dying instead. Remember all that shit on 9/11? People jumping from the burning building?' he said. 'She used the rope from the living room curtain tiebacks. Had tassels on it and everything, singed from the fire, they were. She was hanging from a stair spindle. She must have removed the spacer fillet and put it back before jumping off the stool that was nearby. I reckon she'd thought about it before, though, more than once, probably, maybe even had a dry run. It was all a bit too thought through to have been done during the chaos and panic of a fire.'

'I see,' said Walker.

'Looks like she started the fire too,' said the firefighter. 'Found a couple of one-litre bottles of barbecue lighting fluid on the kitchen worktop, an area that didn't take the worst of the fire damage. Could smell it everywhere too. She torched the place, alright, with you trapped in it. It seems she tried to kill the both of you. We'll need a little longer before it can be declared safe for your officers to enter. And you might need to use a ladder to get to the first floor—the stairs are pretty damaged. Just give us a little more time.'

'Understood,' said Walker. 'Thank you.'

The firefighter headed back toward the building to complete his work while the paramedics lifted Kathy Johnson into a second ambulance that had just arrived.

'Let's get you out of here then, Chief. You can stay at mine if you want. We can recover together,' said DC Briggs. 'We'll watch Trisha. On TV? It's a talk show. It'll take our minds off things.'

Walker felt his eyes go a little wider. He imagined them both lying down in bed together watching daytime TV. 'No, I don't think...'

'I meant with you on the sofa, Jon. You can sleep there. What are you thinking?' said DC Briggs, grinning.

Of course that's what she'd meant. 'Oh. Thanks, but... I think I'd rather rest at home. I appreciate the offer, though.'

'You're welcome,' said DC Briggs, eying him. 'We are a team, after all, aren't we?'

'We are,' said Walker, but his mind had already turned to other matters. 'He wanted to know what role, if any, Alex's mother had played in the murders he'd carried out. Just because they were both dead, it didn't mean they shouldn't find the truth. Plus, there were still a couple of young boys in custody over all this—young Mo and Liam. He had a responsibility to make sure nobody got convicted and punished who shouldn't be. There were still two potentially innocent lives at stake.

'What is it, Chief?' said DC Briggs, hugging and rubbing

CHAPTER THIRTY-NINE

herself, trying to keep warm in the bedtime clothes she'd rushed out in. Walker removed the fire blanket he had wrapped around himself and placed it around DC Briggs instead.

'I just want to take one last look around in there, once it's been declared safe,' said Walker. 'See if there's anything in there pertaining to the case.'

'What? Why? Her son just died, so she went a bit mad, killed herself. The case is over, Chief,' said DC Briggs. 'Isn't it? You don't know when to stop, do you.'

'No. You don't understand. When I went up to the main bedroom, snooping around while she was sitting in the living room, I found something: a wall projector that had a Bluetooth connection,' said Walker.

'I see,' said DC Briggs. 'You're still thinking of those smart glasses Alex was wearing, aren't you?'

'*So?*' asked Walker. 'Could they have been connected?'

'Well... technically, if Alex had a phone to connect his glasses to, and if that phone was networked to another phone, then a projector could also be linked to that to see and hear what Alex was seeing and hearing. I *suppose*. Technically. But I think we're finding things that aren't there now. I told you: lots of people wear those kinds of glasses these days for making calls and listening to music and such. And lots of people watch TV on projectors in their bedrooms. Sometimes, we look so hard we start to see patterns that aren't even there. The human brain is wired to see such patterns, isn't it, as you well know. I really don't think there's anything more to it than that. Anything more would be a bit far-fetched. But... if you want to check it out anyway, you could always look at the phone records of Kathy Johnson. With accessories like that, they tend to be wirelessly connected through a mobile device. He would have to have been contacting her either through a stable internet connection or a mobile network provider. And since he ditched his mobile phone, I'd say that's unlikely.'

Walker smiled. She'd come such a long way as a detective in such a relatively short space of time. He was proud of her; glad she'd taken the step up from being a police constable. But she was still a little naïve, a bit too trusting of people and not cynical enough—but it would come, in time. 'Well get you. Anyone would think *you're* the senior detective.' His smile sank as he thought of those two boys again, and what they might stand to lose if they were jointly convicted of Charlotte Porter's murder. 'I just want to be sure, take one last look around,' he said. 'She did try to kill me, after all. That was weird, you have to admit that.'

'Fine,' said DC Briggs. 'I guess I don't quite understand that part myself. I'll go home, get my work clothes, meet you back here.'

'No. You go back home and rest. I'm fine now,' said Walker. 'It was nothing. I'd have got out somehow.'

'You sure?' said DC Briggs, hesitantly. 'I don't think I'd be fine.'

'Well, I am. You go home and rest. And I'll do the same, just as soon as I've finished up here.'

'Alright then, Chief. I was a bit worried there for a minute. I'm glad you're okay,' said DC Briggs.

'Me too. That *you're* okay, I mean,' said Walker. They shared one last smile, and DC Briggs returned to her car, leaving Walker to watch the firefighters go about their work, waiting for the building to be declared safe to enter.

CHAPTER THIRTY-NINE

* * *

'Don't touch any electrical items, even though the mains electricity is off, stay away from any metals, use the ladder to get to the first floor, and wear these gloves and breathing apparatus,' said the firefighter who was briefing Walker before he could enter the fire-damaged building that had been the home of Kathy Johnson and Alex Wilkinson. 'The structural integrity of the building has at least been declared safe by the Building Control Officer, so you're now safe to enter.'

'Got it,' said Walker, taking the heavy-duty gloves and mask from the firefighter, putting them on.

He entered the building and started looking around. DI Hogarth was already in there having been briefed before Walker. He was donned in the same gear, although it was tighter on him and may have been an XL if they made them in that size. He creaked and shuffled around somewhat uncomfortably, but Walker appreciated the effort and support on this one, what with DIs Riley and Lee undergoing urgent medical care, and DC Briggs needing some recovery time.

Walker didn't know what they were looking for, exactly— but he knew they were looking for any evidence that might suggest that Kath Johnson had been coercing her son into doing the terrible things that he did, or at least that she had knowledge of things about her son that she hadn't told them. He wondered whether she might have been mentally ill too, whether Alex had grown up in a very unhealthy environment that had exacerbated his condition, or even created it. These cases often didn't end well, in one way or another, and Walker strived to at least learn something from such cases, so that future investigations might end better.

Walker carefully climbed the aluminium ladder that the firefighters had installed to get to the first floor and headed back to the main bedroom where Kathy Johnson would have slept, where he'd been trapped. The carpet was blackened charred, and had been pulled up here and there, probably by the firefighters or Building Control Officer, to check the integrity of the flooring. There was no underlay under the carpet, and no gripper rods either, just bare floorboards. It looked like whoever had laid the carpet had done it on a budget, probably even cut it themselves with scissors or a Stanley knife. It wasn't neatly done. He walked over the floorboards and the carpet that was still down, took a good look around. He didn't know what he expected to find. He thought maybe DC Briggs was right—that there was nothing to find here, that he was looking for something that wasn't there.

He was just about to give up and leave when he stepped on one particular floorboard that rocked a little. On inspection, he saw this one wasn't nailed down: it was loose.

Walker bent down, pulled at the loose floorboard with his fingertips, which came up with ease; and then another one next to it as well, and another one. They were tongue and groove boards, so releasing one made the next one loose, and so on, until he came to one that was screwed down properly—so he stopped there.

There were three short lengths of board that he'd been able to remove, and underneath, there was a void just big enough to house a lockable black metal box. He pulled the box out, dusted it off, eyed the keyhole.

'What's this then?' he said to himself, just as DI Hogarth

entered.

'Got something?' asked DI Hogarth, who'd already removed his mask so he could be heard. Walker did the same, pulling his mask down. The bedroom window was still open, and the smoke had cleared now, so they just had to worry about any toxic fumes, but Walker figured a few seconds would be okay.

'Something to hide,' said Walker, trying to open the box, finding it locked. 'I doubt it's valuables—although you never know. You get anything?'

'Nothing,' said DI Hogarth. 'Although I did find a few bags of bondage gear in the spare bedroom—whips, handcuffs, rope, dildos, that kind of thing.'

'Right. Let's get this back to the station then, get it opened, see what we have,' said Walker. 'That will probably be quicker than finding any key in this mess.'

'Okay, Chief,' said DI Hogarth. 'We can do that. But…' He took something out from his pocket, looked like a Swiss army knife only this had *H&H* branded on it. 'Before I joined the force, I was an apprentice locksmith for a time. I still carry these around, just in case.' He started to pull various folding tools out from the device, what looked like tension wrenches of different shapes and sizes.

'Can you pick this lock, Detective?' asked Walker. 'Is that what you're saying?'

Walker's consistently easy-going colleague smiled and nodded. 'I can,' he said, so Walker handed over the metal box, let him get to work on it immediately. Walker really couldn't wait to get back to the station to see what was inside there. He needed to know now.

DI Hogarth set the box on the floor, on a charred piece of carpet that wasn't too damaged. He struggled to get down next to it, huffed and puffed a bit using his hand on his knee to give it a bit more support, but he somehow made it. It didn't take too long, just a bit of fiddling, trying to release the locking mechanism. On the fourth attempt, DI Hogarth twisted his hand and the box clicked open. 'There,' he said, a bit out of breath. 'Got it.'

'Give it to me,' said Walker, crouching down next to DI Hogarth, taking the box.

He braced himself and opened it up.

Inside there were various items, mostly polaroid photographs, a couple of USB sticks, some newspaper articles, and various items that looked like keepsakes—a ring and a couple of bits of jewellery, a hair scrunchy, and, most disturbingly, a small grip-seal bag full of what looked like toenails.

'Holy shit,' said Walker, picking up the bag of toenails, looking at them, then placing them back in the box, picking up some photographs instead. He hadn't seen any properly yet, as the top one was facing backwards, and they were all held together with an elastic band. When he turned them around, though, it soon became clear what the nature of the polaroid photographs were. 'Oh, you poor boy.'

They were photographs of Alex, in various states of distress and torture. As Walker flipped through them, he saw they were in a chronological order, of sorts, with the top photographs being more recent shots, then going back all the way through his youth and childhood. There were many of Alex crying, some where he was tied up, others with him bruised or bleeding, one with one of his big toenails being held with some pliers. He'd clearly been extensively abused over a long period.

'Jesus,' said DI Hogarth, who was also seeing what Walker

CHAPTER THIRTY-NINE

was. 'This is just... awful.'

There was another pile of photos under the polaroid batch, but these ones were printed out on what looked like a standard home printer, probably digital photographs that had later been printed. These were different: young women, all looking similar to the women Alex had attacked, all in states of distress, crying and begging. Some of them were even younger than the current victims. On the back of each photo was a woman's name: Sandra, Ellie, Emma... the list went on. The keepsakes—the jewellery and the scrunchy—Walker thought, were probably taken from them.

'We need to find out who these girls are,' said Walker. 'Make sure they're okay.'

DI Hogarth nodded. 'So, it was the mother?' he asked, seeming a bit confused. 'She made him do all this? Or she just knew about it?' Walker shook his head. 'How do people get so messed up?'

There was one more thing in the metal box: another photograph, this time an old black and white one of a man, stern-looking, looking away from the camera, dressed in a black suit and tie, hair slicked back. Walker turned the photograph over. On the back, in handwriting that was just about readable, it said: *'Now I have the power, daddy. X.'*

'What does it say?' asked DI Hogarth.

'It says that this family had some issues,' said Walker. 'And unfortunately, it's taken this long, and the deaths of several innocent people, for those issues to finally come to light.'

He looked through some more of the stuff, looking more closely at the toenails. Some were stained with blood, but each had a number on—16, 12, 14, 9.... it went on. It was his age. The larger numbers were written on the larger nails, and the smaller numbers on smaller nails. She'd been doing this all his life. It was a miracle the boy hadn't cracked earlier. His life had been one of unending pain and suffering, but he'd somehow managed to adapt.

Walker took out the newspaper articles last. There were only two—new looking. They were reports about the two girls Alex had recently killed. Walker put everything back in the box and closed it.

'We need to take this back with us, get it forensically examined ASAP. And we also need to see what's on these USB sticks, but I'm guessing it's probably digital copies of some of these prints,' said Walker.

'Why do people do things like this?' asked DI Hogarth, now looking horrified at what he was seeing, utterly disgusted, his friendly easy-going nature evaporating in front of Walker's very eyes. 'It's sick.'

'I don't know. I really don't. Let's go, Detective,' said Walker. 'We've seen enough for now. We've got what we came here to get.'

CHAPTER FORTY

Several weeks after Walker found the black metal box under Kathy Johnson's floorboards at her home in Leyland, there had been seventeen women come forward, all remarkably similar in appearance and all with familiar tales to tell.

The latest one had come down to the station—unlike most of the other girls, who'd preferred not to—but her story was just like the rest: Alex had got the young women and girls alone, had punched them in the stomach, either raped or sexually abused them in some way, and then had taken revealing or sexually explicit photographs, threatening to post the pictures everywhere if they said anything to anyone. And none of them had, until now, that is.

He'd been doing this for years, going as far back as primary school, when he'd attacked one girl in the toilets during class time. It seemed that in the age of the Internet and social media, everyone was afraid of something humiliating getting out there, especially young people and children—being particularly vulnerable—and they preferred just to live with their trauma, say nothing, and typically present an idealistic depiction of their life whilst quietly suffering. Apart from the embarrassment and humiliation of coming forward, Walker knew that only one in fifty rape cases recorded by the police actually led to charges being made, and even fewer of these led to convictions, so it wasn't surprising that none of these women had chosen to talk about their experiences until now. *Why would they?* Walker thought. It was sad, and he had to admit it was a part of the system that wasn't working well at the moment. But there was little he himself could do to change that at present. He was just a cog in a much larger machine.

'So, you say he apologised to you when it was over?' said Walker.

'Yes. It was very confusing,' said the girl, called Emma, now eighteen years old, one Walker had seen in the pile of photographs from the black box. 'He seemed to enjoy it, what he did, while he was doing it. But once he was finished, he was contrite, very sorry for what he did, but said he had to protect himself, and that he'd post the pics everywhere if I said anything to anyone. And the look in his eyes: *I believed him.*'

'I see. Well... thank you for coming down and explaining all of this to us,' said Walker. 'It is very helpful. We can eliminate you from our enquiries now that we know you're safe.' He handed her a piece of paper. 'Here are details of some support, should you feel you need it—some talking therapy, CBT, that kind of thing. You might also meet with your GP to discuss any feelings of anxiety or depression that you might have, who may offer you appropriate medication to help with that. I'm so sorry this happened to you, Emma.'

Emma smiled a pained smile and wiped a solitary tear from her eye, before stiffening her back, and standing up. She left the paper Walker had given her on the table in front of her. 'I

CHAPTER FORTY

won't be needing that,' she said. 'Us Chorley lasses are made of tougher stuff. I'm over it.'

Walker picked up the paper, folded it, and then held it out in front of Emma. 'I'm sure you are. But how about you take it anyway, just in case?'

Emma took the paper, stuffed it in her pocket, and walked out of the interview room with her head held high.

* * *

After the near-death experience that DC Briggs had endured, she'd taken a couple of weeks leave of absence to get herself together. The whole thing had shaken her up. It had shaken them all up. But she'd taken some counselling and was now back, ready for action. She entered the interview room Walker was in and sat down opposite him.

'She was the last of them,' she said. 'So many...'

Walker shook his head in disbelief.

'I can't get my head around it,' he said, 'even after all my years of experience, why a mother would do something like that to her child, how social services could have missed this? Two dead girls, Alex too, who was just as much a victim in all this, Benjamin Jackson's suicide, and all those girls traumatised for life. So many. And then we've still got the CPS pushing for a prosecution on Mo and Liam for the murder of Charlotte Porter as well, on the grounds of joint enterprise. If they go down, that will be two more lives ruined, if they aren't already. It's tragic. No wonder us police are a different breed.'

'Is that what you really think, sir?' asked DC Briggs. 'That we're different.'

'I think we have to be,' he said, sucking it up, standing, puffing his chest out. 'How else can we go on. What's next then?'

'Well, we can now visit Mrs Johnson.' Kathy Johnson, despite initially being unable to be resuscitated prior to being put in the ambulance, had somehow been revived on the ride to the hospital. She was badly burned, could barely speak due to damage to her larynx, and had some brain damage due to a lack of oxygen, but she was still alive, somehow. 'I've managed to arrange access to talk to her. I thought you needed it, to put this case to bed, once and for all. You were never going to let this one go without a fight, were you. I'm so glad you stuck with it; I was exhausted. Do you want to talk to her?'

'I want to know why she did what she did,' said Walker. 'So, yes, I want to talk to her, or try, at least. I want to try to understand why she abused her boy and forced him to do these terrible things, if that's what she did. I want to know if she's innately evil, or if she was just damaged in some way too, like he was: broken.'

'Are you sure it's worth it, Chief? She'll either be behind bars or in a high security hospital for the rest of her life,' said DC Briggs. 'There are other cases to focus our attention on now. Is there anything else to gain from this?'

'The *truth*,' said Walker. 'There's always something to gain. We're truth seekers. That's what we do. Don't you forget it.'

* * *

CHAPTER FORTY

Kathy Johnson was almost unrecognisable. Her face had been all but destroyed in the fire—her lips were mostly gone, part of her nose too, her eyelashes and eyebrows decimated, her skin was badly damaged, and she was blind in one eye, which had lost its colour and was milky white. She was lying in bed, one hand cuffed to the railing, staring at the ceiling, impotently. In that state, it was hard to imagine she'd ever had a psychological hold over anybody, that she'd ever been strong enough to hurt someone.

'Mrs Johnson. It's DCI Walker. The one you locked in your bedroom before setting the place on fire,' said Walker, raising his voice slightly to make sure she could hear, still feeling more than a little aggrieved and agitated about it, but trying to remain professional. 'I found the black tin box, the one under the floorboards.'

Kathy groaned and moaned, moving her head from side to side, her heartrate ticking up on the monitor. She was distressed or exhibiting some kind of emotion—be it anger, or remorse, or anxiety. Walked hoped it wasn't excitement.

'Are you able to talk, Mrs Johnson?' asked Walker.

'Bad boy,' she managed to say, her voice all hoarse and scratchy, almost unrecognisable. 'Bad girl too...' She coughed and seemed to laugh, before calming some. She tried to say more, but nothing came out, so Walker reluctantly fed her some water from a paper cup that had a plastic straw in it. She slurped on it, before swallowing and going on. 'Seems it runs in the family,' she said.

'Mrs Johnson, can you confirm for me that you coerced your son, Alex, into murdering those young girls?' asked Walker. 'There are currently two young men on trial, who may go to prison if we don't get the facts straight.'

She spat, but nothing much came out. 'He had a choice. We all do, don't we?' she said.

'But were you in contact with Alex while he carried out these attacks?' asked Walker. 'It's important. We have to know. You've nothing to lose now. Were you involved?' He knew damned well she'd been in contact with someone during the attacks but had no idea who. There were two numbers she'd been in regular contact with, both with no phone records and presumed to be burners—temporary, untraceable, cheap discardable mobile phones often used by drug dealers or cheating husbands, both of which were possible given her lifestyle choices. But calls had been made to one of these mystery numbers the night Charlotte died, and also around the time of the other attacks too. Walker didn't like such coincidences, despite no such burner phone being found on Alex when he died.

Kathy started to sit. It took some effort, and she was clearly in some pain, but she made it, putting a couple of pillows behind herself, Walker not willing to help this time, watching her struggle—maybe even enjoying it a little. 'Why is everything so colourless?' she asked. 'I'm so tired. Can you get me a smoke?'

Walker had prepared some cigarettes for her, just in case he needed some leverage, some motivation for her to talk. 'The doctors said you have some minor brain damage, which may affect the way you perceive the world, including your vision, and high levels of fatigue would also be typical of such brain damage, especially after the injuries you've experienced.' He got out the cigarettes, along with a lighter, and popped them on a unit just out of Kathy's reach. 'If you tell me what I wanna know, I'll leave these here with you, and move them a

CHAPTER FORTY

bit closer before I go. It's your brand, I believe—Marlboro.'

Kathy licked what was left of her lips, but in her present condition, it just looked creepy and made Walker cringe. 'Fine. What do you want to know?' she asked.

'I want to know if you coerced Alex into killing those women,' he said. 'And I want your confession, for everything.'

Kathy started to pull on the handcuffs, manically shaking them, getting something out of her system before calming again. 'Alex deserved what he got. I never hurt him when he was being a good boy—but that was hardly ever. I was trying to discipline him, so he never did anything like this. But it wasn't enough, as you can see. I failed.'

'So, you're saying that Alex was out of control, and that the abuse you inflicted upon him was some kind of attempt at disciple. If that's the case, then why did you document everything, keep photographs? It makes no sense,' said Walker. 'I just... I just want to understand.' He wondered how clearly she was thinking, whether the brain damage she'd experienced was going to make anything she said unfit for use in a court of law.

'What goes around comes around,' she said, laughing again.

'Mrs Johnson. *Were* you talking to Alex while he did what he did?' asked Walker. 'Were you instructing him to do these things.'

'I did love him, you know,' she said, now flipping, becoming choked up. 'Before his father left, I loved him with all my heart. It was the best time of my life—the *only* good time.'

'Your life was difficult?' asked Walker. 'Did you suffer similar abuse?'

Walker got the sense that if she'd had any tears in her tear ducts, then she might have cried at that moment, that the floodgates may well have opened. He thought back to the second champagne glass and the used condom in her bedroom, the mystery male who may also have been involved.

'You have no idea,' was all she said, before the heart rate monitor started to bleep, faster and faster, before quickly flatlining.

'Nurse!' shouted Walker, pressing the emergency button near the bed. 'Nurse! We need some help here!'

CHAPTER FORTY-ONE

Kathy Johnson was revived twice more before she finally passed, taking the awful memories of what had happened with her. She would be buried next to her son, nearby her father—one Tony Johnson—who'd paid for the lots in advance before he'd died and instructed the family solicitor, T. Finch & Sons Solicitors, which was still in operation.

Walker had looked into the history of Kathy Johnson in some depth, but there was no history of social services being involved in her childhood, no official evidence of similar abuse, nothing on record. He'd begun to think she may have been born evil, that there was something innately wrong with her. She'd severely tortured her son and made him kill those young girls. There had to be something wrong with her, no matter what level of abuse she'd experienced. There was no excuse. Not really. Her wiring couldn't have been right to begin with.

In the autopsy of Alex Wilkinson, they'd found he'd been mutilated over many years, with him exhibiting all kinds of scars—the worst being a butchered scrotum and missing testicle, something one would expect more from a horror film than in real life, but there it was. It was a real-life horror. They existed. There were no hospital records of such an operation, and the level of work was suggestive of an amateur removal. It seemed Alex had been physically and psychologically abused over many years, perhaps most of his life. Although he'd outgrown his mother in size and strength, it wouldn't be difficult to imagine that she still had some kind of psychological hold on him after all those years of trauma, and that she'd coerced him into doing those terrible things. The question was, *why*? Had she got some kind of perverse pleasure from doing what she did, and watching the results? Or was it some kind of coping mechanism? Walker still didn't know, and it was nigh time to let go of it, just like DC Briggs had suggested in the first place. She was right. Some things will never be right, and one just has to let them be. Otherwise, you can drive yourself mad thinking about it, getting stuck in an endless loop, becoming a tourist in your own bad memories, and in the imagined ones of others.

Walker put the last of the documents for the case into one final file and closed it, ready to put away for good. He was done. More than done. There were other cases to look at, other investigations to focus his attention on—ones that were more pressing. But before he could do anything, the phone rang.

'Hello. Mrs Wilkinson?' said Walker. It was Dominic Wilkinson's wife, Alex's stepmother. 'What can I do for you? An email, you say, that I must see? Okay. I'll check it right away. Thank you.'

Walker hung up the phone and checked the inbox of his email. It seemed he wasn't quite done with the case just yet. There was one there from Donna Wilkinson. He opened it up.

CHAPTER FORTY-ONE

It was immediately obvious why she'd sent it. There was a photo of her younger self. He'd never met her in person, of course, but there was a definite likeness to the more recent photo he'd seen of her—despite her looking markedly different in style and appearance now. Underneath this old photo, she'd written:

Dear Inspector Walker. This is a photograph of myself taken eighteen years ago, when I first met Alex's father. I saw the pictures of those poor girls who'd been murdered recently and thought this might be of interest. Many thanks – Donna Wilkinson.

The picture of her younger self had an eerie resemblance to the two girls who'd died, and the girl who'd managed to escape with her life, along with all the others who'd come forward. Kathy had clearly been targeting women who looked just like Donna had, back in the day—blonde, slim, hair tied back, ample bosoms but not large, blue eyes, pale. She'd been exacting her revenge, or stopping other women from having their men stolen, or acting on some other twisted value. Whatever it was, she'd used her son to achieve this, and this had resulted in him ending his life as well.

Walker printed the email and placed it into the folder he was going to put away. But there was one more thing he wanted to check. He made a call.

'Dr Johansen? Yes, this is DCI Walker. I worked the Alex Wilkinson case, a former client of yours? Yes, of course. How could you forget. It was awful. I just wanted to ask a couple of final questions, regarding Alex and his mother. Evidence has come to light showing that Alex was extensively abused by his mother. What's that? You'd rather talk in person. 2pm?

Yes, that's great. I'll see you there.'

Walker hung up. It seemed he'd have to put that file away later, put it on hold one last time. He had to talk to the doctor first, get a few final things tied off, and thank him properly for saving DC Brigg's life. She really did mean a lot to him now and he felt very grateful that she'd been unharmed. It wasn't the result he'd wanted, of course, but it certainly could have been worse.

* * *

'Thank you for seeing me at such short notice,' said Walker, now sitting back in the office of Doctor Johansen once more. 'The case has almost reached a conclusion now. I just wanted some more details about Alex, any indication, beyond the files provided, that he might have been abused by his mother as a child, that sort of thing, your thoughts and feelings on the matter. I understand you still have confidentiality rules to adhere to now there's no longer any imminent danger, but since he's deceased, I thought—'

'Confidentiality rules do continue after death,' said Dr Johansen. 'But since this is a criminal case, and I know there are still two young men on trial, I can talk about it a little, especially since there's not much more to tell.'

'That would be very helpful,' said Walker.

'Alex never talked much about his mother, as you can see from the transcripts I sent over. He was very protective of her. Our discussions focussed more on the rage he felt for his father abandoning them,' said Dr Johansen. 'Alex was a

CHAPTER FORTY-ONE

very confused young man, and I still believe he experienced a psychotic break of some sort.'

'I see,' said Walker. 'The autopsy did reveal various scars and bodily mutilations on Alex's body, and a hidden box in his mother's bedroom full of photos suggests that his mother, bizarrely, documented much of this, with young Alex being tied and bound in some of these photographs. It was heartbreaking to see. It's hard to understand why a mother would do such a thing. Did you suspect any of this? Were there any negative signs in his body language when you talked about his mother, any flinches or twitches, that kind of thing? I know it might be hard to remember.'

Dr Johansen tapped his pen on his desk while he thought. 'Look. It's not unusual for a mother of a problem child, especially a single mother, to resort to desperate measures to make their child behave, and to stop them from harming themselves. Some even lock their children in their bedrooms, put bars on the windows, that kind of thing, or handcuff them to a cot. It's a protection mechanism, but one that strays into the realm of abuse. I don't know why she would document this, but all I can say is that it wasn't necessarily for nefarious means, as it first might seem. She may just have been keeping records. Some people do, the good and the bad.'

Walker very much doubted that was right, not with her also keeping photographs of Alex's victims, and with these victims looking so much like the woman who'd taken her man—Alex's father. And then there were the bloodied toenails. Plus, the Doctor's response irritated him—like he was actually defending Kathy Johnson for some reason, blaming the victim. No, this wasn't the understandable actions of a mother dealing with a problem child, Walker thought, it wasn't a protection mechanism gone too far—it was literal torture, sadism, cruelty for the thrill of power. Still, the Doctor had a right to his own opinion, so he tried to let it go.

'Did you meet Mrs Johnson?' asked Walker. 'Alex's mother.'

'I believe I did, on two occasions,' said Dr Johansen. 'She seemed genuinely concerned about her son.'

'What would you say, off the record, if Mrs Johnson also kept photographs of Alex's victims, and what if those victims looked very similar to the woman who Alex's father had left her for?' asked Walker.

Dr Johansen gave it some thought. 'I'd say you might be looking for something that isn't there. The mind tends to see what it wants to see.' Although this echoed what DC Briggs had been saying earlier, coming from him it only served to raise Walker's suspicions. Kathy Johnson's mystery male indicated a possible accomplice—a loose end that Walker didn't like—and Alex's accusations about the Doctor giving him mind-bending meds now also troubled Walker. His dismissal of a victim type just seemed like bad psychology, more wilful myopia than healthy scepticism.

'How so?' asked Walker, wanting to see where the Doctor would take this.

'Well, perhaps Alex was attracted to the same kind of woman as his father. Research is now emerging to show that genetics play a larger role in physical attraction than previously thought. I can only hypothesise as to how she got the photos of Alex's victims, and why she kept them, but this does not prove that she was involved in any way, only that she knew about it somehow, and was keeping a record.'

This speculative scientific handwaving about Alex fancying the same type as his father started to set off some alarm bells for Walker. It was like he was protecting the woman, absolving her of any culpability—which was odd, as if he was covering his own arse, it would have made more sense for him to make a point of how such sadistic abuse, abuse the Doctor might not have known about, could have pushed Alex to breaking point. 'Go on,' said Walker, wanting to see if Dr Johansson might implicate himself further.

'A mother's relationship with her son is very complicated, and vice-versa. She may have wanted to make him face what he'd done, convince him to turn himself in, perhaps. Maybe that's what he was going to do when he went to the police station, and then he had another psychotic break and became violent. It's impossible to say at this stage. And then carrying the heavy guilt of what Alex did, and her failure to stop it, his mother attempted suicide, figuring you'd get away somehow. Or maybe she blamed you for her son's death and wanted you to suffer like he had.'

Walker wasn't buying it. Not one bit. The smart glasses suggested Alex might not have had a psychotic break after all. But without a mobile device with records connecting those glasses to a source, he had nothing. He wondered about how Dr Johansson had come to be there when Alex killed himself. Yes, they had a meeting around that time, but Walker hadn't seen him anywhere around when he'd been commandeering a car. He thought back to the second champagne glass again and the sheaths, the possible male accomplice: if someone was going to manipulate Alex into acting out his mother's sick fantasies, who better to do that than a trained psychologist? Alex had blamed the doctor for everything before he'd killed himself, had called him "the devil"—it had been staring him in the face all along. It had looked like a paranoid delusion at the time, but now it was all beginning to line up. This wasn't a mother disciplining her child. And it wasn't a psychotic break. It was something else—something far more heinous. He couldn't spook the Doctor, though, couldn't risk him going on the run too. He needed to get evidence first, to confirm his theory, get some proof. But he had to act fast. The CPS were pushing to prosecute Mohammad Ali Hussein and Liam Holden for their role in the Charlotte Porter case, were looking for some scapegoats and political relief with all the tabloid media attention the case had been getting—and who better than a young Muslim boy to persecute?

'Well, I thank you for your time, Dr Johansson,' said Walker, not wanting to push any further, to unnerve the Doctor in any way or dent his confidence. 'That will be all. You've been very helpful. I think we can now put this case to bed. I'll see myself out.'

CHAPTER FORTY-TWO

Time was running out, but Walker knew exactly what he was gunna do. Alex's father, Dominic Wilkinson, had mentioned Kathy had seen a counsellor back in the day, around the time she'd apparently been stalking him. "Ramsdale Counsellors" he'd thought it was called. Walker's team had already googled it, found a place in Chorley called *Ramsdale Counselling and Therapy Services*. It was the only name in the area like that. It had to be the same place. He had a hunch if he could find out who Kathy saw all those years ago, it was gunna be the devil himself: Doctor Alfred Johansen. This was a lead that had already been followed up from the Action Book, with the admin staff there saying records had been digitised since 2007, and that all previous records were destroyed in an unfortunate basement flooding incident. However, Walker now had to dig deeper, try to talk to some of the staff there, find out if anyone recognised the name or face of his doctor.

He pulled up outside Ramsdale Counselling and Therapy Services alone in his pool car, the sun having already gone down, leaving a notable chill in the air. It wasn't what he'd been expecting—it was a housing estate, cheap-looking units with this particular one having a small plaque next to the front door with the name of the counselling service on there, and handrails for the disabled leading up to the entrance. He tried the door—it was open—and went in.

'Hello?' he said. Inside wasn't the pristine, clean, stylish office one might expect of such a place. Instead, it was more like a shared house that had been given a tidy up and made to look presentable for a visiting landlord. He walked through to a seating area, where someone was sitting staring at an amateur painting on the wall—one of a landscape that wasn't particularly well crafted in form but had deep and vivid colours that depicted turmoil and chaos. Next to that was an open door leading into an office.

'Can I help you?' came a voice, before a lady peered around the door into the sitting room.

'Detective Chief Inspector Jonathan Walker. I need some information to aid with a case. It's urgent.'

'Oh. Come in,' said the woman, so Walker entered the office. 'I'm Susan. What can we do to help you?'

'I believe a woman called Kathy Johnson may have had some counselling here, some eighteen or so years ago,' said Walker. He took out a photograph of her, one recovered from the fire that had been largely undamaged, an old one, and put it on Susan's desk. 'I know it's a long time, but it's important. Do you recognise her?'

'Well, I'm afraid I've only been here for about seven years,' said Susan. 'But Gill might know more. She's been here from the get-go. I'll go get her.'

Walker sat in the office while Susan went to go find her colleague. If Gill had been here eighteen years ago, she might not only remember Kathy, but also Dr Johansen as well. And if he could get proof that the Doctor had worked with Kathy all

CHAPTER FORTY-TWO

those years ago, or at least that they'd both been here around the same time, then this might be enough for him to get a warrant to search the Doctor's premises, find something more concrete to implicate him.

A woman came in, a bit untidy looking with dishevelled brown hair, but with a friendly face.

'Hi. I'm Gill. I'm just with a client right now. But I understand it's important. Can I help?'

'Yes. This woman,' said Walker, handing the photograph to Gill. 'Kathy Johnson. We're currently investigating a very serious case that she's involved in. Do you recognise her at all?'

Gill carefully looked at the photo. 'Well, I've been here for twenty odd years, and I've seen a lot of people come and go during that time—thousands, probably. She's a bit familiar, but I can't be sure. There are lots of people here who look like her. Susan said this was about eighteen years ago?'

'That's right,' said Walker. 'What about counsellors then? How many of those have you had?'

'A few,' said Gill. 'We're a non-profit organisation, so our counsellors all do this voluntarily. We've had quite a number come and go, but not nearly as many as the clients we've had.'

His doctor also said he did pro bono work. It could have been the kind of place he worked at.

Walker took out another photograph, one of Doctor Alfred Johansen.

'Do you recognise this man?' asked Walker.

Gill looked at it and her face went a shade paler and her eyes a little wider. 'I do,' she said. 'He worked here for a short time. Asked me out on a date actually. I...'

Walker gave it a second. 'What it is, Gill? It's important. We have to know,' he said.

Gill sighed. 'We went out together, and... well, I ended up back at his place. We were both a little drunk, I think. He scared me, though, started strangling me when we were having sex, gave me a safe word first—he didn't just attack me—but he didn't stop right away, and I freaked out. He did stop eventually though, apologised, said we'd both drunk a little too much and taken the fun and games a bit too far. So, I left, as fast as my feet would carry me. He did a few more sessions here, finished his block with the clients he had, but we never asked him back after that. I was just glad to see the back of him. I think he was in the middle of setting up his own practice at the time, as I remember, and had some free time to volunteer as he'd not got enough clients yet.'

'And when was this, exactly?' asked Walker.

Gill gave it some more thought. 'Definitely fifteen to twenty years ago. I think Terry was here at the time too, as I remember talking to her about the incident, so it must have been around 2005-ish, when she was here, as she got married on New Year's Day 2006—I remember that—and then she stopped working here because she got pregnant. She only worked here for a year or so, but we got pretty close in that time. We're still in touch. It was around then.'

'So, roughly eighteen years ago then,' said Walker, more to himself than to her.

'That would be correct,' said Gill.

'That's all I need to know,' said Walker. 'Now, I'm going to need you to sign a witness statement, confirming what you just told me, Gill. Is that okay?'

'Of course,' she said. 'I'm not surprised if that man is in trouble. There was something just not right with him.'

CHAPTER FORTY-TWO

Walker agreed, and his hunch was right, he knew it: Dr Johansen wasn't just covering for Kathy—he was covering for himself. He hadn't helped Alex or Kathy at all—quite the opposite, in fact. He'd met Kathy here, eighteen years ago, psychologically manipulated the both of them over many years, and gradually coerced them into performing the most abhorrent of acts.

'I have to go,' said Walker, in a hurry to get where he needed to be. 'Thank you.'

CHAPTER FORTY-THREE

Walker was heading to the home of Dr Alfred Johansen, flooring the accelerator of the car as much as he dared. He'd already tried his office—his secretary said he'd left shortly after Walker without any explanation, and she'd had to cancel all his appointments for the day. Walker had got his home address and was hoping he'd still be there so he could arrest him, hold him for twenty-four hours, at least, give himself time to collect the evidence he needed to put the bastard away. He already had a used condom at Kathy Johnson's home, which he could use to hopefully get a DNA match, he had the suspect counselling at the same establishment Kathy attended, at around the same time, and he had him treating Alex and suddenly turning up when Alex had DC Briggs in that old warehouse. He had enough to warrant investigating further, at the very least, and if he could just find a burner phone and some other evidence documenting what he'd done, or something similar linking him to the crimes, he'd have him. But all of this hinged on the Doctor having not already run. If he did that, he might never find him.

He got to the address the secretary had given him and looked through the window of the large, well kept, detached house. There was a woman there so Walker knocked on the window,

CHAPTER FORTY-THREE

startling her.

'Excuse me, madam. I'm Detective Walker. I need to speak with your husband, Dr Johansen.'

The woman took a deep breath and came to the front door, opened it.

'What's going on?' she asked. 'I'm Mrs Johansen. Sheila, Alfred's secretary, said he hasn't been in the office all afternoon, even though he had appointments. I've called him about ten times. Is he in trouble?'

'I need to speak with your husband about a very serious matter, Mrs Johansen. May I come in?' asked Walker.

'Do you have a warrant?' said the woman. She was sharp, wily, but obviously very worried.

'Not yet,' said Walker. 'Have you any idea where your husband might be?'

The woman had something in her hand. She handed it to Walker. It was a passport.

'He left this on the table,' she said, before handing one more item to Walker. 'And this.' It was what looked like his wedding ring.

Walker spun around and kicked at a low-lying flower border fence, sending it flying, landing on the grass next to it.

'God damn it!' he said. He'd lost him. The Doctor had got away. It was him. It had to be. It had been him all along. Alex was right. He was a monster. And now, it seemed he was a monster who'd gone on the run, probably taken on a new identity, and was about to start all over again.

'Detective?' said the woman, a tear starting to well up in the corner of her eye.

'I'm sorry, Mrs Johansen, but I'm going to have to take you in for questioning, and we'll be getting a warrant to search your premises, and the place of business of your husband, in due course. Please come with me.'

'But...' said Mrs Johansen. 'We have children, a life together. What's this all about? Where is my husband?'

'This is about the ruining of lives,' said Walker. 'Several of them. It's about unnecessary tragedy, darkness and suffering. It's about the devil himself.'

'What?' she said, not seeming to quite grasp the enormity of the trouble that was about to befall the Johansen family, before Walker snapped out of it.

'Come with me,' he said again. But he had a horrible, slow, sinking feeling that neither of them would be seeing the Doctor again: *Doctor Death*.

CHAPTER FORTY-FOUR

Doctor Alfred Johansen, it turned out, was a sixty-two-year-old practitioner of psychiatry and psychology who'd moved to Southport from Pembrokeshire in South Wales in 2001. At least, he would have been sixty-two if he was still alive. Walker had found a newspaper article containing a photograph of Dr Johansen, taken in 1996, that showed him to look nothing like the Dr Johansen Walker met. This person was already bald, had a squarer jaw, different eyes, a whole completely different face. It was not the same person. That much was obvious. Doctor Alfred Johansen had not been registered as dead or missing, but according to neighbours had simply moved away, telling them of his plans to set up a new practice in the north of England after the tragic passing of his wife, Ella. It seemed that somewhere between Pembrokeshire and Southport, though, the real Doctor Johansen had disappeared, had his identity stolen by whoever the imposter was, the person who'd eventually met Kathy Johnson, it seemed, and systematically manipulated and controlled her for almost two decades—her son, Alex, too.

The problem was that Walker had no idea who this imposter might be and where he might have gone to next. He could literally be anywhere in the world by now, have started a new life, perhaps with a whole new identity, which they may also have stolen. It seemed that the real Alfred Johansen was most likely long since dead, having either been killed by the imposter, or having died somehow and had his body disposed of after all his particulars and belongings had been taken from him. His new neighbours would have had no idea—nobody in the new area would. To them, he'd have just been a new resident moving to the area. In a way, it was brilliant. These revelations had also opened up another case for Walker to pursue, this one a cold case—that of the disappearance of the real Dr Alfred Johansen—and he already had several on the go as was normally the case for a police detective, and especially for a Chief Inspector like him.

After searching the fake Dr Johansen's home and place of work, not much was initially found. He seemed clean—a legitimate business owner and family man. But he'd left some things behind before he'd gone in such a hurry: namely one USB memory stick, and one desktop computer hard drive. Whether this had been a mistake, or whether he was unconcerned about incriminating his discarded identity, was unclear. But computer forensics had been able to recover several deleted files from these storage devices, allowing Detective Walker and his team to piece together a possible narrative of events.

One document that had been recovered was a scanned digital copy of a diary written by Alex's mother. In it, there were direct references to her son, Alex, detailing what she'd done to him, but there was also a common usage of collective pronouns such as 'they' and 'we', which was suggestive of the involvement of someone else. Further on in the diary entries, she also talked about 'The Doctor', which had to be Johansen.

CHAPTER FORTY-FOUR

She noted how this doctor had given her some power back, how he'd helped her overcome what had happened to her.

Although the document was corrupted, from its undamaged contents Walker had been able to decipher the following: Kathy Johnson and a man she referred to as the 'Doctor', most likely Alfred Johansen's imposter, had systematically abused Alex over sixteen years or so in an attempt to both (a) discipline Alex, and (b) give some power back to Kathy. In addition, they'd also coerced Alex into sexually abusing and then raping several women, before graduating on to actually killing two women and almost killing a third, as Walker already knew. Her and the Doctor had also evidently enjoyed some kind of sexual relationship themselves and gained sexual gratification from watching Alex carry out these vile acts. A narrative therefore emerged from the document of control and abuse, of experimentation and long-term manipulation, of a sick one-sided, powerful romance that Kathy could not escape from. She was on a complex concoction of pharmaceutical drugs that the Doctor had given her, and was in a desperate relationship with him that she'd do anything to keep—even hurting and ultimately killing her son. What came across from the writing was that she was obsessed with the Doctor, could think of nothing else, was addicted to him as strongly as any drug, and, like many drug addicts, she didn't care what she destroyed in her path to get it. Reading between the lines, Walker could see that this imposter had taken a very vulnerable young woman, one who, by her own admission, had been extensively physically and sexually abused as a child herself by her father, and then slapped around a bit again by Alex's father before being cheated on.

Unfortunately, Walker had been too late. The doctor, or

whatever he was, had got the hell out of Dodge, as they say in those old American films, and Walker had a feeling he was intelligent enough not to ever be found.

Walker was driving home, getting ready for a well-earned rest after another hard day's work, when his mobile rang. He was waiting at a traffic light, so he checked, just quickly to see who the call was from. It was an international number, coming from the Netherlands. He got through the lights and pulled over, as the phone continued to ring. He answered it.

'Detective Chief Inspector Jonathan Walker?' came a male voice on the line before Walker could say anything.

'Yes, this is DCI Walker. What can I do for you?' said Walker. 'The voice was familiar—too familiar—but he wasn't sure; not sure if he was hearing what he wanted to hear.'

'I just wanted to congratulate you on cracking the case. Very well done, Inspector,' said the man. 'I've seen the tabloids—the court case with those boys, the *Sensational True Story*. You've become quite the celebrity.'

'Dr Johansen? Dr Alfred Johansen?' Walker leaned forward in his seat. 'Or should I say the man who stole Dr Johansen's identity. It's you, isn't it?' He was sure of it now. He had the same slow and precise style of speech. 'You killed him, didn't you?'

'Would you believe that some people still pick up hitchhikers?' said the man. 'Folks really should be more careful.'

'I'll find you,' said Walker, resolutely. 'I'll never give up.'

There was a pause. 'I'm sure you won't, Detective. But I can assure you that you'll never find me. I'm a ghost. I don't exist. I just thought it might be polite to... offer you some closure.'

Closure? He was gloating—simple as. He was revelling in the fact that he'd got away, at least for the time being.

CHAPTER FORTY-FOUR

'Why did you do it?' asked Walker. 'You tortured that boy and warped his mother's mind until it was rotten. Was it fun? Is that all it was to you—a bit of fun?' He was getting angry now. 'You're evil,' he spat. 'That's all you are. Pure evil. You'll get what's coming to you, eventually, whoever you are. I'll find you.'

'Inspector Walker. Are you familiar with the work of Stanley Milgram and his experiments on obedience and authority?' asked the man masquerading as Dr Johansen. 'Fascinating stuff. But the work was never finished, never applied to the real world.'

'And you think you've done that, I suppose,' said Walker. 'You do realise that you're not even a doctor of psychology and psychiatry, right?'

The man on the end of the line laughed. 'I'll publish the study anonymously, online, Inspector Walker, along with a number of others. My work will be important and groundbreaking. So-called "ethical guidelines" have held back the field so much, and many others. It will be used for good. These people wouldn't have led good lives anyway. I know it's difficult to see, from your point of view, but my work was utilitarian. Far more people will benefit from them than those who have suffered. And if I enjoyed my work along the way... well, that's just a bonus, now, isn't it? It's good to enjoy your work, I think. I bid you good day, Inspector.'

The line went dead.

Walker wanted to throw his phone, smash it to pieces, but he also wanted to get as much data from the incoming call as possible, so he restrained himself.

'*Bastard*. You'll get what's coming to you,' he said, but Walker wasn't sure he really believed it.

EPILOGUE

Walker was stopped outside of DC Briggs's house, picking her up in the unmarked Audi pool car they used for detective business. She'd been on holiday for a couple of weeks, taking a well-earned break after the events of the Charlotte Porter case and the investigation that unfolded. She got in and sat in the front passenger's seat, and Walker got moving.

'Chief,' she said, regarding him. 'How've you been?'

'Things are okay, I suppose,' he said. This wasn't entirely true. He'd struggled with the conclusion to the case, had got a bit out of sorts with it. One very dangerous man had got away—the man who'd orchestrated the whole thing—to God knows where, and he was likely to commit further unspeakable crimes if he wasn't caught, which seemed a very real risk with them currently having no leads on his whereabouts whatsoever.

Walker had studied Kathy Johnson's diary in depth now, had scrutinised it, with computer forensics being able to recover more of the corrupted data now that they'd had more time. From it, he'd got the whole sorry story. By her own account, Kathy had been extensively abused as a child by her father, had been perpetually beaten and raped by him, before finally growing up and meeting a man who'd initially given her some hope but also later abused her, before leaving for another woman. She'd clearly, by her own admission, had a very difficult life and had endured much suffering, before meeting who she believed to be one Doctor Johansen, a man who'd claimed to be able to help her regain some power in her life, and to stop her being a victim. He'd done this, it seemed, through a very slow process of psychological manipulation, over many years, getting her to inflict increasing abuse on her own misbehaving son, making him the focus of her rage, making him embody the spirit of both her father and Alex's father—both of whom Alex carried the genes of. They'd tortured and humiliated him together, her and the Doctor, and somehow this had progressed to eventually coercing Alex into harming and sexually abusing young women. Alex must have been terrified of them, of what they'd do if he didn't obey. And they'd watched—at least the last few attacks, with Alex wearing those smart glasses. They'd hooked the feed up onto the wall projector and had sex together while watching Alex beat, rape, and murder these women. In her own words, she said she didn't know why she was doing what she was anymore, only that she trusted the Doctor and his methods, blindly, that he was the only person who'd ever wanted to truly help her. She loved him without question, unconditionally, and she'd do anything he asked—even kill herself, even kill her own son.

'Chief?' said DC Briggs. 'You sure you're okay.'

Walker let out a heavy sigh, trying to let go of what had happened, at least a bit of it, but not succeeding one iota. 'Yeah. My wife called yesterday. Said it's about time we met up, had a chat. Told me the kids miss me—well, one of them, anyhow.'

'Well... that's good,' said DC Briggs. 'Isn't it? That's... really good.'

Walker nodded, head down.

'I'm fine too,' said DC Briggs.

'Oh, sorry. How are—'

'I just said. I'm fine. What we doing today then?' she asked.

Walker tried to shake himself out of it, be professional—be a detective again. 'There's a case emerging over in Blackpool, near the Tower. They thought it was a jumper at first, but now they're not so sure, want us to take a look. They're still cordoning off the area yet—it's Illuminations season, isn't it, so it might take some time to process the crime scene, get things in order. They asked if we could come over in a couple of hours,' said Walker, 'give our opinion at least.'

'I see. Right then,' said DC Briggs. 'I guess we're taking a trip to Blackpool.'

'I guess we are,' said Walker, taking a good look at DC Briggs, eying her up and down. 'But first I want to make a quick pit stop. See how young Mo is doing.'

'Mohammad Ali Hussein? He was a lucky boy,' said DC Briggs. 'The CPS wanted those boys on a platter.'

Getting the charges dropped against Mohammad Hussein and Liam Holden was perhaps the only good thing to come out of the Charlotte Porter case. At least two young lives had now been saved. Walker heard Mo was doing well, had started university, was currently home during the term break. His mother had got in touch, thanked Walker for solving the case, said they'd love to see him and be able to offer their gratitude in person, if he had time. He normally wouldn't once a case was closed, but he wanted to see Mo, see he was alright with his own eyes, that working the case hadn't all been for nothing.

It didn't take long to get to Mo's home in Chorley. They'd been there before of course, although that seemed like a long time ago now.

'Detective Walker!' said Mo's mother, Maira, as she opened the door. 'And DC Briggs. It's so nice to see you. Please, come in.' She perhaps had a few more greys than the last time he'd saw her, but she was friendlier, which was to be expected with the circumstances being more pleasant, and her South Asian accent seemed to be a touch stronger for it.

'Perhaps just for a moment,' said Walker. 'We don't have a lot of time. How is Mo?'

Right on cue, Mo popped his head around his mother. He'd been behind her, just out of sight.

'DCI Walker!' said Mo. 'It's good to see you.'

They came in and sat at the same dining table they had several months ago. There was some tea on the table, already brewed and steaming, and some biscuits.

'Doodh pati chai?' asked Walker.

'You remembered,' said Maira.

'How could I forget. And sweet cumin biscuit too,' said Walker. Maira smiled. 'I've been buying them from the Asian grocer's, over near Chorley Train Station, the one you mentioned when we last visited. Delicious.'

'Oh, that's great,' said Maira. 'At least *something* good came out of all this then,' she said. It was probably meant to be a joke, but her face turned serious, seeming to regret it as soon as it came out of her mouth.

'Well, that's why I'm here, actually. Not the tea and biscuits—although that's good too. I mean to see Mo is doing okay. How are you Mo? You holding up well?'

'I passed my A-levels and got into Liverpool Law School,'

said Mo, proudly. 'I'm already a semester in. It's going well.'

'Congratulations,' said DC Briggs. 'We're proud of you, Mo.'

'I'm going to do my thesis on racism and the joint enterprise law in the modern era,' said Mo. 'I got lucky, because of you, Detective. But many young people like me do not. I'm going to dedicate my career to defending those who are wrongly accused.'

Walker took a sip from the tea, and took one of the biscuits, before standing up. He'd heard what he wanted to hear, and they had to be on their way, get to that crime scene in Blackpool.

'We wish you all the best, Mo. It's so good to see you doing well,' said Walker.

'Lovely to see you,' said DC Briggs, also taking a biscuit.

Mo and his mother waved them off at the front door, before they got headed towards Blackpool and a potential new case.

'It's good to see you too, Constable,' said Walker.

'Don't be getting all soft on me, Detective Walker,' said DC Briggs. 'We have work to do.'

Walker smiled. 'Really. I don't know what I'd do without you. You've been a breath of fresh air. I can't remember the last time I actually enjoyed coming to work,' he said, as he munched down on the cumin biscuit he'd taken.

DC Briggs waved a hand around in the air, dismissing the sentiment. 'Oh, shut up! Just drive, will you?'

Walker smiled again, but this time it was a smile tainted with sadness and regret, the weight of those he'd not been able to save dragging him quickly back down. He put the car in gear and started to move tentatively forwards once more.

A Note From the Author

"Thanks so much for reading my book, *The Pike*. I hope you enjoyed it. Please could you be so kind as to leave a **review** on Amazon? (Goodreads and Bookbub also appreciated) I read *every* review and they help new readers discover my books. In fact, they're invaluable for my career and the continued lives of DCI Walker and the gang. So… please, do it now before you forget! (and I'll keep writing)"

J.J. Richards

SIGN UP to my mailing list at **J-J-Richards.com** for news of new releases and more!

A LANCASHIRE DETECTIVE MYSTERY

THE TOWER

Sometimes you have to be cruel to be kind.

J.J. RICHARDS

DCI Walker Crime Thrillers BOOK THREE

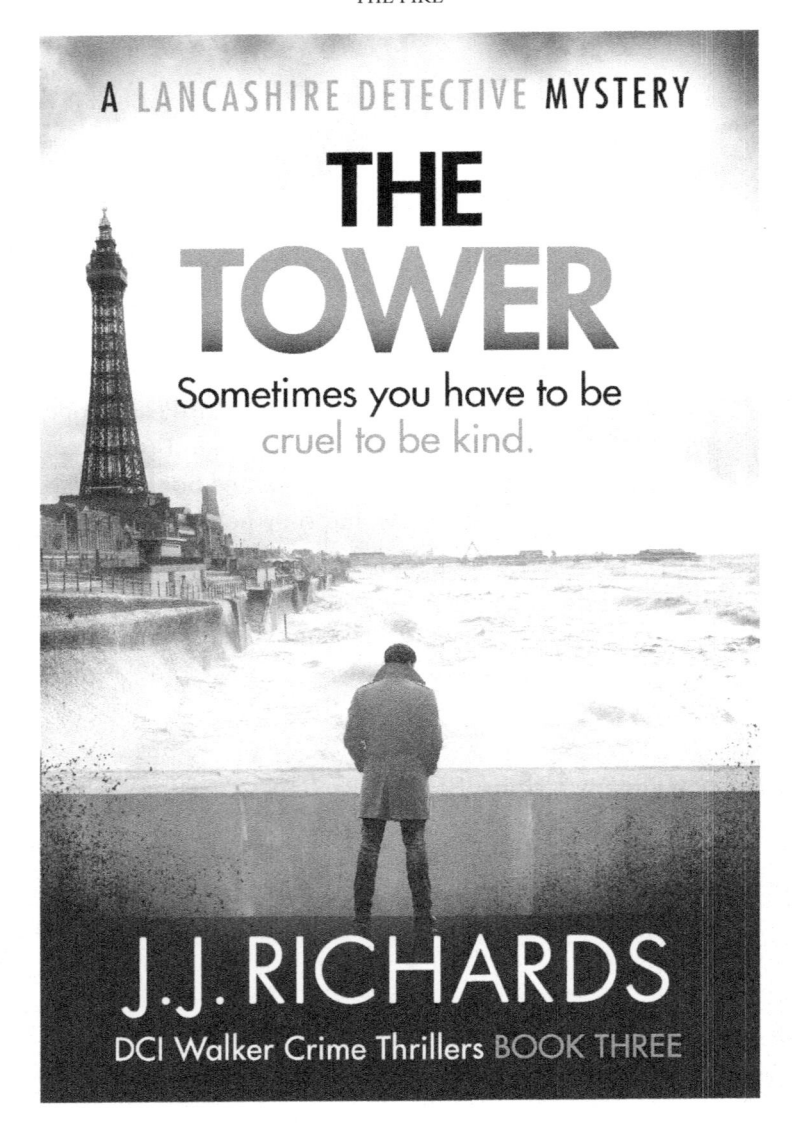

Visit **Amazon** to pre-order a copy of Book Three, today!

Printed in Great Britain
by Amazon